Sorceress

CELIA REES

CANDLEWICK PRESS

Copyright © 2002 by Celia Rees
First published 2002 by Bloomsbury Publishing Plc, London

Second U.S. paperback edition in this format 2009

The Library of Congress has cataloged the hardcover edition as follows:

Rees, Celia.
Sorceress / Celia Rees. — 1st Candlewick Press ed.
p. cm.
Summary: Eighteen-year-old Agnes, a Mohawk Indian who is descended from a line of shamanic healers, uses her own newly discovered powers to uncover the story of her ancestor, a seventeenth-century New England English healer who fled charges of witchcraft to make her life with the local Indians.
ISBN 978-0-7636-1847-6 (hardcover)
1. New England—History—Colonial period, ca. 1600–1775—Juvenile fiction.
2. Canada—History—to 1763 (New France)—Juvenile fiction.
3. Indians of North America—New England—Juvenile fiction.
4. Indians of North America—Canada, Eastern—Juvenile fiction.
[1. New England—History—Colonial period, ca. 1600–1775—Fiction.
2. Canada—History—to 1763 (New France)—Fiction. 3. Indians of North America—New England—Fiction. 4. Indians of North America—Canada, Eastern—Fiction. 5. Shamans—Fiction. 6. Witchcraft—Fiction.] I. Title.
PZ7. R25465 So 2002
[Fic]—dc21 2002023739

ISBN 978-0-7636-2183-4 (paperback)
ISBN 978-0-7636-4229-7 (second paperback format)

2 4 6 8 10 9 7 5 3

Printed in the United States of America

This book was typeset in Centaur.

Candlewick Press
99 Dover Street
Somerville, Massachusetts 02144

visit us at www.candlewick.com

For Terry and Catrin, who came with me

This volume follows on from the remarkable collection of documents known as "the Mary Papers." These were found hidden inside a quilt dating from the colonial period and identified as the diary of Mary Newbury, a fourteen-year-old girl who was forced to flee from England in 1659 after witnessing her grandmother's execution for witchcraft. The diaries described Mary's subsequent journey to America and how she came to join a Puritan settlement. Mary's account stopped in midsentence, when she was forced to leave the settlement or meet the same fate as her grandmother.

Apart from a page or two added in a different hand, the diary ended there, and with it what we knew of the story of Mary Newbury. Even before transcription was completed, I knew that I wanted to know more about Mary's fate. Many people responded to my e-mail appeal, and I

would like to thank all the correspondents
who have helped me piece together the
stories of many of the people Mary encountered. I have tried to incorporate as much of
this information as possible into the text;
where there is too much to include, I have
supplied endnotes. This book is, however,
primarily Mary's story, and she proved to be
the most elusive person of all. So, finally, I
have to thank Agnes Herne and her aunt,
Miriam Lazare, who found her for me.
Without their help, this book would never
have been written.

Alison Ellman
The Institute, Boston, MA

If I am a witch

If I am a witch, they will soon know it. I had never ill wished anyone, but as I fled Beulah, anger and hatred clashed together, sparking curses like steel striking flint. I had done no wrong, so why was I forced to run like a fugitive? My accusers, Deborah Vane and the other girls, they were the guilty ones. Even as they denounced me as a witch, their eyes gleamed with scheming malice. The madness twisting their faces was counterfeit. Who could not see it? "Them that's blind and will not see." My grandmother's words came to me. She was a wise woman, but her wisdom brought her nothing but sorrow. She ended her life on the hanging tree, and now the same fate awaited me.

They searched, and that most diligently. I cowered in Rebekah's borning room, thinking to be safe for a little time, but they demanded entry even there, their voices ringing loud with right and duty. Only Martha stood against them, defying Reverend Johnson as brave as a robin before a striking hawk. They went away reluctantly. I tracked them searching through the rest of the house, moving from one room to the next, their heavy tread freighted with hatred.

I got away, but they searched for me still. I heard them hallooing through the woods, saw their torches, tiny bonfire sparks in the blackness. I heard the dogs baying and yelling. Dogs run faster than men.

Snow started falling soon after I fled the town, icy pellets seeding the wind. It began to come thick, evermore whitening the ground, making it easier for the dogs to pick me out. The first to come upon me was old Tom, Josiah Crompton's hunting dog. He's a gazehound, hunting by sight. Old Tom came leaping out of the brush toward me and threw back his long, bony head, making a sound deep in his throat, somewhere between a yelp and a swallowed bark of triumph. This brought the other dogs tumbling to him. They stood ringed about, tongues lolling, eyes bright.

They had me cornered. I backed against a tree and stared at them, waiting for them to spring. Tom crept nearer, the others following, the circle tightening, then he stopped. He stood, head inclined, his short ears cocked as if harking to some sound. The men's shouting was nearer now. I thought that was what he was hearing and that at any minute he would commence barking, but he did not. He gave me one last look, wheeled around, and made off with all the others streaming after him in a rag and tag mob.

The baying and yelling thinned to nothing. Tom had led the hunt away from me. I was alone again in the forest's frosty silence. I thought to run on, but tiredness overcame me. I sank down, leaning my back against the tree's rough bark, intending to gather what strength I had.

I have been here ever since. The snow is still falling, drifting through the air and making no sound, feathering across my cheeks like angel fingers, weighting my eyelids, settling upon me, covering me like a counterpane filled with the finest down.

I feel no cold, but I cannot move. My limbs have no feeling in them. To sleep is to die, I know that, but I cannot keep awake. Sometimes I almost hope that they might come back this way, that they might find me, but I dismiss the thought as soon as it arises. I'd rather die here than be taken. I'd rather freeze to this tree than be hanged.

Agnes fell forward, cracking her head sharply on the glass. The screen saver jarred and jerked, just for a second, then the monitor went black and she was looking at her own face staring back, eyes dilated by more than the pain in her forehead. What had that been? Vision or dream? She was cold; she was freezing. Her fingers were bloodless and withered, the nails blue. She looked to the window, expecting to see snow falling, but there was nothing. The sky was a clear evening blue.

Whatever had just happened was as real as any experience of her own, anything that she had ever known. She could not stop shivering. She got up and dragged the quilt off the bed. The quilt was serviceable as well as beautiful, a bright Lone Star, Aunt M's farewell gift to her. Agnes gripped the edges tight, wrapping it close around her, but still she could not get warm. Teeth chattering, she went to the window, opening it onto the quad below. Sodium streetlights were coming on, bronzing the leaves on the trees. Across the way, desk lamps were beginning to show in the windows of rows of little rooms just like her own. She closed the window and in the gathering darkness shifted her focus, turning the glass into a mirror. She stared at the face staring back at her.

Agnes put her hand up, sweeping back her jet-black hair. She wore it long, past her shoulders. She was only eighteen, but already a few silver hairs were threading down from the parting. She would have a white streak there, just as her aunt had, and her grandmother before her. She frowned, thick dark brows drawing down. The eyes beneath were gray, rimmed with black—unusual, particularly in her family. The color of her eyes and her faraway gaze had caused her grandmother to name her Karonhisake, Searching Sky.

No one called her that here. To her fellow students, to the staff and faculty, she was Agnes Herne. The only time her tribal name was used was when she was back on the reservation. She did not seek to hide her Native American blood. She did not disguise it; neither did she advertise it. It was who she was. She went home as often as time and vacations would allow, but she'd moved away to go to college and she liked to keep her life in separate compartments.

She had chosen anthropology as her course of study.

"You'll have us all laid out like bugs on a tray," Aunt M had said about that. She'd laughed, blowing smoke through her niece's denials. Then she'd added, "You be careful, honey, or they'll turn you into a spy in your own house."

The cold was receding now, the room returning to its normal temperature. Agnes went to her chair, trying to figure what had sparked the experience in the first place. She stared at the screen saver spooling on the monitor. She'd been sitting over here, thinking she maybe needed fresh air. Her head was aching and her shoulders felt like they'd been crafted out of rock. She must have closed her eyes, just for a second, and that's when it had happened. She shook her head as if that would clear the fog in it. She'd definitely experienced something. She could feel the effects even now. Not quite a vision, but definitely more than a dream.

Nothing like this had ever happened to her before, nothing so intense. It left her feeling dazed. Some deep part of her knew that all her life she had been waiting for this exact moment to happen. Meanwhile her brain struggled on, trying to find some rational explanation.

It had to be a projection from the book she'd just read. She'd been reading it most of the day, cutting classes to finish it, and had been feeling kind of tired and spacy when she went to check the website. She touched a key, banishing the screen saver, and a face appeared, a girl's face shaded in bleached-out black and sepia. She was meant to be Mary, the girl in the book. Agnes found herself pondering who she really was. A model, maybe? Some girl off the street? Was it an archive photograph? An Amish girl? Or an immigrant, straight off the boat, caught on camera before she began her long trek west? Whoever, it was a good choice. The girl was young, you could see that, and there was something compelling about her face. The strong brows, the clear, level gaze, the lips slightly parted as though she was just about to smile or speak.

Agnes printed out the page and tacked it to the bulletin board above her desk. Underneath the face there was a message similar to the one in the back of the book.

> Since the discovery of these diaries,
> efforts to trace Mary Newbury and
> the other people in this account
> have continued.
>
> If you have information regarding
> any of the individuals or families
> mentioned, please contact our web-
> site, www.witchchild.com, or e-mail
> Alison Ellman at
>
> witchchild@candlewick.com

Agnes read the message again, although she knew it by heart. She moved the cursor around until it turned to a hand, first digit pointed to the highlighted address, but she did not click on it. She did know something about Mary Newbury, about what had happened to her, but to click would be a big step, one she was not certain that she wanted to take. Especially not now, not after what had just happened. It was a sign. She knew enough to recognize that. Medicine power ran through her family, like the streak of white in the hair. It followed the female line. Her aunt, her grandmother, and her grandmother before her, each had followed the medicine way.

"If it's gonna come to you, it'll come," her aunt had told her. "Natural as your period. No way you can avoid it."

Agnes hadn't wanted that, either. Now the thing had happened, and she was not at all sure what to do. She stayed for a long time lost in indecision, finger raised, hand crouched over the mouse.

"Keep your mind open and there's no knowing who'll come visit."

Her aunt's voice was in her head again and Agnes looked around, almost as if someone had spoken the words out loud. There was no one there.

The room was tidy. Agnes was a neat person and liked to keep her things that way. The walls were bright with posters and prints; the room was scattered with interesting things she'd collected, stuff she'd brought from home. She'd hoped that the effect was welcoming, but it had taken a while for people to step in and appreciate it.

She'd been lonely here. Very lonely. What friends she had at home had decided to study locally or to skip college altogether, but she had wanted to get a degree and had chosen to come here. That decision had been made almost by accident; there were so many schools, so many courses. She'd wanted to get away and this seemed as good a place as any, but when she got here, it had not been what she had expected. She had a few friends now, in the dorm, among the faculty, but it had been hard at the start. Back then doubts had gnawed at her, eating away at her confidence. She'd kept to her room, listening to the voices outside raised in greeting or fixing meetings, calling down the corridor, shouting out of the windows into the quad. Within days it seemed like they'd all known one another forever, while none of them had discovered that she was even here. She'd stayed on her own, alone in her room, wondering if she'd made the right decision, if she'd even make it through the year.

She'd been lonely plenty of times before, but there'd always been someone there for her, even if it had just been her mom. Here, every face she saw belonged to a stranger. The big city streets had her shrinking within, as if her true self was lost inside another person's skin.

For a while she'd even thought about leaving, but those thoughts hadn't stayed long. She owed people. They'd made sacrifices. She couldn't quit school for no reason. Besides, she was not a coward and she'd toughened up some since then. Now it didn't bother her much if it was the beginning of a warm spring weekend, with everyone gone away. She had not been expecting company anyway.

But someone had come visiting. The girl watched from the wall as Agnes began to tap out her message.

To: Alison Ellman
From: Agnes Herne
Subject: Mary Newbury
Dear Ms. Ellman,
A friend lent your book to me. She really liked it and thought I might, too. She was right about that—I read it all the way through without stopping—but there was something that she couldn't possibly know. One of the reasons that I couldn't put it down has to do with Mary, the girl at the center of the story.

Agnes stopped the rapid motion of her fingers. Typing the next words would commit her to a course of action, and there was no telling where it might lead. Agnes hesitated. When she'd first read the story and realized that there *could* be a connection, her heart had leaped inside her, but then reason had begun to kick in. She'd only glimpsed the things after all, and the stories might be about someone else, not Mary at all. How could she be sure? How could anyone be sure that *this* was the one person out of all the unnamed dead who'd gone before? The more she thought about it, the more unlikely it seemed. Her aunt would know more, but that could be the biggest problem of all.

Even if it *was* Mary, getting the things from Aunt M, bringing them here to the city, taking them to be studied, that would be difficult. Not just difficult— impossible. Because these were special. Sacred. Aunt M, as guardian of such things, would never allow it. She'd led campaigns, started petitions, demanding the return of sacred objects. The way she saw it, most of the Native American artifacts displayed in museums had been amassed as ethnic knickknacks, cultural curios, by collectors who had no idea of their true worth to the people from whom they had been taken. To her, they were so much stolen property.

"What right they got to any of that stuff? Bunch of grave robbers!" Aunt M's voice started up in her head again. "How'd they like it if we started busting up their churches, hauling the crosses off the altar, stealing the chalices and crucifixes? What if we started breaking open their tombs and digging up their dead?"

There was a pause, then the voice came back, even stronger than before.

"You just flat out can't have them. I'd rather toss them in the trash can."

Agnes thought to close the letter right there and then. Instead she found herself typing:

I am Kahniakehaka, Mohawk, part of the Haudenosaunee, the Iroquois Six Nations Confederacy. I live on the reservation in upper New York State, but right now I'm at college here in Boston.

The sky outside was black now, and night had closed around her, making anything possible. Making what she typed, anything she typed, not real. The quilt fell from her shoulders as she added some more.

My aunt also lives on the reservation. She has certain artifacts that seem like the things that Mary could have taken with her when she left the settlement. Much of our history is told in story form, and one of these stories tells of a white woman who joined the people. I can't recall all that much about the story, I'm afraid. I heard it when I was quite a little girl and guess I wasn't paying much attention. Neither can I be certain that this ancestor *is* Mary, but when I saw the message at the end of the book, I knew I had to contact you.

Agnes looked at what she'd just written, hesitating again before clicking on <u>Send</u>. She went to close the window instead.

Do you want to save changes to this message?

She was about to click on <u>No</u> when the picture on the wall caught her. The eyes held hers. She'd worry about Aunt M later. As Agnes stared back, the room began to get cold again.

She reached for the quilt, wrapping it close around her, no longer able to dismiss this as some dream projection triggered by reading the book. This was something else altogether. Even though she had not consciously sought it out, it had come to her anyway. Impossible to deny it. She could still feel the coldness. To ignore such a powerful experience might be positively dangerous. She was medicine enough to know that once a thing like this started, it would not go away. She had to find out what it was and follow. Wherever it took her. Whatever the consequences. She had no choice.

The first step was obvious. She flexed her numb fingers into painful tingling life, then pressed <u>Send</u>.

• Alison •

alison_ellman@theInstitute.org

Alison Ellman was working late at the Institute. An icon popped up in the corner of the screen, informing her, <u>You have mail</u>. She ignored it, concentrating her attention on the task at hand. She had information and files on pretty much everybody now. All the people mentioned in Mary's diary: Martha, who had befriended her; Jonah Morse and his son, Tobias; the Rivers family and their daughter, Mary's friend Rebekah; Elias Cornwell and Reverend Johnson; the people of Beulah; the girls who'd accused Mary; even Jack Gill, the boy she'd met on the boat. Everyone was there. Everyone except Mary. That was the worry.

She'd put it out of her mind to focus on what she was doing, working on a transcript of Elias Cornwell's journals. These were not a complete record;

some parts were missing, but they had proved a good source for what happened in Beulah after Mary fled the settlement. Alison had read through them and everything else that he'd ever produced in her quest to find any reference to his time at Beulah, and to Mary.

Cornwell seemed to have had a soft spot for Mary and hadn't been the first to accuse her of witchcraft, but when push came to shove, he'd joined in readily enough. He never lost his interest in the subject, and New England's subsequent history had offered plenty of scope for his expertise. His theories were pretty much run-of-the-mill—Cotton Mather did it better—but there were one or two references that could have been based on Cornwell's actual experiences. They showed up in sermons he'd given on visits to outlying settlements, ones very much like Beulah. He seemed to think that these areas were most in danger. Alison added a Post-it to those already frilling her computer, to remind herself to follow up on that.

She read through what she had so far. There was only a little bit more to transcribe, and she didn't mean to leave her desk until security made its final rounds and the alarms were set.

Alison leaned back in her chair, her transcription from Cornwell's diary finished. She was glad she didn't have to spend any more time with him. He had not improved as he'd gotten older. He'd just become more pompous, his observations increasingly long-winded and tedious, as he progressed through his various ministries. He'd married Sarah Garner, one of the girls who bore witness against Mary, and he'd certainly kept his young wife busy in the childbearing department. She'd gone from confinement to confinement and had died on the job, so to speak. Childbirth claimed her before she made thirty. Barely ten years after she left Beulah, her young life was over, her body worn out.

The other girls hadn't fared too well, either. Mary's main accusers had been Deborah Vane and her sister, Hannah. According to Cornwell, Hannah had never recovered from her "possession." The temporary madness became permanent in her case. Within a year she was dead of some kind of wasting sickness. As for Deborah, their leader, she'd gotten her way and married Reverend Johnson—but "Be careful for what you wish," isn't that what witches said? This marriage had not brought happiness. After Johnson, Deborah had gone on to Ned Cardwell, but this had not worked out well, either. The record showed a history of domestic violence and disorder. Eventually she left Cardwell and ended up in Virginia. Alison had a feeling that even there she did not prosper, probably finishing up in the stews of Jamestown or some other port.

Maybe there was something inevitable about that, just like the younger sister's going mad, but Alison had a feeling again, feathering the hairs on her arms and the back of her neck, that something else was going on here. Maybe Mary *had* put a curse on them.

Just like in that other, more famous place. The legend of Salem did not end with the witch trials. The judges and the sheriff did not walk away unscathed from courtroom and execution place; they went bearing curses. Many of those involved met untimely ends, so the stories went, and the curses did not finish with them but passed down from generation to generation.

A similar dark stain spread through Beulah's history. With the exception of Cornwell, all the accusers and would-be persecutors had come to a bad end in some way or another. Mary's two main tormentors were dead by the next year's end. Obadiah Wilson, the Witch Finder, choked to death on his own blood. Johnson drowned in shallow water. Indeed, the stain had spread until there was nothing left. Beulah had been obliterated. It didn't appear on any modern map, or any map at all that Alison had managed to find. It had ceased to exist altogether.

Could this have been Mary's work? Could there really have been a curse? Alison rubbed her arms as the goose flesh spread.

"'Bout to lock up, Dr. Ellman."

The security guy's words startled her back to reality.

"'Kay, Lloyd."

It was nonsense, of course. Alison hauled her jacket off the back of her chair. It had gotten chilly, that was all. Most likely the heat had clicked off for the night. She had been studying these Puritans for so long, she was beginning to think like one.

There were logical reasons for every single event. The explanations were evident. Each of these individuals was responsible for his or her own fate, and everyone had to die sometime, of something.

It was not all dark and gloomy. Others in the story had prospered, sometimes in conditions little short of miraculous. Take Jonah and Martha. They had befriended Mary, cared for her, and nothing bad had happened to them, as far as Alison could tell. Jonah had opened an apothecary shop right in Boston, in what is now called the North End. There they had stayed, living out quiet lives in peace and prosperity until both were buried up on Copp's Hill.

The Rivers family, along with Tobias and Rebekah, had experienced far more turbulence in their history. John Rivers had led them clear across the state to the Connecticut River valley, right to the

18

edge of the world then so far explored. Here they had endured all kinds of dangers and difficulties. Rebekah and Tobias had even come under Indian attack in the conflict known as King Philip's War. Their town had been deserted for a time, but they went back. They survived; not only that, they prospered, going on to found quite a dynasty.

Alison had pieced their story together with the help of one of their descendants, and running like a thread all the way through this story was the quilt. It had passed from Martha to Rebekah, and then, according to family lore, it had been handed down through the female line, from daughter to daughter or daughter-in-law. A quirk of family history had led to the quilt's survival, and ten girls in all had received this inheritance. Ten girls growing from child to woman, each in turn fading from maiden to matron, handing on the quilt to a daughter, then aging to crone before death and the grave claimed them and turned them to dust.

The quilt had its very own file alongside all the major players. Alison had information on every one of them now. Everything was cataloged and accounted for, ready for inclusion in the sequel.

If there was ever going to be a sequel.

Working on Cornwell's diary had buoyed her, made her think that she was getting somewhere. Now gloom descended. She was not a quitter, but sometimes she felt like giving up entirely. What was the point in going on with this? The material she'd discovered about the Rivers family, about Martha and Jonah, about Jack Gill—it was interesting, fascinating even, but by itself it was not enough. It could never be enough without Mary. Without her, there could be no second story. Without her there was a void at the center of the whole project.

"Locking up now, Dr. Ellman."

"Be right there, Lloyd."

Alison moved the pointer to shut down her computer. The <u>You have mail</u> icon was still flashing in the corner. She was eager now to finish for the day, but she did not like to put things off and leave them until tomorrow.

To: Alison Ellman
From: Agnes Herne
Subject: Mary Newbury
Dear Ms. Ellman,
A friend lent your book to me. She really liked it and thought I might, too. She was right about that—I read it all the way through without stopping—but there was something that she couldn't possibly know. One of the reasons that I couldn't put it down has to do with Mary, the girl at the center of the story. . . .

Alison sat for a moment, unable to believe what she had read. She even looked away and back again, expecting the words to erase themselves or tumble down to the bottom of the screen.

She read the whole e-mail several times and then got up from her desk and walked around. She went to consult the big wall map of northeastern America, her mind processing information in double time. Mohawk reservation in upper New York State. Her finger went up near the Canadian border. Canada. Mohawk. Iroquois. That put a brand-new spin on everything. She'd thought Native American before, thinking maybe Mary joined up with Jaybird and his band, but she had come up with a total blank—a big nothing. But what if they'd gone to Canada? She'd thought of that too, but without proof of some kind, it would be searching for a needle that might not be there to find. But a link to the Iroquois, to Mohawks? That meant Mary might have passed through Montreal. And that opened up a sudden new wealth of research possibilities. It was not within Alison's province, but that hardly mattered. The knack was knowing where to look, whom to contact. She had friends and colleagues up there. One in particular. She wondered if he'd be on-line now.

She went back to her desk, the beginning of a plan forming itself in her head. But first she had to contact this girl.

To: Agnes Herne
From: Alison Ellman
Subject: RE: Mary Newbury
Hi, Agnes:

Thanks so much for getting in touch! You are the first person to contact me who has promised anything about Mary. We have information on other people involved in her story but nothing on Mary, so anything you have would be a step forward. Would it be possible for you to come here to the Institute and meet with me? Would tomorrow be too soon? Say around 11 a.m.? If this does not suit you, maybe you can suggest a better time.

I am VERY anxious to talk with you—I can't tell you how excited I am about what you have told me.

Looking forward to meeting you.

Best,

Alison Ellman

"Got to set the alarms now, Dr. Ellman. Have to hurry you."

Alison did not look up from her screen. She was already prioritizing websites, collecting threads, composing more messages.

"I could be here all night. So you might as well lock me in. You got coffee?"

"Sure." The guard grinned. "You take it black, right?"

"You got it."

• Agnes •
The Institute Museum

Agnes took a cross-town bus to the Institute, where Alison worked. It was a big colonnaded building set back from a wide tree-lined avenue. Agnes crunched up the graveled drive and mounted the wide steps, not sure whether to go on inside. She'd missed her stop and had to walk back, but she was still early by nearly an hour. She never liked to arrive late for anything, but the journey had taken less time than she had anticipated, and this was on the cautious side of punctuality, even for her. The weather was fine. She could wait outside, sitting on the steps in the spring sunshine, or take a walk around the grounds that led down to the river. Or she could go in and look at some of the exhibits. The Institute was famous for its Native American collection.

Agnes offered the price of admission to the girl selling tickets and thought to mention her appointment with Alison Ellman, but the girl, a grad student perhaps, barely glanced up from the book she was reading. So Agnes paid her five dollars and went to wander through the rooms marked North American Indian Collection.

A gallery ran around the top of the large wood-paneled room. They had stuff from everywhere, from Mexico to the Arctic, but the exhibits had not been thrown together or mixed up in any arbitrary way, as they might have been at one time, but had been arranged carefully in order. The visitor was invited to enter a twisting labyrinth that showed the history of the native peoples from the earliest times to the present. Text panels on the wall explained each era.

Agnes found she'd stopped to read the boards describing the impact of different waves of European arrivals as they flowed across the country. She could hear her aunt talking in her head again.

"Never mind they pretty near wiped us all out. Never mind that. Just as long as they tell us just how it came about, guess that makes it all right."

Aunt M would have some kind of angry comment ready, whatever the curators tried to say.

Agnes went through, following the exhibition in the direction indicated. This took her past northeast woodlands tribes and artifacts once owned and handled by her own people: clubs and tomahawks, strings of wampum, split-ash baskets, birch-bark boxes, cradle boards, and canoe paddles. She went on through goods belonging to other nations, past baskets from the Cherokee, shields and painted tipis from the people of the Plains, then to Navajo textiles and Zuni ceramics, until she found herself under giant totem poles from the northwestern states.

Agnes could hear Aunt M sounding off even louder now.

"Most of this stuff has been got by cheating or stealing, or else it's been looted right out of the ground. They got the remains, too, you know, thousands of 'em, all belonging to our ancestors, stored away in boxes for study, just like a bunch of dinosaur bones."

There were arguments on both sides. The museums saw themselves as holding and guarding a cultural heritage, raising and widening public awareness, facilitating academic and scientific research. None of this cut any ice with Aunt M. She had taken an active part in various campaigns, putting pressure on museums to return their holdings, and with some success. Human remains were no longer on show. There was a growing trend for them to be taken down from the shelves, to be removed from the indignity of lying around in dusty cardboard boxes, stored in compartmentalized trays. The bones of the ancestors were being returned to their homelands for burial, to be put into the earth with proper ceremony.

Artifacts, particularly those with spiritual significance, were also being given back to their rightful owners. Maybe not as fast as Aunt M would like, but the process was happening. Agnes noticed that some sacred objects had been removed from display. There was a little notice explaining the absence of masks and turtle rattles used in the sacred rituals of her own people. A lot of other things were still there, though.

For instance, there was a whole case of kachina dolls from the Southwest. Many people said that they were just that: dolls, carved and fashioned to teach Zuni and Hopi children about the special beings they represented. But these kachinas were old and powerful. They held spirit. Even looking at them seemed disrespectful. These were fetishes and could form part of a medicine bundle, or they could be used in hunt societies and for ceremonies. They didn't just represent a god; they embodied one. Agnes backed away, as though the case were surrounded by a force field. She glanced around at the other people wandering through. Didn't they feel it, too?

She went on past more textiles and pottery, circling back toward the beginning of the exhibition. She stood lost in thought before a glass case of cradle boards and miniature model canoes. A clock chimed in some distant gallery and she looked at her watch. It was nearly time for her appointment.

As she made her way out to the exhibition entrance, an invisible beam or eye set off the low sweet sound of a water drum. The accompanying chants were Haudenosaunee, Iroquois Six Nations. She was hearing the voice of her own people, the People of the Longhouse. What was the song telling her? To go on? Or to go back?

Agnes glanced over at the desk. The girl was busy talking to someone. She could sneak out easily. After all, what *did* she know about Mary? A couple of stories that could be about anyone. It was the objects that went with the stories that made the match possible. Without those, nothing could be proved, and this museum visit had only confirmed what she knew already: her aunt would never allow her to have them, let alone bring them here.

Agnes would have to explain that to Alison Ellman, and how humiliating was that going to be? She turned up her jacket collar and tucked her chin down into her chest. She was partway across the polished wooden floor, making for the heavy glass doors, when a voice from behind her said, "Excuse me? Are you Agnes?"

"I'm Alison Ellman."

The woman coming toward Agnes was maybe in her late twenties and wore casual clothes: a blue shirt and khakis. She was slim and small, shorter than Agnes, and kind of pretty, with short wheat-blond hair.

"How did you know it was me?" Agnes asked.

Alison looked at the young woman in front of her. She was dressed like any student: sneakers, jeans, white T-shirt, denim jacket. She wore an earring in one ear: turquoise beads finished with a feather. Lots of kids wore ethnic jewelry these days, but the beads had a dull finish, suggesting that they were old. She was slender, slight even, still more girl than woman, but she had presence. She stood upright and when she moved it was with graceful ease. She had high cheekbones and clear features; strong brows and a straight nose above a wide, full mouth and a delicately rounded chin. Her skin was the color of clear wild honey. She was tall, taller than Alison thought at first glance, taller than Alison herself. As she inclined her head in greeting, her long hair fell forward, soft and silky, as shiny as a raven's wing. The eyes, though— the eyes were a surprise. They were as gray as the sky on a snowy winter's day.

"I was watching you in the exhibition. You looked at it differently from the other people in there. Apart from that, I just took a pretty good guess. I'm very pleased to meet you, Agnes."

Alison put out her hand and Agnes took it. The girl's hand was long, thin fingered, and strong. Her wrists were circled with power beads and friendship bracelets woven from leather and bright silk thread. Alison made her mind up quickly about people, and she liked this girl; she liked her right away, whatever she did or did not have to say.

"I'm so glad that you could make it. Was the bus OK? No problem finding us? I'm *so* excited about this, you can't guess. It's this way." Alison shepherded Agnes to a door marked No Public Access. "Most of the work here goes on behind the scenes. What you see on exhibition is only a fraction of the whole collection, and our work is, of course, much, much more . . ."

Alison led the way up the stairs, more than aware that she was talking too much already.

Alison's workstation was in one corner of a room banked with modern filing systems and glass-fronted bookcases full of old-looking leather-bound volumes. Alison's area held a computer, a microscope, a light box, and a lamp with a magnifying attachment.

"I'm planning a follow-up to 'the Mary Papers.' I'll show you what I've got so far. I've kind of commandeered this wall."

Agnes followed her down the room past tables piled with document folders and portfolios tied with ribbon. The wall was papered from top to bottom with maps, charts, family trees, computer printouts, photographs, and facsimiles of documents. Yellow Post-it notes covered with small fine lettering dotted the field of print like curling autumn leaves. Agnes read the wall from right to left, then back again, scanning fast but careful not to leave any part out. She knew quite a bit about research and this was excellent work, but she saw more than that. The hand-drawn family trees, the carefully drafted charts, the tiny meticulous printed notes told her that this was a labor of love that bordered on obsession.

"This is a lot of work. Really impressive."

Alison stood, arms folded, peering up at the board through narrow wire-rimmed glasses. She smiled, pleased with the response she had gained.

"I didn't do it on my own. I've had information from all over." She reached forward to readjust a peeling Post-it. "Elias Cornwell is right over here along with what's left of Beulah. The Rivers family is up there alongside the Morse family. There's Jonah and Martha." She nodded to different quarters of the display. "Remember Jack Gill, the boy on the ship? I've even managed to track him down."

"How did you get so much?"

"The response to the book and the website have been excellent—and my own research, of course." Alison laughed. "It is my job, after all. It's not so hard to find out about somebody, even as far back as this. The Commonwealth of Massachusetts is well documented; there are vital records: births, deaths, marriages, along with church records, court records, gravestones, private papers—containing letters if you're lucky. Account books, you can tell a lot from them; probate inventories, wills, what people left behind and to whom and in what quantity; there's also family traditions and superstitions, plenty of stuff. The key is knowing where to look. I owe a great deal of thanks to the Internet, of course, and also the New Englander's love of genealogy."

Alison laughed and stopped. Her laugh was getting a nervous edge to it. She didn't want to go on too much, sensing that Agnes might be drifting off.

Agnes knew that stuff anyway, so she had been only half listening. She did want to know something about the family tree marked Rivers/Morse. It stretched from one side of the wall to the other. Beginning with Rebekah, fourteen generations spread out and on from her.

"What's that?" She asked, pointing to a single blood-red thread snaking through the branching names.

"It's the quilt. It follows the distaff side, the female line." Alison used a pointer to follow the ribbon along. "Starting with Rebekah and going to her daughter Mary Sarah, and to her daughter, and on and on to the tenth generation and this woman, Eveline Travers Harris."

The red line stopped there, although the tree branched up and off to include three, in some cases four, more names.

"What happened?"

Alison pointed up at the names bracketed with Eveline Travers Harris: husband Clarence Edgar, died in France, 1918; two infant children (Etta May, age 3, and Earl Leonard, age 18 months) died of influenza in 1919.

"Eveline herself lived on. Her death was not recorded until 1981. But she never married again."

"So what happened to the quilt?"

"Seems that Eveline never quite recovered from what had happened to her family. She became reclusive, devoting herself to the making and collecting of quilts and other kinds of needlework. Her death broke the family tradition. Her whole quilt collection, which was by that time extensive and valuable, was sold to a private collector."

"So how did it come to you?"

"The purchaser, J. W. Holden, died several years ago. He collected all kinds of things from the colonial period. On his death, the collection went to the Holden Foundation: this guy was so rich he founded his own museum. Anyway, the quilt was eventually cataloged along with everything else, but the box it was in was wrongly attributed to eighteenth-century craftsmanship. It was some time before someone realized exactly how old the quilt inside was. They didn't feel they could handle it, so they called us for one of our textile conservators to come take a look."

"Uh-huh." Agnes was having a hard time concentrating. She scarcely heard Alison's final words. "Can I see it? The quilt, I mean?"

"Sure. They've finished working on it. Come with me. It's not here; it's in the textile area. I thought you might want to see it. I've had it all set out for you to view."

They went through a storage area accessed via swipe-card-activated, air-locked doors. Machines hummed and little red lights winked high on the walls. Alison took Agnes through another door to a room where the textile conservators worked.

The quilt was laid ready for them on a table.

Alison put on cotton gloves before she handled the quilt. She touched it gently, stroking and petting it, as though it were some live slumbering thing. Agnes knew something of the art of quilt making from her aunt and her grandmother. But this was nothing like the bright multicolored patterned spreads created by them. It was not patchwork but all of a piece. The fabric was coarser, rougher than Agnes had imagined it to be. The color was not drab exactly, but the deep blue had dulled to faded indigo. The quilting skill and patterning lay in the stitching, which was hard to see against the dark background. Agnes peered closer. She knew not to touch.

"These are the patterns."

Alison unfolded a large sheet of paper. Released from monochrome, the motifs burst into life: ferns sprouted, feathers fanned, flowers bloomed, leaves intertwined. The designs were strong but simple, like the bead embroidery of Agnes's people. There were other patterns, too; hearts and knots and abstract spirals surrounded stylized depictions of a cabin in a grove of tall pines and a ship at full sail.

"Wow! I'd never have guessed—" Agnes shook her head, the impact the quilt was making on her too hard to express.

"Impressive, isn't it?" Alison smiled. "It's hard to say how precious this is, even without the diary inside it. And valuable? Even the conservator here had never seen a quilt this old before. You could not put a price on it."

Alison spoke on, describing the quilt's provenance, while Agnes continued to stare at the motifs. They were not just a random collection of patterns. They told a story complete with characters: Rebekah and Tobias, Martha and Jonah, even Jaybird. They were all here right along with Mary.

"... like pepper from a peppershaker."

"Excuse me?"

Alison smiled. "I'm sorry to be so boring."

"You aren't at all." Agnes shook her head, embarrassed. "I'm having a problem concentrating, that's all. It's a lot to take in, I guess. What were you saying?"

"At some point the back of the quilt sustained damage. The material the conservator found there was relatively recent and only tacked down, in some places even pinned, and the pins were rusting, damaging the original fabric. It wasn't an integral part of the piece, so she decided to remove it. When she took the back away, that's when she found the diary. The original backing had been scorched, making the fabric brittle, causing weak spots and holes to develop. The diary was hidden in the batting, the wadding between front and back, and it had begun to shake out like . . . ." Alison shrugged, turning her gloved hands palms up.

"Pepper from a peppershaker?" Agnes supplied.

"Exactly. To me, it's like a miracle." Alison smoothed the fabric. "In normal circumstances conservation involves minimum intervention. It would be unethical to interfere or compromise the object. So even if we had *known* the diary was inside, we could not have removed it." She paused again and gave a small smile, as if apologizing already for saying something silly. "It's almost as though it shook itself out. As though it was time. Time to give up the secrets it had kept safe for all that long while. Does that sound crazy to you?"

Agnes shook her head. "Not at all." She looked at the other woman, her turn now to wonder how far to extend her trust. "One time I lost my watch. I put it down and just turned around and it had disappeared. I couldn't find it anywhere. My aunt said, 'It'll come back when it's good and ready.' That's what she believes. To stay lost or be found, it's up to the thing itself to decide."

"I hadn't heard that before, but I guess that's what I think, too. That's why, for me, the quilt is so central. Everything about it is meaningful. Its history, its discovery, everything. That's why I wanted to make it the center of the exhibition." Alison stopped and looked away. The enthusiasm drained from her voice as she added, "Except now I don't think there will ever be an exhibition."

"Why not? You've got a whole heap of stuff."

"Oh, sure. And we've got more than you've seen here and on just about everyone. Except Tom Carter, the old guy who lived in the woods? We've got nothing on him—or Mary." She gave an ironic smile. "Right now, old Tom's not the worry."

Alison was putting on a brave face, but disappointment, anguish even, was clear in her pale blue eyes. Mary was at the center of everything. Without her, all this work, all this research, would come to nothing.

Agnes looked down. She was aware that ever since they'd met, Alison had done most of the talking. Agnes had said almost nothing. Alison was being careful around her, not putting any pressure on her, but she felt the weight of the other woman's expectations. Now was the time to speak up.

"May I see the actual diary?"

"Oh, sure. It's back in the Documents Room. Follow me."

Minutes later Alison laid the sheets on the table, fanning them out in front of Agnes, angling the light so that it was easier for her to see.

"Each individual sheet was conserved and then photographed. The facsimiles are easier to handle. The papers were folded to fit along the channels made by the quilting or into pockets created by the stitching." Alison pointed to lines of wear on the photographed pages. "Some were literally in fragments and had to be pieced together." She moved lightly over the endless hours of painstaking work this had entailed. "After that, the pages were photographed and ready for transcription. The writing was a dream to work out, so that turned out to be the easy part. When we were through doing that, we had to figure out some kind of sequence. The papers didn't exactly come out in page order." Alison stopped, fearing she was losing Agnes. She was talking too much again, out of fear, out of nervousness, as a means of postponing disappointment. "Would you like to see the actual diary?"

"Yeah, I would. Very much."

The pages were kept in individual files, each one cased in a plastic wallet to protect paper that had darkened with age and was crumbling at the folds and margins, as brittle and fragile as unrolled papyrus.

Alison took out the pocket labeled Page I.

The words were closely packed but not crowded, and they looked orderly on the page. The writing was a remarkably uncluttered cursive italic, elegantly executed and surprisingly easy to read. It could have been modern. Only the fading ink gave it away as belonging to a different time. The letters were small but evenly formed. The pen strokes were firm and cleanly curved. Mary had nice handwriting; no wonder Elias Cornwell had wanted her to scribe for him. Apart from the occasional restrained flourish, there was little of the elaborate looping that Agnes had expected to see.

Agnes read to the bottom and then scanned back to the top again. She leaned in to look closer. The page inside the envelope was torn across the corner, so it actually began:

a witch. Or so some would call me . . .

It was time for her to speak.

"Our history is very different from yours." She looked up at Alison. "Or maybe I should say our way of recording it is different. We don't have so much of this." She indicated the pages in front of her and the other boxed materials stacked around. "Very little was written down until recently. But there are stories.

"Each teller tells the story as though it is within their own memory. My aunt used to tell me stories that sounded like they happened to her when she was a young girl, but they were told to her by her grandmother, who had heard them from her grandmother, and so on. That's how the family history accumulates."

"And one of these stories could be about Mary?" Alison hardly dared to breathe.

"I think so. It's hard to work out dates, because it's not as though time is stretched in a long line like so." Agnes threw her arms wide. "It's more as if it's all of a piece. Past, present, future going around and around." She brought her hands together and made a hoop, touching thumb to thumb, forefinger to forefinger. "It's as if the past is out there somewhere and events are still happening, but in a place that we can't access."

"So what is this story? The one you think might be about Mary?"

"It is about a woman who came from someplace else and was adopted into the tribe. She had two sons: one dark, one fair with yellow hair. One son became a renowned warrior, a chief. The other . . ." Agnes frowned. "I guess it doesn't say what happened to him. Anyway, some said she came to the people from Rahwehras, the Thunderer, because she came out of a storm, and she came at a time when the people were sick. She helped to heal them and stayed with them, a powerful medicine woman." Agnes frowned again. "There's some more, I think, but I can't remember it."

"What makes you think she was Mary?"

"There is a mystery surrounding where she came from, and some of the legends say she had eyes that were gray like mine, the color of smoke. The eyes were the first thing I read that made me think there could be a connection. But there's other stuff, too, a whole bunch of clues. My aunt has a box. It's about so big." Agnes linked her hands again to describe a circle. "It's made of bark and decorated with embroidery. I used to study it when I was a kid. It has little knots of white flowers with a line of red strawberries creeping around the edges, and in the lid is sweet grass. Gives a really good scent when you open it—not that I was supposed to open it."

"How old was it?" Alison asked.

"Hard to tell, but it had been made to contain medicine objects. Even Sim—he's my older cousin, kind of like my big brother; he always took the lead when we did daring stuff—even he said not to touch it. But you know kids, right?" For nearly the first time she smiled. It was like sudden sun on a cloudy day. Alison was dazzled. "The more you tell them not to, the more they're going to want to do it."

"So you opened it?" Alison smiled in reply.

Agnes grinned. "You bet. I remember it had this little toggle thing that was tough to undo. My hands were trembling so much I nearly spilled the stuff."

"So what was inside?"

"Not a whole lot, not as far as I was concerned. I was really disappointed. I don't know what I'd been hoping for: gold coins maybe, or diamond rings. What I found was medicine stuff—a bear's claw necklace, wampum strings, and a ratty old neckpiece; but there was also a ring that did look like gold and a locket black with tarnish. In one corner of the box there was a little curled-up bit of paper, worn kind of soft and furry so it looked like doeskin. I didn't pay it much attention once I'd checked it out for secret writing, but now I've been thinking. It could be a corner. That corner." She pointed down at the plastic pocket on the table. "The one that's missing."

"Was there any lettering on it?"

"Like I said"—Agnes shook her head—"no secrets."

"I could see if there is." Alison switched on the magnifying lamp. "Read it, too. There's all kinds of stuff I could do. Match the tear. Match the paper. If we could do that, we could prove she was one and the same person!"

"I think I'm right." Agnes's dark brows drew together. "But I've only ever seen these things once. I'd have to see them again to be sure."

"Maybe you could bring them here?"

Agnes shook her head. "The box and its contents are highly sacred. I doubt my aunt would allow them out of her hands."

"I could see her. Ask her if she—"

Agnes put her hands up to damp down Alison's growing excitement. "I think I better go see her first. She can be kind of stubborn, and she doesn't have a whole lot of time for museums, I'm afraid."

"Do you think you might persuade her?" Alison looked worried.

"I'll try."

"That would be wonderful! You've no idea what this means to me, Agnes. How important it is. How soon can you make the trip?"

"Oh, I don't know . . ."

"You don't want to miss school?"

"It's not so much that. It's a long way by bus"—she gave an embarrassed shrug—"and there's the fare. I'm kind of low on funds right now."

"That's no problem. I'll take you."

"Hey, no!" Agnes was even more embarrassed. "There's no need. I didn't mean that. I wouldn't want to put you to any trouble."

"It would be no trouble. As for need? I think there is. For me, at least. I'm owed time off, and I'm pretty much my own boss. I was thinking of taking a trip to Montreal and maybe Quebec. I've got friends up there, and a colleague at McGill is looking up sources for me. I could drop you off."

"It'd be out of your way—"

"Not by much. I want to see what's up there. The French kept far more detailed records than the English, particularly with regard to indigenous peoples. Mary may have gone to Canada." Alison's voice gathered intensity. "If she did, there could be some trace of her. I've nothing else so it's worth a try. I have to give it a shot."

"If you're sure . . ."

"Different route, that's all."

Agnes took a moment to decide. She had not shared all her doubts about Aunt M. In some ways it could be easier for Alison, because books don't have tongues like knives, and libraries do not as a general rule flat out refuse to give you information.

"OK," Agnes said at last. "As long as you're going that way, I guess I might as well come with you."

After all, a ride was a ride, Agnes reflected as she took the bus back to the campus. She would have to go home sometime, and the sooner she went now, the better. The true extent of Aunt M's stubbornness was not the only thing she had failed to share with Alison. She had told her nothing about the vision. Last night Agnes had hardly slept. Mary had come to her dreams and would not leave her be. She was there all the time now; sleeping or waking, it didn't matter. Whatever Agnes did, wherever she was, her mind was always slipping back to the girl.

She was the reason that Agnes had set out so early, out of nervousness, as if she were on a first date. Then, on the bus, she had filled Agnes's thoughts so entirely that she missed the stop and had to walk back. What had Alison said—"You looked at things differently"? Agnes saw the truth of that. It was as if her gaze was being directed by someone else.

Agnes had felt herself zoning out while she was with Alison. At some points her attention had been strongly focused to the exclusion of almost everything, but at other times she was hardly listening. She must have seemed ill-mannered, and that wasn't like her one bit. She meant no disrespect to Alison. She shared her fascination. She knew how Alison felt because she was beginning to feel that way herself. In the short time they'd been together, she had sensed the older woman's hunger for information, her fear, and her elation.

Talking to Alison, looking at all the stuff, soothed the spot, but the ache did not stop. Agnes also had to find out what Mary's story was. Even that might not be enough. For Alison it was still some kind of intellectual exercise, but for Agnes it was on a different level. Agnes sprinted down the bus, in danger of missing her stop again. She was involved in a way she did not fully understand. Getting Mary out of her head might take her to places she did not want to go.

Agnes knew before she walked through the door that Aunt M had called, so it was no particular surprise to find the light on the answering machine blinking on and off. That kind of thing had happened before. If she had psychic ability, it had confined itself to minor synchronicity. Until yesterday.

"Hi, Agnes. It's me. If you're there, pick up. . . . OK, so you're not there. I called to say go see the woman. Then come see me and I mean *now*."

Agnes smiled. Aunt M knew already. Her psychic sense was at a much higher level. Agnes need not have worried about what to say. She thought the message was finished, but it went on.

"Oh, and until you get here, make sure you wear the earring."

Agnes's hand went to her ear to find the earring already there. She must have put it in this morning without even thinking. She knew what it meant. These beads had power; her aunt had brought them back from the desert and made the earring for her. The brown-barred feather was from *teiakoiatahkwas*, the hawk, a spirit feather there to protect her. But from what? Mary could not mean to harm her, could she?

• Alison and Agnes •
On the Road

"All set?"

"Sure."

Agnes threw her bag into the back and swung herself into the passenger seat of Alison's little car.

"Pretty much an easy drive," Alison said as she
pulled into the traffic. "We take the Mass Pike and
turn right."

They were strangers to each other, with many
miles to travel together. Agnes felt uncomfortable in
the sudden intimacy of the car interior.

"I brought some stuff you might want to look
through." Alison did not take her eyes off the road.
"In the door pocket next to the maps."

Agnes fished out a couple of files and began to
study them right away. Having something to read
meant she didn't have to talk.

She went through Alison's transcription of Elias Cornwell's diaries and then went on to the file marked Jonah and Martha Morse.

When she'd finished, she turned to Alison. "Do you think they ever met?"

"In Boston, you mean? I guess it's possible. There's no mention of it, but that doesn't mean it didn't happen. There's just so much we can never know."

"I wonder what he'd have said, Elias Cornwell; I wonder what he'd have said to them? He'd be kind of embarrassed—don't you think?"

"Nothing, is my guess. Beulah was not a good time for him. I think he'd prefer to ignore the whole business. Draw a veil over it."

Agnes nodded. She thought that way, too. She opened the Rivers family file. Alison checked the road signs as they loomed up and over their heads.

"We're following pretty much the same route the Riverses would have taken all those years ago. They would have taken the Long Bay Path, an old Indian track leading clear across to the Connecticut Valley. The quilt must have gone the same way, loaded on the back of a cart." Alison waved a hand out the window at the six-lane highway and the fast-flowing traffic. She laughed as a giant tanker rolled up and past. "Kind of different, huh?"

"I guess."

The road was more than a trackway now, and

monster trucks had taken over from bullock carts, but trees still lined the route either side for mile after mile. Sometimes the trees gave way to show other vistas—hills, for example—but pretty soon the trees would close in again. Signs of habitation were relatively few: rooftops glimpsed from a rise, white spires poking through the canopy. Traveling the green corridor made Alison feel timeless.

"Huh?"

"I said, turnpike coming up."

Alison looked up. They were nearly in New York State. She'd driven almost a hundred miles without really noticing.

"Maybe we better stop. I need to check the map."

"There's a place up ahead."

Alison pulled over and took the next exit.

"You want coffee? You hungry? Do you want to eat?"

"Iced tea, please. No, I'm not hungry. Thanks all the same."

"Bought you a muffin anyway." Alison came over to the place Agnes had chosen to sit. The traffic droned on, even through the thick plate glass.

Agnes crumbled her muffin, eating it slowly bit by little bit. Then she sat back and gazed out of the window, her fingers tugging at the earring she wore in her right ear.

"I like the earring," Alison commented. "Meant to tell you yesterday."

"Oh, thank you." Agnes smiled uncertainly and put her hand down in her lap. She could hardly tell Alison she hadn't even known she was wearing it then. She doubted that the other woman would understand.

"Where did you get it?" Alison sipped her coffee.

"Oh, er, Aunt M made it with beads she brought back when she went to the desert one time."

"Aunt M? This is the one you're going to see?"

"Yeah."

"What was she doing in the desert?"

"She goes to stuff—powwows, tribal meetings— she travels all over."

"So what does she do?"

"She's a medicine woman." Agnes hoped to make it sound like an everyday job, like working in a gas station or something.

She did not succeed.

"You didn't tell me!" Alison put down her cup and stared at Agnes. "That's fascinating! What does it involve, exactly? I've always wanted to know."

"She's, uh, a healer, an expert in native herbs and healing methods. She has her own business. She even sells on the Internet now. Sim set up a website for her last year. She has other power as well, aside from healing. Spiritual power. She spent years studying under different people, gaining knowledge, learning the traditional ways. She teaches, too. There's lots of interest now—people come to her for spiritual development, to go on a vision quest, or if they need spiritual guidance."

"I see. A pretty powerful lady."

Agnes nodded. "It's her life's work, I guess. It takes her everywhere, up into Canada and down to Mexico."

"That where she got the turquoise?"

"No. More like Arizona; she has friends among the Navajo. Or maybe Nevada—she goes there sometimes."

"She has friends there?"

"Yes, and . . ."

"And?"

"My mom." It was out before Agnes could stop herself from saying it. "They're sisters, but very different."

"Your mom? She doesn't live on the reservation?"

"No." Agnes shook her head. "She's in Vegas."

"Las Vegas! Hey! What's she do there?"

"She's a croupier." Agnes frowned to dampen the excitement her words were creating. "Sounds glamorous, but it isn't."

"I didn't know . . ."

"Why should you?" Agnes looked at her watch and stood up. "Hadn't we better go?"

"Yeah, you're right."

Alison followed Agnes out. Without meaning to, she'd stepped over some kind of line between them. They were back to being strangers traveling in the same car.

Agnes picked out another file and began reading as Alison negotiated the turnpike and took the turnoff to Albany.

"How'd you find this stuff about Jack Gill?"

"Huh?" Alison was in the driving zone again.

"Jack Gill, how'd you find out about him?" Agnes waved a file marked Jack Gill.

"Accident. I was over in Nantucket. With a friend, just for the weekend. I hadn't even thought of following up any of the people mentioned in Mary's account of her life. Just transcribing the diary pages was enough. I knew that I wanted to make them into a book, but that would be about Mary. What happened afterward, to Mary herself, or anyone else for that matter, hadn't really crossed my mind.

"I was down by the harbor when the name jumped right out at me: Richard A. Gill, Ship's Chandler."

"What did you do?"

"Went in, of course. You know, it's funny, but I felt as though I'd been guided there."

"By providence?"

Alison grinned. "Exactly. I'd just finished the section of 'the Mary Papers' that dealt with Mary's meeting Jack on the ship."

"Do you think they ever met again? It would be great if they did, don't you think?"

"Yeah, but that would be like in a novel. In real life that just doesn't happen." Alison hit the gas and overtook a line of local traffic. "You can trust me on that one. Those two never met again. I know that for sure."

"How? How could you?"

"It's all in the file."

Agnes took that as a cue to read for a while.

"So he *didn't* die like Mary saw in her vision, all smashed up by a monster whale?"

"No." Alison shook her head. "He died in his bed."

Agnes turned sharply, the disappointment clear on her face. "So where does that put the prophecy?"

"That's what I thought. First time out and Mary doesn't even make it to first base." Alison smiled in sympathy. "I didn't want the old guy to see it, but I was devastated."

"So first time around, she fails?"

"Read on and you'll see. I guess precognition is an inexact science."

"This lucky piece the Gills carried? The one they always took to sea with them. It was . . ."

"Half a silver coin."

"Like the one he gave Mary?"

"Other half, I'd say. Looked like it anyway."

"You *saw* it?"

"Uh-huh. He had this kind of little museum. It was right there in a glass case on a little velvet cushion."

"What was it like?"

"Smaller than I expected, and worn wafer thin from all those vest pockets. It was drilled in one corner as if it had been hung from a cord or chain."

"This Richard Gill, did he get it out for you to see?"

"Yes, he did. He opened the case with a tiny key."

It was hard to describe what Alison had felt when he reached in and took it out. The rush of emotion had surprised even her as she held this whisper of silver in the palm of her hand. It was so light and thin; there was no sign left of a head or letters—any embossed pattern had worn off altogether. She had held it for just a moment before giving it back, relieved to have the silver token out of her hand. She was afraid it might melt from the heat of her skin, afraid it might crumple. It seemed too fragile to be metal, too thin, as frail as a winter leaf.

"I've never been there," Agnes said. "To Nantucket."

"Haven't you? You'll have to come with me next time. Meet Richard. You'd love him. He's a real sweetie."

Alison stopped herself from going on, thinking the girl might refuse her invitation, but she didn't.

"Yes, I'd like that." Agnes smiled at her. "It'd be good."

• Alison and Agnes •
The Old Mohawk Trail

They were coming up to a point where decisions had to be made about the best route to take. The scenic choice would take them up through the Adirondacks. The faster option followed the interstate.

They stopped again to eat and look at the map.

"This route from Albany to Buffalo takes the old Mohawk trail." Agnes traced it with her finger. "Did you know that?"

Alison shook her head.

"It's kind of a weird thing to think about. Like you were saying about the trail the Rivers family took." Agnes went on as she studied the map. "These highways follow routes already worn deep into the land before Europeans even got here."

"I was thinking of taking that road anyway." Alison smiled. "That's decided me. Come on. There's still a long way to go."

*   *   *

"Have you always lived on the reservation?" Alison asked.

"No," Agnes answered, and then, thinking that was maybe too abrupt, added, "I used to just vacation there, but one year, around about when I was eight or nine, the vacation became permanent."

"What happened?"

Agnes was silent for a while, as if deciding whether to speak or not. The highway still stretched on for mile after mile.

"You don't have to say. . . ." Alison didn't want to crowd the girl.

"It's OK. Mom and Dad split up. He was in the army and we moved around a lot. When he left the army, he couldn't get a job. He and my mom used to fight about it all the time. One day he went out saying he was going to look for work and didn't come back. My mom sent me to stay with Gram and Aunt M while she figured out what to do and" —Agnes shrugged— "I didn't go back. Seemed I didn't fit in with the plans Mom had. She took off for Vegas, got a job in a casino, and I stayed on the reservation with Gram, Aunt M, and Sim."

"Do you see her? Your mom, I mean?"

"Oh, sure," Agnes lied. "My dad, too."

"But you don't live with either of them?"

"I prefer not to. Dad's got a new wife. She's OK,

57

but . . ." Agnes shrugged again. "My mom? Well, I'm too old for her, I guess."

"How's that? Too old for what?"

"I make *her* look old, to be more accurate. She had me when she was very young, but an eighteen-year-old daughter gives you away when you're trying to pass for thirty."

Agnes scrunched down in her seat, folding her arms around herself, conversation over. There were no more files to read, so she stared out of the passenger window at the passing scene. Alison probably thought she was asleep. Agnes let her think it. She did not intend to sleep if she could possibly help it, but she was done talking for the moment.

All those files. All those people. What if she herself was reduced to a file, what would it consist of? What did she have to show for a life so far lived? A birth certificate, school reports, a high school diploma, a bunch of grades and SAT scores. That would be about it.

What of the memories that couldn't be measured like that? Her mother's scent when she went out: perfume mixed with cigarettes. Her father's morning smell of after-shave and fresh-laundered poplin. Her happiness when they were together. Her misery when he left. The way she'd waited and waited, all the while knowing he wasn't coming back. He'd smiled that day and called her "Short Stuff," just like always, but she'd seen the tears in his eyes and he couldn't look at her as he waved goodbye.

What about the places they'd lived? Her file would contain quite a bunch of addresses. Army bases where the houses were all set out as neatly as a parade ground. Row houses that smelled of damp. Ratty apartments with narrow halls and thin walls and steps out front to go sit when the quarreling got too much to bear.

All the schools she'd attended had merged in her mind into one long corridor. She'd rarely stayed long enough to make a friend. Now all the faces jostled together, as anonymous as the rush hour. The mean kids and the nice ones. The ones who thought she was Hispanic; the ones who knew she wasn't; the ones who didn't care either way. The kids who treated her like a breathing museum exhibit, expecting her to do dances and bring war bonnets to show-and-tell, when all she wanted to be was a regular kid, just like everybody else. In one place even the teachers were racist. Her mother had taken her out straightaway. Agnes had been proud of her that day.

After Dad had left, Agnes thought they'd be OK together, her and Mom. That was why it had hurt so bad to be left on the reservation. She'd taken it really hard. She remembered the exact time she found out that Mom was not coming back for her. It was on the day appointed and she was out on the porch, listening

59

for the car. It was late, almost night. She'd been watching all day. The cars went up and past, and none slowed down to turn into the yard. All the stars were out by the time Aunt M called her into the house. She could still taste the anger, bitter on her tongue like a mouthful of copper. She'd known before Aunt M spoke. Maybe she did have power after all.

Her anger grew, making her blind to everything. She hated the reservation. She wouldn't speak to Aunt M and Gram, but they were both women of wisdom and patience; they knew she'd come around, so they set to wait her out. Meanwhile Agnes fought every kid in her class who even looked at her funny. Sim made her stop that. She'd gotten herself surrounded by big kids: the brothers and sisters of her classmates had finally caught up with her. Sim had come up behind her, and she thought he'd fight beside her. Instead he wrapped his arms around her, binding her fists with his.

"You can't beat the whole world, Agnes," he'd said to her. "You got to know when to fight and when not to, and this time I advise you to quit. Any of these kids done stuff to you?"

Agnes shook her head.

"You do stuff to them?"

Agnes shook her head more vehemently.

"To their brothers and sisters?"

It took a while, but Agnes nodded.

"That case, I'll talk to them. You go on home now."

Sim had saved her that time, and plenty of times after. He'd even squired her to the prom when her date failed to show up.

That was a life, not dates and records, certificates and papers. In Agnes's mind the reasons for taking the trip had begun to change. The objects that Alison wanted so badly were ceasing to be the major concern. To Agnes they had become just that: trinkets, inanimate bric-a-brac. Even if they had belonged to Mary, so what? She had to know more than they would be able to tell. What mattered, really mattered, was the story, and how was she going to access that? There was only one way, and for that she had to prepare herself mentally, conserve her energy.

• Agnes •
The Reservation

Alison drove on past the sign that said they were on reservation land. They were in a separate nation now, and this took them outside certain state law and tax systems—sales tax, for example. Alison took advantage of that by filling up at the first in a line of gas stations that lay along the road. She dropped Agnes here and turned the car around. She still had a long drive to Montreal and was anxious to press on, but she'd scribbled down a list of contact numbers for Agnes to call after she'd talked to her aunt.

Agnes took the paper and stuffed it in her pocket as she watched the red taillights fade away. It was kind of strange to be on her own again, and it was cold outside the warmth of the car. She began to walk toward a group of buildings centered around a truck stop: a smoke shop selling discount cigarettes and a couple of small gift shops stocked with Native American souvenirs. Tax-free goods were a big draw. Folks who stopped by for those could be tempted to buy gift items also. One of these other stores belonged to Aunt M: Nature's Way: Natural Medicine and Herbal Healing—Miriam Lazare. But it was dark.

Agnes turned away from Aunt M's store and thought to go into one of the tourist places; she knew people there, but at the door she turned aside. Her aunt's house was not far, and she didn't feel like talking to anyone else right now. There was a distance between her and everything around her. Her head was filled with a low-grade background buzz that would not go away. Even her vision seemed distorted, as if she was looking through Vaseline-smeared lenses.

When Agnes got to her aunt's place, the lights were out. Sighing, she leaned her head against the side of the porch. She had not been expecting that. She let herself in with her key and looked around. There was no one home, but a note taped to the refrigerator told her to go to the casino.

What was she doing there? Agnes had long given up trying to figure out Aunt M, best not even to speculate. She just shouldered her pack and headed off down the road to where the casino sign spilled candy-pink light into the darkness.

Nation status also put the reservation outside of

state gambling laws, and the casino did big business now. Agnes walked past the vehicles lining up for valet parking and on to the main entrance.

She recognized the guy at the door as Rickey. She'd dated him briefly in her last year in high school. Inquiries about her aunt got a puzzled expression, but he told her Sim was in. He'd know where Aunt M was.

Rickey held the heavy glass doors for Agnes and she went in. Rows of slot machines lay in front of her, each bank topped with dollar signs: American one side, Canadian the other. No one took the slightest notice as she passed. Eyes stared straight at the lit-up, flashing squares, checked the spinning reels. Fingers worked on buttons; hands moved from cups of coins to slots and back again. It was a quiet night, so far anyway, and the atmosphere was as subdued as the lighting. The only sound was from the machines bleeping and the occasional chunk, chunk, chunk of a payout. The blackjack stations were even quieter, each in its own pool of light, some empty, some occupied.

No one turned to look at her; the gamblers did not even speak to one another. The task at hand took up all their interest and concentration. There was a tension in the air—she could feel it. Making and losing money was a serious business.

Agnes trod the pistachio-green carpet, following

the lighted pathways past the crap tables and the roulette wheels, making for the area at the back where poker was played.

Sim would be here. Poker was his game. He was much admired. People would stop by just to see him deal, see him handle the cards in his easy left-handed style. Agnes remembered the tricks he used to show her out on the porch when they were kids. The way he could make the cards ripple and flow like one continuous unit. "Watch real carefully," he'd say, but she could never watch closely enough to see how he did it, how he could make a card appear inside your pocket, how he could pluck it from behind your ear.

Now he made a living from it. Poker was a game that required skill; it was not like playing slots. No tricks were allowed, no cheating either, but he'd kept his conjuror's sleight of hand and ability to distract. He could always read the other guy, anticipate his thinking.

He won, too. Not here—that would be against the rules—but when he went visiting other places: Vegas, Jersey City, or other nations with gambling operations, like Foxwoods or Turning Stone. Sim went with his uncle Jeb, who ran the casino here, and he generally sat in on a game or two. He knew how to balance gain against loss. "You gotta quit while you're ahead and that can be hard, but that's what you have to do." He generally got up from the table with more than he took to it, and he was generous with the money he gained in this way. He'd given some to Agnes for her college fund.

Agnes could see him from across the room. He was wearing the casino uniform green tux jacket, a gray dress shirt, its white frill front bordered with black, and a western-style string tie. His long black hair was tied back in a ponytail, accentuating his knife-blade cheekbones and thin-faced handsomeness. He'd grown a mustache since Agnes saw him last, a line on his upper lip not much wider than his tie. It looked as if it had been drawn on with eyebrow pencil. It made him look older—she guessed that was why he'd done it—but was wrong for his face. His tilted black eyes did not as much as flicker in her direction as she approached the table. The copper skin of his brow creased in deeper concentration. The cards took all his attention.

In fact, Sim had seen her as soon as she'd come in, although he made no sign of it. He dealt. He checked the bids, no bids, he checked the cards being picked up and put down, and he checked her out. She was thin. Too thin, tired, and troubled looking. Kind of jittery, like she was on something, but knew that would not be the case, not with Agnes.

She knew better than to interrupt when he was working. He was due off in fifteen minutes. He would be free to speak with her then. Her business was not with him but with his mother. He could sense her agitation from clear across the room.

"Your cousin's here," the waitress whispered in his ear as she passed drinks to the customers.

"I know it. Tell her I'll be over when I finish up here."

When Brad took over as dealer, Sim eased himself up from his place at the table and headed over in Agnes's direction.

"You're too young to be back here. Over twenty-one only. How did you get in?"

"Used to date one of the doormen." Agnes drew on the condensation beading the sides of her glass.

"Which one?"

"Rickey."

"Lacrosse Rickey?"

"That's him."

Sim nodded, as if taking in this information. Agnes scowled. He was nearly eight years older and protective of her, as if he were her brother. Sometimes she liked it, but it didn't give him the right to give ratings to the guys she dated.

"I'm looking for Aunt M." She turned her glass around and around on its coaster, setting the ice clinking like little silver bells.

"Well, she ain't here. You know what she thinks about the casino."

"I thought she was all for it."

"Says she prefers the old bingo days, that they were more fun."

"What about the money it generates? Gambling is helping to pay me through college."

"Yeah, I know, I know, and for medicine and housing, a place for the old folks to go. But there are plans for more expansion, and she worries where that will take us. She wants to know how long before we all fall to squabbling and fighting like a pack of dogs over a pile of meat, or before some real big hound comes along and drives us all off."

"Do you think that'll happen?"

"You can't stay still." Sim shrugged. "If we don't do it, somebody else will."

"She been active about it?"

"Let's say her views are known."

"That where she is? At a meeting or something?"

Sim shook his head. "She's up at the lake."

"Looking Glass? What's she doing there?"

"Waiting for you. I gotta take you. You set? Finish your drink. We need to go. Gotta get something first, though."

He stood up and led her past the gaming tables, down through an avenue of slots to the smoke shop.

"Carton of Marlboros, please, Denise."

The woman behind the counter pulled one down for him. He passed it to Agnes.

"I don't smoke." Agnes gave him a puzzled look.

Sim laughed. "They ain't for you. They're for her. You gotta give tobacco, remember? When you go see the medicine woman, tobacco is the traditional gift. I take it you're not just here on a family visit?"

Agnes shook her head.

"So put them in your pack and let's go."

She shrugged and followed him to the parking lot.

"How'd you get here, anyway?" Sim asked as he unlocked the doors to his battered, mud-spattered pickup.

"Woman called Alison Ellman gave me a ride."

"All the way from Boston? Some ride."

"She said she didn't mind."

"Where's she now?"

"She went on to Montreal."

"She must like to drive. What she do?"

"She works in a museum." Agnes grinned at Sim's expression. "You wouldn't think it to look at her. She's different from the average."

"She cool?"

"Yes. I guess she is."

Sim nodded, taking that in. "Excuse the mess," he added as Agnes maneuvered herself into the passenger seat. "Me and some of the boys took a trip up to Kahnawake."

Agnes cleared the empty candy wrappers and chip bags and found a place for her feet among the crushed and crumpled soda cans that littered the floor. Sim took off from the casino parking lot, and it wasn't long before the reservation sign loomed up and passed. The scattered houses were thinning, the pools of porch light placed more sparsely. Once or twice a dog barked at their passing, but they were heading into darkness, the only ones on the road. The night was cold, and Sim had turned up the heater. Agnes struggled out of her jacket. He'd also turned up the music. Some local band, Native hip-hop: a soft, insistent voice, merging and emerging, backed by what could be a water drum. The effect was kind of hypnotic. Agnes made her jacket into a pillow and stared out the window. The moon was rising. A sliver of moon, white as bone, shone through the bare-leafed birches. It flashed in and out of view, in and out, in out, now you see it, now you . . .

"Hey, Agnes, you like this music? Agnes?"

When Sim got no reply the second time, he looked over to see how she was doing. She seemed to be sleeping. So he turned the volume down, his quick fingers fluttering to the rhythm of the background beats as he spoke softly along with the track.

• Mary •
The Snowstorm

Movement behind the snow's swirling curtain, a shape forming, gray on gray. It looked like a dog, leaping this way, that way. I thought it was Tom back again, but this creature was bigger in the chest and head, the muzzle longer, the eyes smaller, the space between them broader. This was no dog. This was a wolf. Great paws reared and fell, throwing up puffs of powdery snow. She was female; I saw her dugs as she pounced again and again, seeking some small creature, a rabbit or a mouse perhaps, trapped beneath the surface. She was toying with it, waiting to seize it, to snap its neck between her long white teeth.

I blinked the snow from my eyelids, trying to see better, and she, alert to the smallest of movements, left off her pouncing and came forward. The red tongue hung from her open mouth. Her breath plumed in the freezing air. Suddenly I knew. There was no mouse, no rabbit. I was the hunted one. She had come for me.

She looked at me with yellow eyes, head to one side, as if deciding whether to kill me now or later. I wished for now. I beckoned her to me. I would rather die fast than slow.

She approached bit by little bit, crouched low to the ground, like a dog herding sheep. Finally she was in front of me. I thought she would take me. Now. I could feel her breath, hot on me, smell the rankness of it. I closed my eyes, ready for the bite. It never came. Instead of ripping out my throat, she licked my face again and again. Her rough tongue melted the ice glaze from my cheeks, chafing sensation back into skin numbed beyond feeling.

She pulled at me, tugging at my coat, worrying my sleeve. Night was coming on and the snow was getting thicker. She was trying to tell me that it was time to leave, that I must follow her. I tried to stand, but I could not walk. My feet had lost all feeling. They would not hold me. As soon as I tried to take a step, I tumbled headlong in the snow. This happened again and then again, until I felt what little strength I had ebbing from me. She looked at me, head to one side, for all the world as if she was judging the situation, deciding what to do, and all the time the snow fell faster and faster until I could hardly see her. It was as if the very air thickened like a sauce to a seething whiteness.

At last she stood up. I thought she would leave me then, for night was upon us, but she did not. She began to turn around and around, like a puppy chasing its tail. This seemed no weather for games, but then I saw what she was about. She was creating a den, a depression in the snow. She carved deeper and deeper until she had hollowed out a veritable cave. When she was satisfied, she came to the place where I was and began pulling me across.

I could barely crawl but managed to get to the spot. She fussed around me, nosing the snow back and pawing at it, as nice as any goodwife tending to her house. At last she seemed satisfied. She gave a large yawn to show this was so and stretched out as if in readiness for retiring. I pulled my satchel to me and tried to undo the catches, but my fingers were frozen, as unbending and useless as wooden pegs. I had to use my teeth, but at last I got it open. I fished inside for bacon and bread soaked in grease, the provender given to me by Sarah Rivers. I had not thought to eat before now. I unwrapped the cloth and tossed the bacon to her. She did not gulp it down but accepted it carefully, holding it between her paws and chewing at it most delicately. I held the bread between my wrists, tore on the crust of it, getting it into my mouth to melt and chew bit by bit.

Food brought some warmth and strength back into me. She finished the bacon and curled up next to me, her back to the driving snow. I huddled in the shelter of her body, snuggling into her long winter coat, reaching my fingers through the coarse guard hairs of gray and black to clutch the soft fur that lay thick and white underneath. Her body gave off great heat. I held my face against the pale soft fur of her chest and neck and tucked my feet up into her belly. I felt better than I had since I left the settlement. Her warmth brought life to me—and hope.

We lay curled around each other as night fell and the wind howled, forcing the snow up and over us until we became a mere hump, a drift among drifts.

The next thing Agnes knew, a bunch of smoldering twigs was being wafted under her nose. She jerked back with a yell from the pungent burnt-herb smell.

"Easy!" Her aunt held her gently cradled. "Easy now."

"I thought she was just sleeping," Sim said, a deep frown arrowed into his forehead. "I had the heater up high, but when I reached over she was so cold."

"You weren't to know. Help me get her into the house."

Sim carried Agnes in his arms and laid her down on the cot in the corner. He remembered sleeping there when he was a kid. He covered her with the worn patchwork quilt, brushing back a wing of her hair, touching his hand to her cheek. Her skin felt warm now, he noted with relief. She looked so vulnerable; he'd hate it if anything hurt her. His mouth moved in a silent charm to keep her from harm. He loved her like a sister and had been looking out for her ever since she'd move back to the Res, and before that when she used to come on vacation.

Sim stepped away quietly into the middle of the room. The cabin never changed. His great-grandfather had built it solid out of thick-sawed beams caulked between with moss and clay to keep the winter winds away. It comprised one room, with a kitchen lean-to out back and a porch at the front facing down to the dock.

Most of the furniture had been made by the old man as well. Sim had never known him—he had died long before Sim was even born—but Sim always felt especially close to the old guy. He was called Karonhi-ahkeson, Along the Clouds. The name had been passed on at the midwinter naming ceremony; it was Sim's name now. Sim was glad that nothing changed in his cabin. There was no electricity; the interior was lit by soft oil light and heated by a wood stove. He looked around. It could be when he was a kid. It could be a hundred years ago. He liked to think that if the old man stepped back, he would know his place straightaway and still feel right at home.

Aunt M came in carrying Agnes's bag and jacket. She laid the coat over the back of a chair. As she did so, she suddenly bent forward, carefully hooking something off the collar.

"What's that you got?"

"An earring." She held it out for him to see. "Must've got caught when she took off her coat."

She went over to the cot where her niece was sleeping.

"She be OK?" Sim's frown returned.

"She'll be fine now she's with me. You want something? I got coffee on the stove."

"Nah, I'm good. I'm meeting Joanie. I'd better be getting back. Here." He reached into his pocket and took out his cell phone. "I want you to have this." He held up his hand to ward off her protests. "I know you don't want phones up here, but I'd be happier, OK?"

To his great surprise, she took it from him.

"How do you use it?" His mother regarded it suspiciously.

"The way to use it is simple. Press here to switch on, punch in the number, and then press this one, see? Any problems, anything you want, you call. You promise me?"

His mother nodded and put the phone in her pocket.

• Agnes •

Looking Glass Lake, Day One

Agnes woke in a strange bed; the mattress was lumpy, the frame narrow. She put her hand out to grab her watch off the table, and her fingers closed on empty space. She opened her eyes and saw bare boards instead of carpet. She had no idea where she was. Panic grabbed at her stomach; then she looked up. Bundles of sage and braids of sweet grass hung from the shelf above her bed along with a couple of rattles, one made from a gourd, the other from a turtle shell. Right alongside them hung a tobacco pouch made from a whole otter skin, the claws engaged to act as catches, folded nose over chin. Either she'd been transported to some shaman's den, or she was at Aunt M's place.

"How are you this morning?" Aunt M saw she was awake and came over with a cup of some steaming brew. "How many times has it happened?"

Agnes knew what she was talking about.

"Twice. Just before I contacted Alison and on my way here."

She had an idea she was just confirming what Aunt M already knew.

"Drink this." Aunt M handed her the cup. "How are you feeling?"

"Strange." The black herbal tea smelled good but tasted bitter. "Kind of tired. And empty. Like part of me is not really here."

It was hard to explain, but everything seemed flat around her. Her life seemed pale, with no meaning. It was like waking from a dream and wanting to stay dreaming. It was a desire, but more than that, a need. A kind of hunger. Agnes wanted to be back with *her*.

"Hmm." Aunt M sipped her own tea and thought for a minute. "You did right coming to me. She might be kin and mean you no harm, but . . ."

Aunt M did not have to say it; fear and concern showed in her eyes. The dead don't see the value we place on this life. She might just take the girl with her when she left next time. One more episode like that and Agnes might not survive.

"You know why I've come?"

"Sure do. And you know what I'll say, don't you? Can't be close as we are and not know what the other one's thinking on most given subjects."

"So the answer's no?"

Aunt M shrugged. "Depends on what you want. My guess is things have moved on. This Alison woman, she still wants the medicine objects, but you're not sure you want that now. Am I right?"

Agnes nodded. No matter how hard she tried to disguise her thinking, Aunt M always knew.

"In that case, I got to tell you, she's powerful. You can't go unprotected. That's why I put the quilt around you that first time it happened."

"And the earring?"

"That, too."

"How did you know about Mary? Was that more shaman stuff?"

Her aunt cackled. "Not really. Saw that Alison Ellman on the History Channel, talking about this project, asking for information about her. Read the book, too. We got stores up here, you know."

"So you think there could be a connection?"

"Between this Mary and Katsitsaionneh, our own Bringing Flowers? I'd say most certainly. From the story; from what she brought with her. I even held a ceremony using the ring and the locket, figuring that she's kin and if we have the gift of medicine power, it has come from her in no small measure. I thought she might come to me, but instead she went to you."

"Why? Why did that happen?"

Her aunt thought before answering.

"Words are powerful. Hers had been hidden for

all that time. Suddenly they're alive again and out in the world. You are near the age she was when she wrote them; that could be the reason. These dreams you've been having, these visions, how do you know she does not dream of you? What happens in our world can reach into the spirit world, too."

To Aunt M, the spirits of those no longer living were perceptible presences, alive to her in the everyday, the world they inhabited as real as ours.

"She's using me to tell the rest of her story?"

"Maybe she wants to tell her story to you."

Her aunt stood up and beckoned Agnes to follow. They walked out into the waking morning and the clamor of birdcall. Agnes had forgotten how beautiful it was here. The sun had risen through a gap in the hills, and it was shining now down the length of the lake, rendering the mist banks luminous, turning the water to chased silver. Trees crowded the shore. Spruce and firs showed in the lake like reflected shadow. Stands of birch, trunks as bright as platinum, slender branches misted with new leaf, dipped toward the surface of the water like girls preparing to wash their hair.

"Take your clothes off. You're going in."

"What!" That was not what Agnes had expected. She looked out at the water. The spring had been exceptionally mild even up here, but there was still ice out there. "The water will be freezing!"

"Won't kill you. When we were kids we used to have to break the ice to go in. This is not going to be easy, Agnes. If you're going to do it, we gotta toughen you up."

Agnes did as she was told. She bathed naked, not that a suit would have made any difference. The ice had retreated from the margins of the lake, but the water was so cold that at first it numbed her completely and she thought that she would not stand it. But she was a strong swimmer, and when she struck out from the shore, the numb feeling left her, to be replaced by exhilaration and a sense of sheer amazement that she was actually doing this.

She swam out as far as the old diving deck and then turned for the shore. She got out when she felt the numbness creeping back. Her aunt was there with a towel. She led her back to the cabin for breakfast: coffee, and pancakes laced with syrup Aunt M had collected herself. Her aunt sat across from her, dressed in a man's plaid shirt, corduroys, and work boots. Whenever Aunt M came up here, she always dressed for practicality. She wore her hair in two braids. She'd had a white streak since she was young, like Agnes; now she'd pick a braid off her shoulder and remark that the rest was growing to match it. Her face was tanned from being out in all weather, and although she could look quite severe, she was smiling at Agnes. Even though her aunt wouldn't say it, Agnes knew that she had passed some kind of test. Aunt M could be gruff, tough too, but right now her black eyes sparkled. In that moment Agnes loved her more than she loved any other person, and she knew Aunt M loved her. It felt good to be here with her, better than ever before.

Agnes was not exactly sure what was going to happen, but she'd figured that they'd get started right away. Pretty soon it was clear that would not be the case. After breakfast Aunt M wanted chores done around the cabin. It had been shut up all winter and leaves had sneaked in, along with twigs and dust and the odd mouse leaving droppings about. So floors wanted sweeping, the old hooked rug needed beating, the windows were smeary, and the bedding could do with an airing now that the sun was out.

There were logs to be split for stove kindling and to be carted from the pile and stacked next to the fireplace. The day promised warmth, but Agnes was told to get a fire going to warm the place up after the long cold of winter, and dry out any damp that might have crept in during the spring thaw.

Agnes swept around the rockers that stood on either side of the hearth. She wiped down the oilcloth spread on the table under the window and pushed in the straight-backed chairs. A shelf ran the length of one wall. Agnes dusted over and around the battered storage canisters and rearranged the books. A mix of old maps, seed catalogs, and mildewed herbals stood next to a selection of well-thumbed paperbacks fat with damp. They were propped up by a pile of stones from the lake, some round, some oval, smooth as eggs.

While Agnes worked, Aunt M buzzed about doing what she called "a bit of brightening," tacking up pictures out of magazines as well as bright woolen blankets woven in stripes and zigzag patterns to cover where the whitewashed wall was webbed and meshed with cracks.

"There. That's better!" She stepped back to admire her handiwork and then stepped forward, brushing her fingers over the flaking surface. "Needs a fresh coat, but I guess that can wait for another day."

When they had finished, Aunt M brewed up more coffee. She made it the old-fashioned way, setting a chipped and blackened pot of blue enamel to heat on the wood stove, watching it until the brown liquid splurged through the thick glass dome on the top.

"Got no milk or creamer left," Aunt M said as she poured out two mugs. Agnes stirred in sugar from the bowl on the table to sweeten the brew.

"Oh, I forgot. I brought you these." Agnes reached in her pack and laid the carton of cigarettes on the table in front of her aunt. Aunt M took the traditional gift of tobacco, nodding her acceptance.

"Thanks, but I quit." She turned the red-and-white box over in her hands. "Smoking's bad for your health, didn't you know that? Take 'em to Jake over at the fishing shack. They're his brand. He still uses 'em. Says he's too old to quit."

"That's clear across the lake! There's still ice out there; I saw it."

"Won't be a problem if you go carefully. You can get me some bait while you're over there and I need some supplies. Here." She handed Agnes a list. "If you go now, you'll be back by dark. If you're not, I'll put a light out on the dock—just head for that."

Agnes dragged the faded orange plastic canoe from under its tarp cover and took it down to the water. She climbed in gingerly, arranged the apron around her, and used the paddle to shove herself off against the lapping water. It was a long time since she'd been in one of these. She hoped her stroke had not deserted her. It was a calm blue day with no wind to speak of, and she glided over the water, guiding the boat through and around the remaining cakes and plates of melting ice. The stroke, the steering, came back as natural as riding a bike. She began to revel in her newly remembered skill on the water, even though her back hurt from the cramped position and the handle of the paddle chafed her hand, breaking the blisters raised across her palm by a morning spent chopping wood.

Jake accepted the cigarettes with thanks and sent her off with a couple of cans of worms and colored maggots.

Agnes went from his bait shack to the small store that supplied the boats and the summer folk, waited for the boy to fill out her order, and toted the paper bags back to the boat, stowing them in the nose and tail. She had to be careful; the extra weight meant the canoe rode lower in the water. Her hands hurt more now, making her progress even slower.

The sun sank in the west, its rays flooding across the lake until it seemed her paddle dipped and dripped liquid gold. She went on, working her way toward the farther shore as dusk thickened and the sky's blue deepened above her. White mists came up from the lake, rising around her like wraiths. She guided the boat with care through rafts of ice, feeling the chunks clunk against the sides of the craft before floating away again.

She took the canoe to a patch of clear water. Here stars showed above and below her, and the moon shone like a silver coin cast onto the rippling surface. She let the canoe float, stilling its movement as far as she was able, so as not to disturb the heavens reflected around her. If she kept motionless in just this way, it was almost impossible to see where the sky ended and the lake began. Above her blazed the Milky Way: the Spirit Path, the Ghost Road, the way taken by the dead on their journey to the west. It opened before her like a diamond highway.

It was getting cold. The creeping mist and the near-freezing water chilled the air around her, but she did not feel it. She lay for a long time rocking in the boat, looking up at the silent intensity of the stars. It was said that each one was a campfire lit by those who had made the journey across the sky to the place where the sun sets. How many of her people had gone that way? The number was as countless as the leaves that grow in spring and that fall at the end of the year. Was it possible to reverse the journey? For a soul to leave the land of the dead and come back to the living?

The need to know was strong within her. A fish rose near, rippling the water, breaking the spell. She turned, startled by the sudden sound, and halted the boat's drift. Still reluctant to disturb the tranquil surface, she dipped her paddle with careful motion and made for the steady light winking on and off at the distant dock.

Agnes knew that she was being prepared for a vision quest, but she was beginning to find all the chores just a little tedious. She'd been given them for some kind reason, but she could not be bothered to figure what the purpose was. Some kind of testing thing, to do with humbling herself to another and also discipline.

This morning she'd been sent to swim in the lake again, and it hadn't gotten any warmer. After that she'd been piled up with plastic canisters and sent to collect water from a cold spring deep in the woods. The water was supposed to have healing qualities, and the spring never froze over, no matter how cold the winter, nor did the water get stale or brackish. The spring was called the Place of Clear Water. White trappers and hunters call it Witches' Well.

It was past noon by the time Agnes found the place. She filled the two plastic water containers and then bent to bathe her face, cupping her hands to drink. As she leaned over and gazed down into the deep pool, light caught on coins, white pebbles, quartz crystals, even a bead or two. Offerings to the Mother, for the water springs from her and flows free and pure to give us life. People had thought that from the very first times. Agnes had never really believed it herself, but she reached in her pocket and threw in a dime, offering her own prayer of thanks as the coin winked once or twice in the sunlight before sinking down to the depths.

Agnes set off, staggering a little from the weight of the full canisters. She was probably supposed to be looking out for medicine signs right now, searching the forest for arrowheads, special stones, twigs crossed in a certain way, so they'd know whether Agnes was ready to undergo whatever ceremony her aunt had in mind for her.

Agnes refused to do any such thing. She did not want to turn this into some kind of cheesy vision quest, like something her aunt might put on for the city folks who came to her for "spiritual devel- opment." Anyway, signs had to come unbidden, in Agnes's opinion, or they were not of any value.

Snow still clung here and there, up to a foot in areas of permanent shadow, but it was low and dirty. Now that the sun was high, Agnes found herself sweating. The water carriers weighed heavy, and to add to her discomfort, the little black flies were coming out. Not as many as there would be later in the year, but enough to make her wish she'd packed some bug spray. The little black gnats formed clouds around her head, biting her neck and sticking to her sweating skin. With a water carrier in each hand, she could not even slap them off.

A blue jay called close by, answered by another cry. She shied instinctively as it broke from cover and swooped above her, and swore as the screw top popped off the canister and water slopped all down her pant leg.

Her aunt said nothing when she got back to the cabin, just took the carriers from her. Agnes waited to see what chores she should do next. Aunt M set the water down and slowly walked over to where Agnes stood by the door. She reached up and plucked something from the crown of Agnes's head and from her shirt collar. Then she opened her hand to show two blue feathers. She smiled.

"It's time. Come with me."

A fire burned on the far side of the yard. Flames leaped, transparent in the sunlight, causing the air to waver like a mirage. Flat rocks lay heating at the ashy white center of the hearth. The heat was intense as Aunt M led Agnes past the fire toward a low dome built half into the hillside.

"Take off your clothes," Aunt M instructed. "Go in."

Agnes did as she was told, stripping down; then she moved the stick that held the skin flap in place and stepped into a dark space smelling of earth and pungent smoke.

The floor was marked out with white quartz rocks laid in a circle, radiating from a central boulder like the spokes of a wheel. Low wooden platforms, strewn with blankets and animal skins, lined the walls.

Agnes seated herself on one of these. She had never taken part in a sweat lodge ceremony before; she'd never even been in a sweat lodge. It was rather like a sauna, both in principle and function, but she had a feeling that whatever went on inside was likely to be a little different from anything that happened at the local health club.

Sweat lodge ceremonies were not traditional to the Haudenosaunee, but Aunt M was not averse to adopting and adapting the practices of the other peoples. The ways to wisdom were many. She did not see one religion, one nation, or one people as having a monopoly on the truth. Her own path had led her to different teachers from different traditions. She had brought what she had learned back with her, introduced it into her practice, and used her medicine power to help, to serve, to teach those who came to her. If the sweat lodge ceremony was Lakota, what did it matter?

The flap pushed aside again. Aunt M came in, using a forked stick to push a white-hot ash-flecked rock into the center of the circle. She maneuvered it into a depression just below the white quartz boulder. Then she left and returned with another and placed it on the other side, and then others until there were six in all. One for each direction, one for the earth, and one for the sky.

She returned for the last time and addressed Agnes.

"In here I am Kanehratitake, Carrying Leaves, and you are Karonhisake, Searching Sky. We left Miriam and Agnes with our clothes at the door. D'you understand me?"

Agnes nodded.

"Good. Now. Speak when I tell you, do as I say, and don't interrupt. Is that clear?"

Agnes nodded again.

"Very well. Let's get started."

Aunt M unwrapped the sacred pipe and filled it with tobacco from the otter-skin pouch. The pipe was short, the bowl and stem of polished black stone. It was of an unusual type, and very old. Aunt M lit the pipe and offered the smoke to earth and sky and the four directions, then offered the pipe to Agnes. Agnes took a puff, trying to hold the smoke inside her, but it made her eyes water and she had to try hard not to choke on the thick, acrid stuff. Her aunt rested the pipe in the center of the circle and pinched herbs from the bundles suspended from the ceiling. She cast the leaves on the hot stones, where they writhed, curling and withering before igniting in tiny puffs of fragrant smoke.

The lodge was heating up. Aunt M let the door flap down and covered the entrance with a blanket. They were engulfed in a blackness so total that Agnes could not see her hand in front of her. All she could see was the hot stones shining crimson in the darkness, suffusing the quartz boss at their center, filling the rock with a deep fluid rose-pink glow.

Aunt M sprinkled water with an eagle feather, and the temperature rose still further until Agnes didn't know if she could stand it. Sweat broke out all over, plastering her hair to her scalp, riveting down her body, dripping from her eyebrows, pouring like tears all down her face. She sat up, feeling that she would faint, and was hit by another wave of heat as Aunt M sprinkled water again.

She was failing the test before it had really started. She wanted to shout into the suffocating steamy blackness, tell her aunt that she could not take it, could not stand it. She was not ready. All this was alien and terrifying in some deep way. She wanted to plead, to be allowed to leave, but the words would not come out. Her throat constricted, pushing her voice back down to her chest, and her tongue lay heavy in her mouth.

When they started, Aunt M had been as gruff and down-to-earth as she ever was, but now she was different. Agnes had not known her like this before. She was speaking in the old language, and she sounded like someone else, someone who would not like being interrupted. Silenced, Agnes stared at the central quartz stone. The pink glow was waxing and deepening; the surface flickered, mothlike shadows playing across it, as if something were moving deep within it, testing for a place to get out.

Her aunt spoke on, intoning and chanting, calling on the spirits until the words seemed to hang in the air, dancing there like dust in sunlight. Behind the words came a drumbeat, deep and clear, as constant and near as the beating of blood in the ear. The turtle rattle scattered its sound to the four directions, and bare feet thudded on the ground, going around and around in a ritual dance.

Agnes made one last effort to get up and leave, but it was too late for that. She could no longer resist what was about to happen. Any strength that remained was draining from her. She could no longer sit upright or keep her eyes open. She collapsed backward on the bed, the slippery silk of animal fur and the soft roughness of woolen trade blankets against her skin. She felt at one with the heat and darkness, as if she had become part of it, or it had entered her. It was as if she had no weight. Her limbs felt loose at the joints. At pelvis, hips, spine, the bones, muscles, and sinews seemed to be disengaging one from another. There were no limits to her. She was unraveling from the inside, becoming nothing, part of everything.

Agnes closed her eyes in the heat and steam of the sweat lodge. She woke to air that was dry and cold around her. She was no longer Agnes, or even Karonhisake, Searching Sky. She was no longer American or Haudenosaunee. She was English and her name was Mary, and she woke to find that she was dying, freezing to death.

The snow had stopped falling and the wind had dropped to nothing. I woke in an ice cocoon and lay, still curled, surprised to be waking at all. The sky arched above me, diffused to milky blueness by the thin crystal crust formed by our breath. It was like being inside an egg.

I woke alone and listened for the wolf's return. Where had she gone? Why had she left me? Without her I would die, was surely dying already. I could not move; this ice cave would be my grave. To save me and then desert me—the thought struck me cruelly and set tears forming to slide down my cheeks and glaze my face. I was about to give up, consign myself to my fate, when I heard a voice speaking as if in my ear:

"Be of greater faith. Do not doubt that I love you.

Just because I cannot be with you, does not mean that I love you less."

Then I heard something else and not from the realm of the spirit. It was coming toward me. I thought it was her, coming back to me, but then I huddled in my pit, holding my breath as if even breathing could cave the roof of delicate crystal and give me away. No dainty-stepping wolf would make that sound. The snow creaked and creaked again with the steady tread of man. Not many, but more than one. There were no accompanying calls and shouts as the tread came nearer. Except for their heavy trudge, they moved in silence. Each step was accompanied by a swishing sound of powdery surface snow. Not boots. Snowshoes—such as the Indians wear.

My ice shell cracked and broke. I looked up, expecting to see the face of a painted stranger, and I saw Jaybird looking down at me. He stood wrapped to the eyes in raccoon skins. I didn't know how he came to be there, how he found me in all that white wilderness, but I knew that it was he.

My face was a frozen mask. I could not even smile as his sloe-black eyes widened in gladness. I stared back, thinking that my mind deceived me, that this must be a dream, one last glimpse of the life I wished before the cold claimed me and I went into the final darkness.

The arms that reached down for me were real enough. His white teeth showed in a grin as he dropped the edge of his fur cloak and bent to pull me from my icy sepulcher.

He knelt, brushing the snow from my face; then he shouted and another figure came up behind him. His grandfather, White Eagle, wrapped in a bear-skin. He stepped forward, his lined face cracking into a smile. He bent down, touching my face, my nose and cheeks. Jaybird pulled his fur-lined mittens off with his teeth and tugged at my sodden sheepskin mitts. He held my hands between his own. His grand-father pulled off my boots and examined the flesh of my hands and feet as he had felt my face. He said something and stood. Jaybird tenderly fitted my hands into his warm mittens and rubbed my bare feet, breathing on them and chafing them between his hands.

"What did he say?"

Jaybird smiled. "He says she cared for you well."

"How did you find me?"

"Last night Grandfather dreamed he met a she-wolf in the forest. He rose before first light and told me to prepare for a journey, to bring furs and spare moccasins and mittens. We found her waiting in the clearing below the cave. She turned, wishing us to fol-low her, and she led us to you."

"How can that be? She kept me from freezing. She was here with me. I don't understand."

"There are many things that are hard to understand."

He continued rubbing my feet until the blood returned. The pain was so acute that I cried out.

Jaybird smiled. "That is good. The feeling returns like fire and ice together, but it is good. Here. I brought these for you to wear."

He reached inside his furs and brought out a pair of winter moccasins, with rabbit-fur lining and fitting like boots to the knees. They were warm. He must have carried them tucked next to his skin. He put them on for me, deftly fitting them on my frozen feet.

I had been utterly numb; now returning sensation brought a flood of emotion quite as painful as the burning I felt in fingers and toes. I clung to him and he wrapped his fur mantle about us, lending me the warmth from his body as I sobbed out my relief and joy. He wiped the tears from my face and tucked the raccoon robe around me, then turned to build a fire.

"They will see the smoke." I feared what would happen if fire brought men from the settlement.

"They will not come in this." He nodded to the drifts all around. "They would sink to their hips. They do not have shoes for snow." He set me by the fire. "Do not get too close. The blood must return slowly."

He crammed snow into a little iron pot and set it to heat. He reached into a pouch and brought out leaves, which he crushed and dropped into the heating water. When it was ready, he poured it into a clay beaker.

"Drink that and eat." He gave me a strip of dried meat pounded with fat, pungent and sweet with juniper and berries. "Chew it slowly."

He left me then to help his grandfather cut branches and saplings to weave together into a carrying frame. When it was ready, they wrapped me in the furs, the raccoon cloak and the great bearskin, tucking them carefully all about me, and strapped me to the frame. They kicked snow over the hissing fire, burying it and smoothing the ground around. They strapped their shoes back on, and White Eagle swept a branch over the clearing so no one would know we had ever been in it. Then Jaybird fixed the burden strap across his forehead and pulled me along.

I was cold to the very core—even the furs did little to warm me—but the jolting rhythm of the journey soothed me and I must have slept. When I woke, it was toward evening. The first stars were appearing, and we were at the base of a great cliff face. I recognized it as the place of their winter cave, but I could not see how we would get to the level of it.

"You must leave me here. I'm too weak to climb—"

"We cannot do that."

Jaybird cut me off, and he and his grandfather stood, heads cocked, listening intently to a sound borne on the wind, one howl answered by another, distant, then near.

I started in fear, thinking the noise might be made by dogs from the settlement.

"We must get you up there." Jaybird began to undo my strapping. "Settlers are not all we have to fear. Mohawks have been raiding deep into our territory. They may reach us even here. Each moon they grow bolder, even in this time of great cold."

A yelping howl sounded again, this time very near. I froze as a gray form emerged from the trees at the edge of the clearing. It was a wolf, and a big one. As she came closer, I realized that I knew her. She must have followed us here. She sat on the snow, yellow eyes watching. White Eagle spoke to her, his tone one of deference, humble thanks, and reverence. He took a pinch of tobacco from his pouch and threw it up into the air, so that the wind would carry it to her.

"What is he doing?"

"He is thanking her. He offers tobacco to her because she is spirit, *manitou*, very powerful and special

102

to you. To be chosen by such a one is to be greatly honored. Grandfather thinks . . ."

But I did not need it explained further.

I looked at her and the yellow eyes blinked and shone bright in recognition. I did not need White Eagle to tell me who she was. This was my mother. Just as my grandmother could go into a hare, so my mother had taken the shape of a wolf to save me yet again from the malice of men. I inclined my head and uttered my thanks, sorry that I had ever doubted her. She gave one last low whining cry, and then she turned and melted into the shadows of the forest.

Night was coming on apace and the cold was getting bitter. Jaybird hoisted me over his shoulder and started up a narrow path, zigzagging across the face. The way was steep and stony; sometimes the path disappeared altogether, and he was forced to climb from rock to rock. I feared many times that my weight would be too great for his strength, that he would drop me, or that he would slip and that we would both tumble down into the abyss, but he kept on climbing, slowly and methodically, and at last we approached the lip of the cave that was their winter shelter. His grandfather must have taken another path, for he was there before us and helped pull me onto the rocky ledge.

The cave was as I remembered it. A wide mouth opened in the mountainside and led into a chamber so large that its margins were lost in shadow. White Eagle crouched down to feed fir twigs and cones into the red embers of the fire, adding more wood as the kindling caught and setting stones to heat.

Jaybird carried me to a low bed spread with furs. He removed my moccasins and gloves. I tried to struggle up. It was not fitting that he should do this for me, but my fingers were next to useless in their clumsiness. I could not unclasp my cloak, let alone manage the hooks and buttons and fastenings on my other clothes. I told him to leave it, but he shook his head.

"They are wet."

He stripped me of my sodden outer clothes, but I told him that I could manage the ties on my undergarments. He turned his back as I finished undressing. I slipped naked between the thick furs, and he brought more. I thought I had begun to thaw, but I was suddenly taken by violent chills and fits of shivering until my teeth were rattling.

Jaybird wrapped hot stones in deerskins and slipped them into the bed with me. White Eagle came to look at me, then went through to another chamber. He returned with a white bearskin and threw it across me; then he took small bunches of herbs and birchbark folds of powders from his pouch. He pinched leaves from the dried bundles and crumbled them into a black trade kettle, then emptied the contents of several packets. I could smell the spice of sassafras and powdered sumac as he stirred.

He tasted the infusion and sweetened it with honey; then he withdrew, leaving Jaybird to tend me alone. He brought the hot drink to me. When I could not hold the cup and my teeth clashed against the rim, he held my head steady and tipped the liquid down my throat. Still I could not get warm. Jaybird replaced the cooling stones with newly heated ones. He tucked the white bearskin more tightly around me. The bear who owned it lives far to the north and has the thickest fur of any creature; Jaybird told me this, but it could have been a threadbare blanket of the meanest stuff, for still I could not get warm.

Jaybird built the fire higher and higher until the flames leaped. Animals and men leaped with them. The figures carved and painted on the walls seemed to be moving, stepping down from their places, until the cave was filled with gods and spirits in an endless round. As they danced, so they chanted, a song with no end and no beginning. I was gripped by a feeling of such awe and amazement that my shivering broke out anew.

Jaybird was at a loss as to what to do, how to tend me. Finally he gave me the warmth of his own body. He came into the bed with me, fitting his limbs along mine and giving me his heat. It was then that the drumming started, beating slow, then beating fast, slow, then fast. As did my blood. So did my heart.

The drumming grew faster and faster and a flute sounded, sometimes slow, shrill, and plaintive, but then playing higher and higher, up and up the register, until I could scarcely stand it. Then the playing broke off. The antic dance stopped. The world ceased its spinning and I was no longer cold.

I must have slept again, for when I woke, Jaybird was no longer with me. His grandfather pointed to the mouth of the cave and then to a figure painted on the wall: a huntsman bent and crouched, his body as taut as the bow he carried. In front of him stood a deer, front legs splayed, antlered head bent, cropping the ground all unsuspecting. I nodded. I understood. Jaybird had gone hunting.

I went to sit up, then remembered that I was entirely naked. I looked about for my apparel, but it was nowhere to be seen. The old man inclined his head to me as though he sensed my predicament.

He left me then, presently returning with a pile of clothes. He shook out the different items and laid them out on the bed. The garments were creased from long folding, and he smoothed each one out with a gentleness of touch, as though it still held the warmth of a wearer well beloved. The clothes were very fine, of the softest white doeskin, richly worked. His long thin fingers fluttered over the soft hide, straightening the decorated borders, touching the beading and embroidery work on yoke, sleeves, and hem, moving in remembrance and recognition, like the fingers of a blind man.

He withdrew, leaving me to dress. I dropped the tunic over my head and wrapped and belted the skirt around my waist. I pulled on leggings secured at the knee with a garter, and pushed my feet into a pair of moccasins. The fronts were decorated with woven moose hair and porcupine quills, four red-petaled flowers set in a circle around what looked like a small white bird. They could have been made for me; they fitted exactly.

When White Eagle returned and saw me, he smiled. He smiled rarely, but he smiled at me then. He looked at me for what seemed a long time, and then his dark eyes clouded, the gladness replaced by sadness. He said something in his own language, and for a moment he seemed sadder still. Then he abruptly departed, disappearing into a small antechamber and leaving me to wait alone.

I braided my hair, for I had no cap to wear to hold it back. I needed no looking glass to tell me how my own people would describe me. They would regard me with horror, turn from me with despising pity, although I was the same person as when I dressed in white linen or gray kersey. I sat at the mouth of the cave awaiting Jaybird's return, pondering the changes that had come upon me.

I was as much a wife to him now as Rebekah was to Tobias, although there had been no one to solemnize or sanction our union. I could not return. Ever. I would not wear the letter of shame upon my sleeve, and I would not risk having both of us be branded on the cheek and whipped from the town. I would live here with him. I would not risk punishment for something that is no sin.

I thought on the words of Ruth of the Moabites.

Intreat me not to leave thee, or to return from following after thee: for whither thou goest, I will go; and where thou lodgest, I will lodge: thy people shall be my people, and thy God shall be my God:

Where thou diest, will I die, and there will I be buried: the Lord do so to me, and more also, if ought but death part thee and me.

The wind moaned and screamed past the cave, and the snow fell in a wild whirling mass, obscuring the bleak winter landscape spread out below. Despite the weather raging before me, I felt great peace and comfort flowing through me.

The fire at my back warmed me; the clothes White Eagle had given me fitted my body like a second skin. Just like Ruth in Judah, I felt that I had found my people, that I belonged with them.

Jaybird returned, mantled in snow. His eyes widened at the sight of me, but he said not one word. He left the deer carcass he carried over his shoulders and called for his grandfather. They spoke together in low tones. I could not understand their speech, so I watched their faces to glean what went between them. Jaybird looked at me, full of puzzlement, even apprehension. What could I have done to offend him? All the joy I felt at his returning drained from me, and I watched even more carefully to see what fate had stored up for me now. Without him I was truly lost. That was the least of my reasons for despairing. I was in the grip of emotions I had not known before and that I had no name for. All I knew was that he meant more to me than life itself. If he did not want me now, I would have no other. If he turned from me, I would go to the entrance of the cave and dash myself on the rocks below.

Such extreme actions would not be required. As Jaybird listened, his expression cleared, gradually becoming one of understanding. I could breathe again.

Jaybird slung his fur robes on the bed and indicated for me to join him by the fire.

"He does you great honor," he said as he built up the blaze. "More than you know. Those clothes you wear belonged to his daughter, White Bird. She was his youngest and his favorite, the child of his second marriage. She was called at first Little Bird, because she laughed and trilled in her cradle board as it swung from the bough. When she grew, she seemed to run before she could walk; she seemed to fly over the ground, just like a bird."

"What became of her?"

"She died in her fifteenth summer. From the spotted sickness, as did his wife and his other children, including my father, and also my mother, my brother, and sisters. Nearly the whole tribe perished. White Eagle blamed himself. He was *powwaw*, medicine man; the people looked to him to cure them. But the spirits deserted him, and he had no power against the white man's sickness. He could not save any, not even his daughter, who was so dear to him. All he could do was bury his people with proper ceremony and make them ready for their journey to the great god Kiehtan, to live in his house in the southwest.

"Those were the clothes prepared for White Bird's wedding. She should have been buried in them, or else they should have been hung from the trees around her grave place, to stay there until they turned to dust." He looked over to where his grandfather was sitting watching us. "He says White Bird came to him in a dream and told him that her everyday clothes would do very well for her journey to the spirit land. She said he must keep her best clothes, the ones made for her wedding. For one day they would be needed. One day another would come to him naked and he must clothe her and she would be a daughter to him."

"And that one is me?"

"Your coming fulfills the prophecy. There are other signs, too. The ancestors have accepted you. The Wolf Mother protected you, showed herself as your guardian spirit, which makes you of her clan. Grandfather will make the mark upon you, just as I wear this." He turned his cheek to show an oval back picked out in black, with a blunt head, stubby legs and pointed tail. "It shows I am of the Turtle Clan." He looked away from me, and his voice became a whisper. "It means it is permitted for us to marry."

"That is good." I reached up, tracing the pitted lines against the smoothness of his skin. "Because we are married already." I held his hand, my grip tightening. "Do you not feel it so?"

He smiled shyly, still with his eyes cast down, the long curving lashes brushing his cheeks.

"The ancestors danced at our wedding, did you not see them? Did you not hear them?"

I nodded, suddenly as shy as he was.

"White Bird was there to give her blessing. Grandfather heard her flute."

So it was, and so it was to be. From that day on, we lived as man and wife.

· Mary ·
Living in Eden

The world changed with the year's turning. Winter released her grip on the land. Water gushed down the mountain and the snow receded, the white carpet creeping back toward our mountain fastness. As it retreated, so the leaves greened the forest and settled over the trees like a gauze mantle. Birds flew from the south, blackening the sky day after day in their journey northward.

As the days grew warmer, I would join Jaybird in the climb down from our cave, to hunt, to fish, to gather what the forest provided. He taught me to use a bow, and to kill, but he taught me that there was spirit in all things. To him, all life was sacred. He would stand in solemn prayer before the creature whose life he had taken, saying, "We are sorry to kill you, little brother, but our need is great. We do honor to your courage and speed and your strength."

He taught me his language, and much else besides. We found delight in all around us, bathing in lakes and streams, standing under waterfalls, wincing in the rushing cold. We wandered hand in hand through dappled glades, collecting strawberries, plums, sweet wild grapes, feeding them to each other, stuffing our mouths with them until the juice ran down our faces, dripping off our chins, running down our throats. All the time the woods rang loud with Jaybird's laughter. Each day was a delight, and each day saw my love for him grow until it knew no bounds. He could charm honey from the bees, climbing high into the trees to lull the wild, fierce, buzzing creatures into giving up their treasures. He would steal away their combs, brimming and spilling sticky, dark sweetness, and carry them to me.

We found mountain meadows and lay in the long grass surrounded by the nodding heads of flowers and bathed in the sun until I was as brown as he. I thought we were in paradise; we had been brought to a very Eden and left to walk in the garden, another Eve and another Adam. I had never in my life known such bliss, such happiness.

Nor would I again, although I did not know it then. We lived each day without thinking of the morrow. Sunrise to sunset seemed to stretch beyond the normal span. I wished that I could stop time's measure altogether, slow the sun in his course and make each day last forever. Such a thing is impossible. As much as I wished to hold it to me, each moment slipped through my hands, dropping away as sand through the hourglass.

I did not spend all my time with Jaybird. I might be wife to him, but I was also daughter to White Eagle, and his pupil. Reluctant as he was to be out of my company, sometimes Jaybird had to leave me to my tuition. This was conducted in the cave's inner chamber, a place forbidden to him.

It was a place full of mystery. The walls were reddened with ocher like the womb of the world. It was painted and carved all about with figures, as the cave was without, but these were *manitou*, of the spirit. Shrines cut into the walls marked the four directions, and White Eagle gave offerings to the gods who dwelt there. Great disks looked down, one rayed, one smooth, one for the sun, one for the moon. Forktailed thunderbirds soared and flew between the two. Animal spirits stalked and prowled behind ancient hangings rendered by time as fine as cobwebs.

Patterned in stripes and zigzags, they were brought by the first people and were said to come from the southwest, from the house of Kiehtan himself.

It was a holy place. I felt the hairs on my arms and neck stir with fear and wonder the first time I crossed the threshold, far more so than in any church I had ever entered.

I felt more. I felt near to my grandmother; I felt as if I had come home to her. For she had believed in the holiness of all things. The sun, the moon, the rain and wind; the earth, the mother from which everything springs. She saw the divine in all things growing; in all creatures who walked, crawled, flew, or swam; in every living thing upon the earth or in the sky, in river, lake, and sea. She would honor all in prayers each night and morning. It was for believing this that she was hanged.

If she had lived, she would have instructed me in the mysteries. Now White Eagle took this upon himself.

"The spirit is strong in you. I know this to be true. You were born to walk the sacred road, and I am here to guide you. First I must tell you a story."

He did not speak straightaway. He sat perfectly still; such stillness was a lesson for me to learn. His body was slim and muscular, as lithe as Jaybird's, but his face was scored and mapped with lines and his braided hair shone like ropes of tarnished silver. His

118

dark, hooded eyes were hard to read in the shadows of the cave, but I saw a great sadness as he looked into the well of the story he was about to tell. I guessed it to be about his daughter, White Bird. He looked at me, and his unhappiness seemed to double itself. I could not think why one such sadness should be shadowed by still another.

"Jaybird has told you that my daughter died."

I nodded.

"What he has not told you, because he was too young to know, is that I brought her back again from the land of the dead to dwell with me again."

"How?"

"I followed her. She was one of the first of the people to fall sick. I was *powwaw*, medicine man. My wife pleaded with me to save her and I did all I could, but I had no power against the white man's sickness. The sickness spread from one to another with such speed, like fire through a dry cornfield, and I could do nothing. I watched by my daughter's bed from the day to the night to the day again. I could feel her slipping away from me. Evening came and I must have dropped into sleep, for when I woke, it was black night. I saw her get up and go out; she moved with ease and there was strength in her step as if the sickness was no longer upon her. I rose, but she bid me go back; three times she told me and then she left, making me promise not to follow.

"I could not keep my promise to her. I stepped out and saw her white shape enter the forest. I went after her, following the trail she had taken through the trees. The leaves were thick with their full summer growth, and it was so dark, I could hardly see where to place my foot.

"The trail led to a broad track I did not recognize. I looked up, thinking to see my way by the stars, but there were no stars. The sky was empty. I looked down to the ground. It was stamped bare by the tread of many feet, and when I looked around, I saw men and women of different nations all traveling together; some were old, but many were young, with babies in their arms and children following.

"They went in silence and did not look at me. I went along with them, always going west. In front of us, the sky constantly thickened to night and no light showed in the east. Many passed as I journeyed on, and I recognized some of them: my eldest son, his wife, people of the tribe who had lately died. Always the throng grew greater. They flowed down the road as a great river. I had not known, I could not have guessed that the sickness had taken so many. I searched all through that vast throng but could find no sign of her, until at last we came to a vast plain, and here I could see many fires winking alight. I had come to the place where the people rested before they entered Kiehtan's great house. I passed from fire to fire, searching each face lit by the cold white light of the stars, and at last I found her.

"I took her in my arms. She seemed to weigh nothing; it was as if I carried empty clothes. I turned and ran from the place, back down the road we had traveled. The crowd grew thinner as we went until there was nobody left. I stopped awhile to rest, and when I looked up, I saw a gleam in the sky. The sun was coming up as I carried her back into camp."

"You saved her? Saved her from death itself?"

He shook his head. "My joy was brief. I laid her down on her bed and covered her with the finest furs, black wolf and lynx. She lay between life and death, with only the faintest fluttering of breath. In the days that followed, she got no worse, but she got no better. All around, my people were dying, calling for my help, but I did nothing. I would not leave her side—even though I knew by then that I had done the gravest thing, what you would call a sin. I felt shame and fear. What little power I had possessed left me, and I became as nothing, for I had deserted my people in their needful hour and had sought to take the place of the gods, to cheat death itself."

He stopped speaking then and stared into the small fire burning itself to ashes in the middle of the room.

"In the end I had no choice. I snuffed the life from her myself, putting my hand over her nose and mouth, and this time I let her take the journey alone. That night she came to me in a dream and told me not to grieve for her, that I must learn the lesson of acceptance. She told me to keep her wedding garments against the day when one would come who would take her place in my heart.

"I did as she asked. I kept her clothes and brought them here. But acceptance?" He raised his hands together in a gesture of despair. "My heart was twisted, wrung with pity for myself, and blackened with anger against the gods. I could not go back to my people."

I wanted to ask him what he did and where he went in his time of great sorrow, but he turned from me, setting his face to the west. I knew better than to disturb his silence. At last he spoke.

"I followed my feet and they took me north to the land of constant snow, where all is either light or darkness. I dwelt among the people who make their houses from ice. They taught me the proper way to move between worlds and the secret language of the animals. Still I wanted to know more, so they took me across the great ice roof of the world to a distant land of forests. The land of the Tungus, who call their holy people shaman. I learned much from them. They taught me that true wisdom comes only through suffering. I became as one dead so I could return to life again. I wanted to bring my new knowledge back to my people." He smiled then and his smile was bitter. "But when I returned, there was no one left. The village belonged to the white man. It had become Beulah under the chief man John Son. Go now. Jaybird is waiting for you."

The time I spent in the chamber was like dreaming. In the center stood a large basin, perfectly round and carved from some soft stone. I knew its purpose, but I was wary to try it. I did not want to know what was going to happen. Visions of the future might ripple the surface of my perfect present like wind across a lake.

One day White Eagle sent me to fetch water from a special spring. He used this to fill the vessel as my grandmother once filled her scrying bowl. Then he bid me look in. Only by facing what I saw there would I stop being afraid.

I saw strange things. Sometimes what had happened, as in a dream of remembering, sometimes a glimpse of what was to come. Sometimes the things I saw had no explanation. At first I had no skill to direct the vision; scenes came unbidden and made no sense to me. I saw a city of stone built between a rocky crag and a river black and wide. I saw a city of light with buildings made of crystal studded with diamonds bright. I saw a woman's face gazing back at me. I did not know her, but she knew me. Her look was one of fear and love mixed with deep concern. She reminded me of Martha, although her hair was gray and braided the Indian way. She was dark-eyed and dark-complexioned and seemed to be dressed in a man's apparel; a shirt checked in bright colors. I puzzled mightily over who she could be, or what she could want with me. Sometimes I met my mother dressed in velvet as I first saw her. She whispered urgently, and I listened avidly. Her story affected me deeply, but when I returned, I could not recall a single word.

I grew in skill—sight and knowledge coming together—and one day the bowl showed me what I most dreaded. Something was about to happen that would threaten my state of perfect happiness.

I saw a runner on a forest track, the shadow of leaves dappling his back. His body glistened with sweat and the bear grease smeared on his skin against the bite of insects. He ran without sound and was swift. The vision held other meaning. It was like a tiny crack in a perfect glass that would spread and branch until all was shattered. I turned away, sick at heart.

"Someone is coming."

White Eagle saw him, too.

"He will be here when the sun is at its highest point in the sky. We must be ready."

✻   ✻   ✻

Jaybird reached for his weapons as a voice hal-
looed from below. He went to the lip of the cave, bow
drawn, then he relaxed the tension, unnotching the
arrow. He beckoned for the visitor to climb up.

A young man, Jaybird's age or slightly older,
climbed up to the cave. His face was painted and
feathers dangled from the back of his hair, which
stood up in a crested wave. He was clad only in a
breechclout and moccasins, but he was armed with
bow and arrow and a knife hung from his belt.

Jaybird stepped forward to greet him, hugging
him like a brother. The young man knelt before
White Eagle.

"Grandfather, I have been sent by *sachem* Hoosac.
He has asked for your counsel."

"Why? He has other *powwaws* and people to
advise him."

"None as great or as wise as you. Settlers have
come. They say our land is theirs. They offer goods
and wampum. They have papers and say we must sign.
They say we must—"

"Who says?"

I had stayed in the shadows, but now I stepped
forward.

The young man's eyes went wide. "She is Yenguese!"

It was the word they used for English.

White Eagle looked at him. "She is also Jaybird's wife and pupil to me."

The young man's eyebrows rose even farther at the wolf mark White Eagle had etched into my cheek with sooty pigment and a sharp flint, but he addressed his question to me.

"What is your counsel?"

I spoke then. "Accept nothing from them and do not sign their papers or put your mark upon them."

"What she says"—the young man looked from White Eagle to Jaybird—"it is your word, too?"

White Eagle nodded. "As you say, she is Yenguese; she knows their ways."

"Very well. I will return and tell Hoosac what you have said."

The young man went, running off into the forest. White Eagle withdrew into the Chamber of Visions and did not come out again that day.

"We must leave. Go after him. For I fear what Hoosac will do. He has not the wisdom of his father and he is greedy. He might well trade all for a handful of trinkets. Besides, the year is turning. Eyes of a Wolf will need the company of other women. We should not stay for another winter here."

Jaybird looked at his grandfather, then at me, his face breaking into a smile. White Eagle knew, or guessed at, something I had told no one. I was with child.

Agnes stirred and groaned in her sleep, but Aunt M knew not to rouse her. Aunt M opened the flaps to let in the air. The day was cooling to evening. She dipped water from an earthenware pitcher on the floor and sprinkled water over Agnes to cool her hot skin. All the time, she sang her song as she fed the fire outside and put more stones to heat. When these were hot, she brought them to replace the ones cooling at the center of the lodge. She let the flaps fall back and threw herbs and then water over the stones, humming her song low now and softly to herself.

She cast more water on the glowing stones, filling the darkness with steamy heat, then sat down to watch her niece. Agnes had lost all sense of herself. Her breathing was even and deep as though she had gone to a state beyond sleep. If her skin was pricked, cut with a knife, she would not feel it. She lay insensible to the world around her, as if she'd been carved from wood or stone.

Aunt M had helped many people on quests such as this. Ever since a childhood vision had marked her out as a special person, she had been open to the spirit world. Back then, when it first happened, Aunt M had felt wonder, fear, and confusion, pretty much as Agnes had. Her grandmother had helped her, acting as guide and protector. Aunt M had learned from her wisdom; she called on her now to bring strength to herself and Agnes. Aunt M had gone on to help others, to act as a contact between seeker and spirit. She saw it as a service, and she was proud to give it; but she had never worked with anyone she loved the way she loved Agnes. Fear for the girl welled up inside her, seeping into her concentration, threatening to dissolve her resolution to stay calm and not to interfere with what was happening here. She fought hard to banish it from her mind. To intervene would be to put her niece at very great risk. Agnes had gone beyond her power to help or hinder. She had gone to a place where only spirits could reach.

Aunt M watched on through the night. Watch was all she could do, apart from making sure that her niece was comfortable, that her body did not take chill. It was cold now. Aunt M pulled on her old plaid shirt and went out to set fresh stones to keep the lodge warm. Then she went to Agnes and tucked a blanket around her.

For a moment the girl's eyes flared open, but it was not Agnes looking back at her. These eyes were a lighter gray, more heavily flecked with gold, the irises ringed and striated with black. Eyes of a Wolf, isn't that what the Pennacook called you? A good naming. The eyes closed and Agnes sighed. Aunt M continued looking down at her.

"You sought her, and you found her. All I ask is you do not harm her. Or I will . . ."

I will what? Aunt M knew she could do nothing but watch and wait it out. She burned a little sweet grass and pinches of tobacco to honor the spirit and then set herself to watch again, sitting on the opposite side of the lodge from Agnes. She had placed Agnes in the west, the seat of woman power, the home of the spirits, the place of dreaming; she herself sat in the east, the seat of the shaman, the place of mystery, of mirrors and echoes. She sat hardly moving, as immobile and ageless as a wooden carving. She began to hum soft and low, then to chant. She sang to keep Agnes from harm, to lend her strength, and as her song went on, she beat out time with a turtle rattle.

Agnes came back to her just before dawn, just as the forest around echoed with the first birdcalls. Aunt M went over to her, helping her up. She rose with difficulty, her legs wobbly, giving at the knees. She felt unused to her own body, as though she'd been ill and in bed for a long time.

The very early morning cast its pearly light over everything as they left the sweat lodge. Aunt M led her down to the water's edge. Agnes did not mind the swim this time. The water was bitingly cold, but it was refreshing. It woke her body, if not her mind.

Her head was still some other place. Aunt M wrapped a towel around her and led her back to the cabin. Agnes lay down on the bed, suddenly weary. Her mind began sliding away. She was becoming Mary again; this time she felt it happen. There was something else. In the second it took to slip into Mary's skin, she knew that she was not a girl anymore but a mature woman.

The life was hard, but what life is not? The words come slowly. I rarely think in English anymore.

The child I carried in my womb from the mountain was preparing for his winter quest, the time when he would go to the woods as a boy and come back a man. My son, Black Fox, had already earned his name through stealth in hunting. Fierce and skillful in the games the boys played, he had done as much as a boy could do to live up to White Eagle's prophecy on the day of his naming, saying that he would grow up to be a great warrior and a chief. My mother's heart had swelled with pride at that moment, never doubting that it would be so.

I had my place. I was accepted as Eyes of a Wolf, wife to Jaybird, mother to Black Fox and Speckled Bird. I worked with the other women in the endless round of sowing and planting, tending and harvesting.

I learned to cure skins and work them to softness. I did not mind the work. I found it no more or less arduous than the work to be done around a settlement homestead or an English cottage. A woman's work is never done, here as anywhere, but with one difference. We worked all women together with no husband, father, or overseer to chivvy, chide, or criticize. We helped one another, and there was often much laughter and high good humor. No man told us what to do. No man would dare. The children ran around scaring crows or played where we could see them. When he was younger, Black Fox would sit with Speckled Bird, fashioning dolls from cornhusks for her while she made a village from leaves.

Each time of the year brought different work, and it might have gone on in that way until I was old and gray and a grandmother. A life at least as good as any other. But trouble was coming from the south like the scent of smoke blowing on the wind, like the smell in the air when the forest takes fire.

A night since, there had been a sign, a portent, one so full of foreboding that it set the hair to creep and the flesh to crawl. A shadow had passed over the moon, turning her face to blood. Then, as we watched, the shadow seemed to mass and take the shape of a warrior's scalp lock hanging from the back of a bloody skull.

White Eagle was needed to augur this, and I had been sent to ask him what it meant. He was of a great age and lived more and more in the world of the spirit. He had little use for this world and longed to leave it. He had withdrawn from the life of the village, saying that he had no more counsel to give. Ordinarily his wishes would have been respected, for he was revered by all, but the scalp-lock moon was a sign that could not be ignored.

I was one of the few allowed to approach him. It was rare for a woman, but I was now a *powwaw*, and a powerful one. He had taught me all he knew, and although I took little part in ceremonies, my counsel was heeded, and I was needed as a healer, as my grandmother had been before me. From White Eagle I had come to know the use of every bark, root, and leaf in the forest, but it was not just that. I had the power in my hands, more than when I was a girl.

"It must come from here." White Eagle formed a fist and thumped his chest. "As well as here." He tapped his brow.

I learned to tend well and sick alike and was skilled in treating the illnesses that came from the white people. The spotted sickness, which was the name for smallpox, and the agues and fevers that ravaged whole villages. I did not succumb, so I could nurse the sick and prepare the dead for burial.

But I was more than a healer; I had other powers. I was feared for the same reason as the ones called witches: I could summon spirits, I could change my shape to that of an animal; I could harm as well as heal; I could kill as well as cure.

White Eagle chose his camp carefully. Few would risk crossing ground this holy, this sacred. I trod carefully so as not to disturb the dead, brushing through their tattered clothing that hung from the trees like cobwebs.

There was no smoke rising as I approached the clearing. His wigwam was empty. His fire was cold. The camp was swept clean and left neat, but his few possessions had disappeared. He had gone. We would have to face the future without him.

I journeyed back to the village with a heavy heart, reluctant to be the bearer of such bad tidings, to pile one omen upon another. I arrived when smoke was rising from the evening cooking fires, wisping up from longhouse and wigwam. Soon families would gather to talk over the day and to eat together. I stopped on the hill above the settlement. Several men on horseback were leaving, picking their way down the narrow track in single file. Horses and hats gave them out to be English.

I waited for them to be well on their way before starting down the hill. I took care never to be seen by any of them. I did not want it to be known that one of their own dwelt with the native people. Not that they would have noticed. I was a native woman and therefore invisible. Nevertheless, I made sure to stay in the gardens or keep to the wigwam when Yenguese came to the camp, be they neighbor or trader.

I could see Jaybird coming back with the other men from the hunt. They had been successful. Bulging game bags and bundles of fur and feathers hung from their belts, and they were laughing, carrying a deer slung on poles. Speckled Bird ran out to meet her father. He swooped on her, scooping her up, carrying her under his arm as if she were a creature he had caught in the forest. She giggled, wriggling with delight. It was a game that they had played since she was a tiny child. He swung her around and up on his shoulders, although she was eight now and her legs dangled to his belt. She held his braids like a horse's reins and kicked him in the ribs, none too gently at that, to make him paw the ground and canter for her. He stopped at her command and looked up at her; they both laughed at something that she said and I laughed with them. Something of the sort had happened almost every day since Speckled Bird crawled from her cradle board. She was his favorite and he spoiled her. He would deny her nothing.

I stood and watched, the smile dying on my

mouth. I knew this was a moment caught in time. The last of its kind. A moment to be savored and kept in the mind; a moment not to forget.

Beside Jaybird walked Black Fox. He was nearing fourteen years and big for his age, almost as tall as his father, and puffed by the importance of being part of the hunt. He was trying to speak of serious things and resented his sister's interruption. She had taken Jaybird away from him. Black Fox was my first-born and darling of my heart, but a mother's love was not enough. He wanted his father's respectful atten-tion. He stared down to the ground, trying to master his anger. In a moment he would stalk off by himself. His playfulness had gone from him. He wanted to be a man, although he was still boy enough to sulk.

In the distance, across the other side of the snaking silver river, lay another village. Smoke was ris-ing from there also, curling up from stone chimneys to lie in drifts in the still July air. The settlements hid from each other behind high stockades, but for years they had lived in peace together, even friendship. I looked down and my sadness deepened. That time was about to end.

I had never been near the English settlement, although I could see how it grew and developed. I could see the pattern of the lives they led there, and it reminded me very much of Beulah. Soon husbands would be returning with sons beside them, just as

John Rivers had; mothers would stand at the door, like Sarah, calling for their children to come in to supper. I had lived in an English settlement and an Indian village and reflected on how little really divided them in the things that matter: home, hearth, and family.

Both groups believed in dreams and portents. The scalp-lock moon shone down on all alike, and they would have looked back with equal disquiet. A time of trial approached, and both would look to some great spirit for guidance and blessing. Be it God or Manitou, what did the naming of Him matter?

For months past, runners had been arriving, sent by Metacom, *sachem* of the Wampanoags, whom the English called King Philip. The present quarrel lay between Metacom and the men of Plymouth, but the grievances he held were common ones. Everywhere the English settlers were encroaching, cheating the Indians out of their tribal lands, fencing in hunting grounds. But the trouble went deeper, for the Puritans would brook no difference in beliefs. They wanted the Indians to deny their own and become Christian. They wanted them to stop their wandering way of life and exchange buckskin for broadcloth, breechclout for breeches. They wanted them to live in permanent settlements, like the Praying Indians, and yoke themselves to the plow.

Finally it had happened. Metacom had broken out of his tribal lands, burning settlements, killing soldiers sent to protect them. Signs lay along the trails, cut into the bark of trees for all who passed to read; but to the settlers, the war would come all unexpected, just as rain falling in distant mountains surges down the rivers to flood the plains.

The Englishmen I had seen leaving the village must have been frightened, shocked at the news from the south. They had come for assurance that the like would not happen here. Although the *sachem* was minded to offer those assurances, some among the English company had been arrogant and swaggering, threatening what would happen should the tribe join Metacom. This caused anger, among the young men in particular. The joy of a successful hunt was forgotten. I entered a camp torn with dissension, full of tension, and full of fear.

That evening a council was called. I was asked to join them around the council fire. I was a *powwaw*, one whose dreams and visions are true. I had been apprentice to White Eagle. If he could not be there, I would stand in his stead. I was also Eyes of a Wolf. They all knew my story. I knew the ways of the English, for I was once one of them.

The longhouse was crowded, the air thick with smoke from the fire that burned in the center and from the pipes of the men seated in a circle about it.

Hoosac, the *sachem*, sat with his brother Coos, who was *muckquopauog*, war leader; across from them were his *ahtaskoaog*, principal men and elders. The clan mothers were there, too. I took my place beside them.

Firelight flickered over faces set and grim, gleaming on muscle and skin. There was a stranger among us. His hair and dress proclaimed him from a different nation. His face was painted for war. He was a Wampanoag sent by Metacom. He bowed and asked permission to address the people. When he received the *sachem*'s assent, he began to speak.

"Metacom sends his greetings and many wampum belts." He held out the wide bands of purple and white shell beads. "He sends these to show his love for the Pentucket people. He says he will fight alone if need be, but he is calling on you as his brothers; he is calling on all of the nations to band together to help him drive the English from the land and back into the sea."

When he had finished, Hoosac thanked him for his words and the wampum and turned to his council, wanting to know what others thought.

"I say this." Coos spoke from his place on the *sachem*'s right-hand side. "We must fight. Metacom has called for our help and we must join him. It is time we rose up against the English. It is time to take back what is ours and send them back to their wooden ships."

"It is too late for that. There are too many. We should have done that when they first came to the land." Hoosac turned to the stranger. "Besides, Wannalancet says that we should keep out of this quarrel. This matter would not have arisen if Metacom's man had not killed another and then refused the punishment set for this by the laws of the English."

There was nodding all around the circle. Wannalancet was *ketasontimoog*, chief *sachem* of the Pennacook. Hoosac's band owed allegiance to him.

"Why should we obey their laws?" The Wampanoag sneered. "They are cowards. They are soft. If we take arms against them, they will run from us like a bunch of women! If we do not fight, how can we live as men?"

There was nodding at that also. Then I spoke.

"They are not soft. They will fight fiercely, and they can be more ruthless than any of you guess."

The Wampanoag warrior glared at me. I was a woman and a Yenguese; he did not consider that I should be heard at all.

Hoosac saw the look he gave me.

"All who are invited to council have the right to be heard," he said, his tone mild but full of authority. "You have spoken; now it is her turn. That is our way."

"And she says the truth." One of the old men,

Black Feather, spoke up for me. "Who can forget how the English dealt death to the Pequot people? I was a young man then, but I remember when the news came of what the English had done to the Pequot at Mystic Fort. They attacked at dawn, firing the encampment and killing any who sought to flee: men, women, children, shooting them down with muskets. Four hundred all told. The slaughter was so great that even the Narragansett and Mohegan, who were allies of the English and enemies of the Pequot, even they were shocked and made sick by it."

"Black Feather is right." Another elder spoke up. "And it didn't end there. The English did not rest until all of the Pequot were dead or dispersed. They were thorough."

I spoke again, telling them about when I was a child and England was rent with civil war and how fiercely they had fought one another, brother against brother, neighbor against neighbor. How in Ireland, Cromwell had put entire towns to the sword.

"And these were Yenguese, their own people?"

I nodded.

Hoosac shook his head at such savagery. He was getting on in years now, a gentle man and cautious. The thought of war did not fire his blood as it did his younger brother's. He would want to keep his people out of the fighting for as long as he could.

The debate went on, but Hoosac had decided. The tribe had no quarrel with the English hereabouts. They would not commit themselves, not yet anyway. They would wait and see.

The *sachem*'s decision was not heard by everyone. The crowd in the longhouse had been thinning. The Wampanoag warrior and Coos, the *sachem*'s brother, had already left, and other young men had gone with them, slipping off into the night, determined to join the fight.

Life went on as usual through summer toward the autumn. We hoed and cared for the plants growing in the gardens: corn, pumpkin, beans. We made mats from the bulrushes, prepared hides for clothing and moccasins, smoked and dried fish and flesh for the winter months. But the work was done without the usual leavening of humor. The mood in the gardens was subdued, as it was in the village. When the men were away fishing or hunting, the women went about their tasks almost in silence, hardly noticing what they were doing, each one lost in endless calculation of what this war could cost them. Even the children ceased their chatter and playing and looked to their tasks scaring crows, carrying water, picking pests off the growing corn—for every ear grown and safely garnered was insurance against hunger and want.

Even when the men were about, the atmosphere barely lightened. The hunt returning was generally a time for feasting, a time of plenty, but now there was little rejoicing. We dried and smoked the meat the men brought us and put it into storage pits, while the men clustered in groups, talking in low tones.

On past summer evenings, after we had eaten, Black Fox and Speckled Bird would sometimes play together outside our wigwam. He had taught her knucklebones, a game with five stones I remembered from home, showing her how to toss them up and catch them on the back of her hand. He liked to carve things and had fashioned dolls for her, or made stick figures for her village, helping her mark out paths with the pretty stones and shells that she collected. Speckled Bird's village changed with the season. Now a palisade of sharpened sticks bristled around it and a war post stood in the center, a squat stump of wood, stained red as if by blood.

Black Fox rarely found time to play with his sister now. Most nights saw him slipping from our wigwam to join other firesides where the talk was of war. In the daytime he went to help the men who were look-ing to their weapons, making and fletching arrows, working the blades of their tomahawks on whet-stones, grinding the edges to wicked keenness, keep-ing everything in sharp repair.

All summer long it was as if a storm were brewing. The war flickered like distant lightning, playing across the mountains to the south, to the west, to the north, then all around. News of the fighting growled in our ears like thunder. Each day the atmosphere grew more ominous. The war was coming upon us, like it or not.

• Mary •
The War Trail

It came at the time of the green corn harvest when
the first corn was brought in from the gardens. The
kernels were plump and fat with milky sweetness and
were roasted and boiled with fowl and venison. Plums
and grapes and different berries were mixed for a
pudding with cornmeal and maple syrup. It was a
time of plenty, a celebration of earth's bounty.

Coos, the *sachem*'s brother, turned this time of festival into a war dance.

He came back from the fighting in the south a
honed and hardened warrior, with a fresh scar seam-
ing his face from ear to chin. He had his war band
with him. They were honored, given the best place at
the feast, the choicest of meats. After the feasting was

over, he stood up, arms outstretched, and addressed the men about him.

"My brothers, I bring greetings from Metacom . . ."

He went on to describe Metacom's triumphant progress and his own part in it: the soldiers killed, the towns burned, the settlements sacked. Black Fox leaned forward, drinking in every word he said. Coos called for warriors to stand up and join him. First one man, then another moved to form a circle. He asked who else would come to him. Black Fox stood up to join the dance.

"You cannot join! You are too young!" I called out to him, but he walked away as if he had not heard me. I turned to Jaybird. "You must stop him."

"It is too late. He has been accepted."

Jaybird rose from where he was sitting.

"*You* cannot!"

I held his arm, but he shook me off. He was moving away from me now.

"I must! Would you see me dishonored? Shamed by my own son, a boy of barely fourteen summers? If he is prepared to take the war trail, I cannot stand by like an old one."

A deep-throated shout went up as Jaybird joined the other men, for he was a skilled hunter and tracker and had proved himself a courageous and cunning fighter on the war trail against the Mohawks. In normal times I would have been proud of him, but now I rued his prowess and wish him lame, sick, weakly—anything to keep him here with me.

I saw my anguish reflected on the faces of other women as their men rose to leave their hearths and fires and gathered at the center of the village.

Flames grew and sparks flew up into the dark night sky. The *powwaw*s shook their turtle rattles, an empty, ticking, scratchy sound, and then the drums started, beating out a steady and strong rhythm. The war dance was starting. The ground shook with the thump and stamp of feet. The firelight shone on the dipping, swaying dancers, turning their sweating skin and muscle to burnished copper. Then the chanting began as each warrior added his song to the rhythm set by the drums beating and the feet stamping. War cries rang out, inhuman shrieks, like the calls of owls or eagles. Coos raised a ball-headed club with a great spike on it, smeared with vermilion as if blood were already upon it, and struck at a quintain set in the center of the circle. Other men smote the post in turn, while still others held their hands to the sky to bring down the spirits.

Jaybird and Black Fox merged in with the others. I could not tell any man apart in the whirl and turn. They were all caught in the drumming and chanting, blind to those outside them, moving as one thing, like a monstrous snake or serpent. Women and children could only stand and watch in resignation, for they knew that once joined, there could be no leaving. The only honorable way to quit the dance was death.

The dancing went on far into the night, but I was too sick at heart to watch further. I withdrew to our wigwam and lay alone on our sleeping platform, gathering the furs about me, but I could not sleep. Speckled Bird woke, wanting to know what the noise was. I took her in my arms and held her to me, rocking her to sleep to the rhythm of the war dance.

Jaybird came to me as day was dawning. I nearly cried out; he had to put a hand over my mouth. For a moment I failed to recognize him in the darkness of the wigwam lit only by the embers of the fire. He was stripped for war. His head was shaved save for a single crest of hair running from front to back; his face was painted half red, half black. I would not have known him except for the gorget he wore about his neck. I had made it as a wedding gift to him, threading beads and shells together. The half-silver coin at the center glittered against his throat as he bent to touch Speckled Bird's sleeping head.

He gathered me up and held me in his arms and kissed me for one last time. I wanted to whisper my love to him, to beg, to implore, to plead with him, but I remained silent. My heart was too full—words would make the tears spill—and I would not shame him by weeping.

Black Fox was outside, his head shaved also, his eyes ringed with black like a raccoon mask. The sight of him, I must confess, caused my tears to spill. He was just a boy and much too young to go with the warriors. In my eyes he was still a child, my child, but I knew that I could not keep him. My woman's words would not be heeded. I could not make him stay; he would follow anyway. All I could do was give him my blessing.

I might never see them in life again, but they left without a word being spoken. To break custom would be a bad omen, and among Jaybird's people there is no word for farewell.

• Mary •
Dreamtime

I slept alone, with Speckled Bird on the opposite couch from me. At first she slept beside me, but I disturbed her with my dreaming. I did not dream of Jaybird and Black Fox, for their trail was closed to me. Instead I dreamed of Beulah.

I had dreamed of it before. Dark dreams of ruination. Grass growing on tracks that had not seen traffic these years past. It had become a desert place, the forest growing all about, busy taking the village back. Saplings thrust through floors and fallen beams, vine and creeper slowly engulfing the houses.

I had wondered often and pondered long on the fate of those I had left there. Over the years I had dreamed of them also. I had woken in their worlds.

I had walked in from the muddy Boston street, the air laden with sea, stepped into the shop of Jonah

Morse, Apothecary, and sniffed the air, bracing as medicine, laced with camphor, licorice, and sulfur. I had caught the scent of rosemary and sage blowing through from the physick garden planted behind the shop. I had heard the bell ring behind me, seen Martha look up from the counter, surprised to see no one before her, her green eyes as sharp as ever, but her dear face older, more lined, her cheeks withered and puckered like the skin on a winter-stored pippin. Just then Jonah would come from his dispensary, his white shirtsleeves protected to the elbow by black guards. He appeared smaller, bent in the shoulders, and peering about him through small wire-rimmed eyeglasses, wondering what, or who, had called him from his scales and his furnace and his bubbling alembics. Martha would shake her head at him and hurry to secure the door that had blown open for no reason.

That is what I'd seen in my dreams before, but now the shop stood empty. Dust lay on the floor and lined the shelves. Where Jonah and Martha were I could not tell, but I feared that death had claimed both of them. I woke with my face wet, for I would have liked to see Martha again. She had been good to me, and I had loved her well.

I settled to sleep again and my dreaming eye turned to John and Sarah Rivers. I saw them prosperous, their children grown. Sarah stood at her window, staring through glass, and I knew her thoughts were on Rebekah.

I had dreamed of Rebekah before. Seen her as a woman with growing children about her. Seen her with Tobias in the house he had built for her. A substantial dwelling, two stories, wide-fronted, the boarding beginning to weather, the heavy shingled roof sloping down at the back. He built as solidly as ever. Stout barns flanked the house. They lived now in a fair valley, with lush land all about them, a mill turning on the wide restless river. I saw Tobias standing on a wharf, watching as wide flat-bottomed barges laden with timber were seized by the swift current and taken downstream. The river carried his wealth.

I dreamed of Rebekah now. But this dream was different. The strongly built dwelling stood shuttered fast. No smoke rose from the broad brick chimney. From the outbuildings came a plaintive lowing, cows in need of milking, but no one stirred from the house or crossed the empty yard. Scorching and charring patched the exterior, showing that the house had been under attack. There was tension in the air, a sense of waiting. Birds called sharply from the forest, first one, then another, a blackbird's dinning, a blue jay's empty chatter.

The whole scene lay bathed in the first light of a golden autumn morning. The forest, crowding near, lay as yet in darkness. Figures crept from the margin, first one man, then another. They kept to the shadows, then spread out. Some moved toward the barns to steal away horses and cattle. Others held brands and brushwood ready to set fires at the base of the wooden house and finish the burning. A few snaked close to the ground, holding hatchets and tomahawks to hack at the doors and shutters.

At some unseen signal, panels slid back high in the barns and suddenly the front of the house bristled with musket barrels. Smoke puffed amid sharp reports sounding like the cracking of dry branches. The Indians were caught by surprise in a murderous crossfire. First one man fell and then another. The answering arrows pattered harmlessly as the shutters shot back into place.

The Indians regrouped for another attack and began to creep forward again, dragging burning brushwood with them, but again they came under fire from the barns. The leader signaled retreat. His men fell back, but one lay trapped behind a water butt.

Before, they had seemed a group of strangers, but now I could see all. I could see close and far, as one can in dreams. I knew who the trapped one was. I had carried him in my womb, I had loved him and guided him, watched him grow from boy toward manhood. Now he lay in the dust, his black-painted raccoon eyes wide, panting like an animal, the dust stirring with each shallow breath. He looked small and slight.

Too young to be here, too young to fight. A life scarce begun was over. We are sorry to kill you, little brother . . .

I would have done anything, given anything to save him. "Be careful what you wish"—that's what my grandmother had taught me, but I forgot her counsel and summoned all my power. I sent myself out to him, but another was there before me. Jaybird turned back. I saw his face painted half red, half black. He came running, drawing fire to himself. The first musket ball hit him in the shoulder, the second in the back. A third spun him around again while the boy stayed where he was, as still as a rabbit before an ermine, his eyes rimmed with white within the raccoon black. I went out to him again, lending him my strength to take flight. At last he stirred. While the musket balls puffed up the dust around him, he got to his feet and fled.

Jaybird stumbled on into another volley of fire. He went down on his knees before them, arms flung out, head flung back, then he fell to the ground. The fleeing boy looked back, raccoon eyes turning. He would have run to his father, the fallen one, but one of the other warriors caught Black Fox and dragged him away to the forest.

All was silent for a while. Then, first in ones and twos, then in a crowd, men came from the house.

They clapped one another on the back, laughing and grinning, filled with the joy of being alive while others lay dead. They deployed themselves among the fallen, kicking this one, turning that one, as if these were animals killed for sport. One or two took out knives and knelt to the bodies, bent on taking trophies. A woman ran out then, commanding them to stop. She was tall and slender. I knew that it was Rebekah. I sent my spirit out to her. One of the men was standing over Jaybird with sword raised as if to hack off his head. I would not see my husband despoiled.

She went over and bent to look closer at the warrior stretched on the ground before her. Bidding the man to stay his hand, she stood to address all of them. She was a woman of substance and standing; her word was respected. Under her direction, the dead were taken and left at the edge of the forest.

I knew that the dream was true. I was in mourning even before Black Fox came back carrying the gorget from his throat.

"He died well." Black Fox put the necklet into my hand. The silver was tarnished, the beads and feathers soaked, dyed black with his blood. "It is for you. I took it so you would know. I am a man now, Mother. I will take care of you and Speckled Bird."

His voice broke over the last words. He was too full of grief to say more. I cried, weeping openly. Such displays of emotion disturbed him, but he did his best to comfort me. We stood together, united in sorrow for a father who had been greater than any other and a husband dearer than life itself.

The returning warriors brought the war with them like a pestilence.

"You are harboring fugitives." The English words rang harsh through the cold air, clashing together like chains. "Also, it has come to our notice that you have a white woman here."

The captain rode at the head of a column of militia, twenty, perhaps thirty men. His message was relayed by a man whom they had brought with them, John Samson. He wore shirt, waistcoat, and breeches, and carried a musket; only the loosely flowing length of his hair betrayed him as Indian. He was working in their service as a spy and scout. He had told them of the returning warriors and of my presence in the camp.

Without the wiles of him and his kind, the English stood little hope of winning this war. They would blunder from one ambush to another, led on by an enemy that kept appearing and disappearing like so many will-o'-the-wisps, flitting from swamp to forest. They were not used to this skulking kind of fighting. They liked to take a stand and face their enemy out in the open. They liked to fight on solid ground. But they were learning and learning quickly, helped by tribes with scores to settle.

"Unless you give them up, the white woman, too, it will go badly for you. You have until dawn tomorrow."

The captain looked around. His words were met with silence. No one stirred; no one looked in my direction. My head was covered, my face smeared with ashes, and I kept my eyes fixed to the ground. He waited for a response. Getting none, he sighed his impatience.

"Mark me. Dawn tomorrow."

He wheeled his horse and cantered toward the gateway, the troops and their Indian helpers following at a trot.

Hoosac ordered the warriors from the village, and I went with them. We would have a cold and wet time of it. A cutting wind blew from the north, and the hills around were obscured by dark rain clouds. Speckled Bird was already flushed with fever. A night out in the open with the year turning toward winter could only make her sickness worse. My judgment was snarled by grief and sorrow, or I would never have left her, but I thought she would be safe in the care of Hoosac and his wife. I trusted them to look after her and thought that she would be far more comfortable in the warmth of the longhouse than out in the weather with us.

We set up temporary shelters on higher ground above the village and prepared to wait it out. We did not want to put our people in danger. When the soldiers came back at dawn to search the camp, they would have no excuse to mete out punishment on our account.

They did not wait until dawn, and they needed no excuse. They came before there was any light in the sky. We woke to the sounds of attack, to the scent of smoke on the wind, the glow of fire. We ran to the edge of the craggy ledge and looked down on the village. All was confusion. Men were already in the stockade, firing into the wigwams at any who lay inside. Some were shot where they slept, others as they tried to escape, scurrying like rats from a burning barn, only to be cut down. Men, women, children—it made no difference. As the soldiers went through the village, they set fire to each dwelling place. The rush matting was wet only on the outside. The inside layers made excellent tinder. Flames leaped up and sparks flew out as the frame poles and timbers cracked. Soon all was ablaze.

I cast about frantically, trying to see through the fire and smoke. Terror seized me, squeezing my heart, my throat, taking the breath from me. Fear so great I could not see clearly. Black Fox started forward but was dragged back.

"Wait! There are too few of us." Coos, his war leader, held him back. "We can do nothing yet."

We watched as the troop retreated, herding before them those they had not killed, taking them captive. They stopped just outside the burning village to bind the hands and rope the captives together by the neck. Black Fox stood by me, and we strained to see if Speckled Bird was with them. I could tell by their size that some were children, but could not tell if any were her.

"Did you see?" I asked him.

Black Fox shook his head. "But we will find her. I will kill any who harm her. They will pay fortyfold for what they do this day."

Coos called his warriors together. "We will track them. Hope to catch them unawares."

"I will go down to the village." I had already started out.

"It is too dangerous." Coos frowned. "They may send men back to rob or spoil the storage pits. I cannot spare men to go with you."

"I do not ask it. I am Eyes of a Wolf. I go alone."

"No!" Black Fox stepped forward. "I will not let you."

"You are my son," I said gently, "but you cannot command me."

"I will go with you then."

I shook my head. "Your duty lies elsewhere."

The war band was heavily outnumbered already. They needed every man, and he was the best scout they had. He could get right into the midst of the English without any of them noticing him. He could be within feet of them, inches, and they would not know it. They would be lying with their throats cut before any of them realized that the enemy was near. That was his special magic. Coos could not spare him to go down to the village with me.

"Come," Coos urged him. "We must hasten, or they get away."

"Very well." Black Fox turned to me. "But be careful. We will meet back here."

I went down while the buildings were still smoldering. Tears blinded me, set me stumbling so I fell several times on the track. I thought of my life here, of when I first came with Jaybird and White Eagle, me showing the first swell in my belly, how proud we were. I thought of my friends among the women. And my own special one, my little Speckled Bird. There was no one there to see, so I wept openly. How

161

careless we are with happiness when we think it will last forever!

The dead lay all about. Unarmed men, children, women—they had died where they fell, scrambling from sleep. Many had not even left their wigwams; their homes had become their pyres.

I thought, at first, that Speckled Bird had escaped. I pulled aside the charred mats from the side of the longhouse and picked my way through the smoldering interior. I could find no sign of her, although I found others enough to fill my heart to the brim with sorrow.

I thought she must have been taken prisoner and that Black Fox would find her and bring her back to me. Then I saw her. She had sought to escape, running on her swift little legs, but then she must have stumbled. Her foot was still caught, tangled in a fallen cooking frame. She lay as if sleeping, her face clear of any injury, but the dark bloom of blood haloed her head. I knew that she was dead.

I sat on the ground, as frozen and numb as when Jaybird first found me cast out in the forest. I wished that he had left me there. I wished that I had died that day. I remembered White Eagle's extra look of sadness. All those years ago, he had known that this would happen. Such knowledge is a grievous burden. No wonder he longed to leave this world.

I was so lost in grief, I did not hear him until he was upon me. I did not even hear his horse.

John Samson. He slid from the saddle and walked toward me. His step was silent. Even though he was dressed as a white man, he still wore moccasins.

"I knew you'd be back, Eyes of a Wolf. I know why they call you so. I had no use for your whelp, but you—you are worth money."

"Come no closer." I stood and loosened the tomahawk at my belt. "Or it will be the worse for you."

"What can you do, a woman alone?"

"You are a traitor to your people and a killer of children. You do not deserve to live."

"What will you do? Put a spell on me?" He laughed. "I have heard you are strong in sorcery."

"Do you want to see?"

I gave him the wolf in me. His mocking smile died and he paled as a snarling she-wolf took my place. I could have killed him myself, torn his throat out, but I dislike the taste of blood in my mouth. Instead I kept him rooted as I assumed my own shape again. He stood before me motionless as a statue, seeing nothing, hearing nothing until the tomahawk landed with a splintering thud in the center of his chest.

He looked down then, as if he were thinking, "What is that doing there? It was not there before." Then he pitched forward.

I left him with his blood making rivers in the mud and gathered up my Speckled Bird.

I carried her back to the burying ground high on the hill above the ruined village. I laid her beneath the trees, the yellow and red leaves falling upon her, and then I went out to follow the men who had done this to her, to all of us. I saw as if I was a bird, a hawk flying. I saw the column of men making their way to the river. The straggling line of captives was slowing them down. I could see Black Fox and the warriors pursuing. I could lend them my strength, but if the column reached the river, their chance of surprise was lost. Across the river was open country. Once the soldiers gained that, they would have a safe run to the township. They had to be stopped.

I held a thunderbird amulet that White Eagle had given to me. I called on his power now. It had been raining in the mountains for days, weeks now. The night before, we'd seen the lightning flash, heard the thunder roll. Huge black clouds had emptied themselves of rain, filling every freshet, every stream. Now was the time for all that water to find its way downriver.

It came as a pulse, a surge, small at first, but soon it turned into a great wall.

It caught the first horsemen at the fording place. Horses lost their footing; men went down and were swept away in the furious churning mass of water. The rest turned back in confusion. That was when the warriors struck. I heard the screams of men and horses; I saw the blood spray through the air like rain-drops. I rose higher and higher until I could no longer hear, no longer see them. Then I came back to Speck-led Bird.

I chose a place under a strong, young, straight-growing silver birch. The trunk shone bright and the small yellow leaves pattered down on both of us as I took off my beads and bracelets, the gifts that Jaybird had given me, and laid them about her. I took White Eagle's thunderbird amulet and put it on her breast, closing her fingers around it. I cut my hair with a knife and put the thick braids about her shoulders. I stripped bark from the trees and wrapped her before laying her facing the east in the way of her father's people. Then I scattered the earth upon her and said my last farewell.

The story White Eagle had told in the cave came back to me. I knew now why he had told it. He had known that the days would bend toward this one, even in the time of my youth, in my first love for Jaybird, before Speckled Bird was ever conceived. Wisdom and knowledge are born of suffering. I understood that now as I threw the earth down upon my lovely child.

I squatted long at the foot of her grave in the pose of those who want to bring death upon them-selves, with my knees drawn up and my head resting on my folded arms. At first I meant to follow her, take the journey that White Eagle had taken, but I understood the lesson of his story. Such things are not to be. Instead I prayed fervently that Jaybird would stop in his own journey along the way of the dead. That the thongs of his moccasins would snap, and as he bent to mend them, his Speckled Bird would come to him, a quick flying thing. He would sweep her up and carry her on his shoulders, as he had so many times in life, so now in death, and they would go forward together to Kiehtan's great door.

I smeared my face with ashes from some long-dead fire and set myself to watch through the night to the cold light of dawn.

I traveled in dream to White Eagle, climbing back toward the mountains. If ever I needed him, I needed him now. At length I came to the great rock face that rose up sheer to the Cave of the Ancestors. It had been snowing, the first snow of winter, and the gray rock was banked by thin drifts carved by the wind into delicate flutes and ridges. The cold was biting, just as it had been when I first came to this place. I saw now what I had not the eyes to see then. The cliff was carved with strange devices: whirling shapes, circles and spirals. Some had been there since Moses walked beside the Nile, since Noah prepared his great ark. These were not man's doing. They marked the place as spirit, *manitou*. They were carved by the first beings to show the beginning and end of things.

White Eagle was waiting there for me. He was dressed for a journey, a quiver of arrows and a bag of rations slung at his belt, his bow across his back. Black and vermilion painting stood like a mask on a face as white as his snowy hair.

He uttered no word of greeting. He touched my face, his hands trembling like leaves as he wiped the tears from my cheeks. He took me in his arms and held me as tenderly as the father I had never known. I felt his frailty, his bones as thin as a bird's beneath his clothes.

Then we sat down with the towering cliff above us and he talked to me.

"We cannot win this war." He drew a map with a stick on the ground. "I see a land with no place for us in it. I have looked for an end to the white men coming, but I see none. They are like the snow at the time of white frost forming." He held out his hand to catch at the sparse drifting flakes. "At first there are few; they scarcely cover the ground. But if you look, you see each is different, and as the days go on toward midwinter, more and more fall down, and more and more, until the world is white with them. The people long then for the sun's returning, for warm spring rains to fetch it away. Yet for us there will be no thawing. It will be winter all year-round." He looked up at me, his dark eyes fathomless. "They will make this land their own, and there will be no room for us.

They will not stop coming until the land is quite filled up. You know. You who were born among them. They will seek to claim you, but you cannot go back. Neither can you follow the road to the west, however much you might want to take it. It is closed to you until your own time comes, and you have many years yet. You have spilled heart's blood, my daughter, and the wound is fresh within you, but you must go on; the people need you. Your life is with the people now." He raised his eyes to the sky, then looked to the mountains retreating northward. "Go to our Pennacook brothers. If you need me, I will guide you. Take this as a sign that I will be with you."

He took an eagle feather from his hair and gave it to me, then stood and helped me to my feet.

"Now is the time of leaving. I must go from here. Soon the forests round about will ring with the white man's ax. His plows will tear the land. One day he will hollow even this mountain, taking the stone to build and to burn in fires. It is time for the ancestors to sleep. Let the earth take them to her."

He stared up at the rock face. He blinked and the ground quaked under our feet and rocks began to tumble. When the dust had cleared, there was no cave. It was as if it had never been.

He held up his arms. His hands no longer shook and trembled. Then he walked away, setting off west to the place of the setting sun. With each step he seemed to grow straighter; each stride he took was longer, until from a distance I would have taken him for a young man going back to his village, a successful hunt completed. I was about to lose yet another of the ones I held dear to me, but I did not seek to stop him, or call after him. How can you stop a spirit?

I stayed at the burying place until the captives came
back. They were escorted by the warriors riding on
horses that they had taken from the soldiers. Coos,
the war leader, came first, large bulging baskets slung
over his saddle. On the top I could see a hand; it was
turned up and open, as though ready to receive a gift.
The base of the carrier oozed and dripped, the fibers
soaked and blackened with blood. It was the custom
to take the heads and hands of enemies.

The sun went down, staining the western sky red,
as Hoosac collected what was left of his people and
made temporary camp in the woods. The sunset was
matched by an equal glow to the north. Across the
valley another town was burning.

Hoosac posted watchers as we buried the rest of
the dead. Then the warriors built their fire away from

the rest of us. They would talk of their triumph far into the night, telling their exploits again and again, until they became part of each man's story and each man had a part in the story. Thus it would pass into the memory of the band.

Black Fox did not join them. He had come back full of foreboding when he did not find Speckled Bird among the captives, and when I told him what had happened to her, he took it very hard. Tears melted the paint on his face, streaking it down his cheeks. He took me in his arms and we clung together. I offered what comfort I could, but he went from me, his sorrow beyond sharing even with me.

We found him the next morning watching by her side. He had tended her grave most carefully, heaping up the earth and piling rocks upon it so no animal could despoil it. He had combed the country far and wide, collecting stones and shells from river and lake, arranging them in ways that would please her. As in life, so in death, he had made toys for her, whittling soft pine into a doll, dressing it in cornhusks. He had fashioned little figures from sticks and hung them up in the trees, to turn and twist in the breeze, as he had done above her cradle board when she was a baby. He stood now, facing east, still as a statue in the first pale rays of the rising sun.

*   *   *

We left soon after dawn, going by way of the village. What could not be salvaged from the wreck was broken, burned, and scattered, the ground sewn with ashes. As we went I saw people taking special note of all they saw. They knew they would not return to this land anymore. Every tree, every stone, each fold in the hills, the exact curve the river took through the valley, each part of the homeland was committed to memory, as one who feels blindness fast approaching might strive to learn the face of a dear one before the darkness descends.

I had seen the look before, on the faces of those who took ship from England. I thought of John Rivers and Tobias and the men of Beulah. They were fierce and tenacious, and there was no going back for them either. They would not give up what they had come here for. They had guns in plenty, besides, and their people did not fall ill and die. This was a fight to the finish, and I did not need White Eagle to tell me who would win.

The way north took us past the neighboring English settlement. Behind the broken stockade, smoke still curled from houses left to burn through the night. The devastation wrought there was equal, if not greater than, in our own village, but it gave me no satisfaction. I felt torn between two peoples. Rebekah and Tobias could have been living here, or John and Sarah, or it could have been myself.

The ground was scuffed, the half-frozen mud pocked with hoof marks and the confused trampling of many feet, leather shod and booted. They must have taken prisoners with them, but moccasins make little imprint.

"Nipmucs. A big force. They went off to the west."

The trail led down to the river, marked by a spoilage of plunder: torn articles of clothing, a cast shoe, a child's doll. There, a low screening of willows masked a ghastly sight. Mist crept in from the river and lay like a shroud over the bodies of women and children with the morning frost white upon them; their blood broken into lumps of crimson. All of them had been scalped.

"To slay all!" I looked around, appalled.

"They do not slay all. They took those who could walk, who would survive the journey." Black Fox continued to gaze at the sorry heaps. "These would hold up the march. They have far to go to reach safety and must move quickly. Is it better to wait until they can walk no farther, then leave them to the wolves or to perish in the cold?"

"But these are babies. Little children! It is cruel."

"*War* is cruel. How can you say that, Mother? You saw what they did to our people, to Speckled Bird."

He folded his arms and looked at me accusingly. His face was fresh painted; his narrow crest of hair newly dressed with feathers earned in the last skirmish. The tears he had shed over Speckled Bird had washed away what was left of his childhood. He looked older than his years, much older, and ever more ferocious, but he was my son. I would not be intimidated.

"We can at least offer them burial."

"Let them bury their own." He turned away. "We must hasten on unless you wish to join them. Troopers may be on their way, even now."

"There may be those alive." I looked toward the settlement. "In need of succor."

"With the Nipmucs?" His laughter rang out, hard and mirthless. "I think not."

• Mary •
The Settlement

I was determined to enter the settlement and see if there was anyone left alive there. I was joined by others, who came not to help, but to glean what the Nipmucs had left, searching for food, for blankets, anything that had not already been taken. War was making us into birds of carrion, scavenging among the destruction.

In many of the houses, the roofs had burned and beams had fallen, but walls and floors remained relatively intact. Men and women lay where they had been struck down. Each one was scalped and beyond my help.

I crossed the threshold of a house near the center of the settlement. The door lay twisted, broken on its hinges, shattered and splintered by blows from a hatchet. The roof was gone; the house lay open to the elements. Halfway across the floor the body of a man lay trapped under a cross of burnt and fallen beams. There was nothing I could do for him. He was dead even before the roof fell down on him. A blow from a war club had crushed his skull like an eggshell.

I stepped over him into a mess of smashed plates thrown from an overturned table. Over in the corner, slashed bedding smoldered, chests from England gaped open, their contents spilling. Broken pots littered the cold, ashy hearth. Beneath my feet was a trap door, leading to a root cellar. I did not want to join in the scavenging, but we needed food for the journey, for our own survival.

I pulled up the trap, thinking I might find their place of winter storage. Instead I found a boy. He was lying on his back, a great gash on his forehead. I knelt down beside him. The wound was deep and encrusted with black, but fresh blood seeped from the ragged edges. He lay insensible, pallid unto death, but a faint pulse beat in his neck. He was alive.

Black Fox came to see what I had discovered. When he saw, he took out his hatchet and his scalping knife.

"No!" I held his arm. "He's no more than a boy. He will not die."

I was determined to save him. There was too much death around me already, and I was a healer. It was my duty to preserve life, not take it. I bid Black

Fox to lift him out into the open. A stream ran through the village. I carried water from it to bathe his face and clean the filthy wound. His eyelids fluttered open. The sight of us set him swooning again, but I resolved to take him with us. I made a traveling frame for him, binding him to it, then bid Black Fox to tow it while I walked behind.

When we stopped and camped for the night, I bathed his wound again. He was still insensible, so I left him strapped to the frame and scoured the woods around for what I would need to heal his wound. I scraped gum from the balsam fir and gathered oak leaves and yarrow to clean and heal the cut, white willow bark to stew and infuse to take away the pain. When I had what was required, I hastened back.

The others had made camp, putting up temporary shelters, cutting poles from the surrounding forest, and laying on rush mats that we had brought with us. Black Fox had made a shelter and was seeing to the fire. The boy was still strapped to his frame. I untied him and put him on the bed of leaves and fir branches that Black Fox had prepared for me.

"I made it for you. Not him."

He stalked off, offended that I'd spurned the care he had taken, but I had real hurts to tend, not just injured feelings. Black Fox would come back, given time. I set a pot to boil over the fire to infuse the bark

I had collected, and set about dressing the boy's wounds. He still lay insensible, despite the pain I must have been inflicting on him.

"Do you think he will recover?" Black Fox asked when he returned.

He regarded him with cold curiosity, as if this were a dog or some other injured animal I'd brought in to treat. The boy's face was still deathly pale; freckles stood out like a spattering of mud over his cheeks. Black Fox's expression darkened. He knelt, looking closer.

"He is speckled. As speckled as . . ."

He twisted away, the pain of loss upon him again. Then he took out his knife and grabbed a hank of the tousled fair hair. It was dirty and tangled but gold shone here and there.

"No." I held his wrist. "You will not do it."

"Why should he live, when she is dead and left to lie in the cold earth?"

"Life replaces life. He is just a child, like she was. Speckled Bird was ever kind-hearted and would want us to take care of him, to let him have her bed and place at the fire."

He gripped his knife tight and continued to stare down at the white skin and fair hair.

"I know it is difficult for you. Their blood runs in your veins, too. It is hard to be caught between two peoples."

"For you, Mother, maybe. Not for me. I am Pentucket."

He looked at me then, his dark slanting eyes alive with a mix of hatred and pride. I thought he would defy me, but he did not. He put his knife by and pledged not to harm the boy. He then left to sleep elsewhere. He promised so easily because he thought the boy's life lost already, but I knew that it was not. I made a makeshift pallet across from him, but I slept little. I tended the fire and kept my eyes on him, watching on until morning, hoping to save one life out of all those lost.

The boy woke as dawn streaked the sky. His eyes opened, blue and unfocused. He made no sense of what he saw, but he was awake long enough to sip the decoction I had prepared and to take a little broth before he slipped back into unconsciousness.

I worried that the blow that had rendered him insensible might have robbed him of his wits as well. Even the bumping of the traveling frame did little to rouse him. On the next night, however, he seemed a little better, well enough to sit up and take in the world about him. His eyes widened in very great wonder at my presence and what I was doing traveling with savages. His fear decreased when I spoke to him in English.

"I knew by your eyes you weren't one of them. How came you among them? Were you captured?"

"A story for another day."

"How came I to be here?"

"You were hurt. You must rest now and get well."

He frowned as if trying to remember who he was and what had happened; then he winced at the pain, for although it was healing, his wound was still tender.

"Do not distress yourself. You must rest."

"How can I?" He struggled to sit upright. "Who are you? What is your name?"

I told him.

"No, your proper name. Your English name."

"No one has called me it for many years now, but my name is Mary."

"Then that is what I will call you."

"What is your name?"

He thought, wincing again at the pain in his head. He closed his eyes; tears came from the sides.

"I do not recall."

"Never mind. Drink this." I gave him a draft from my small stock of sleeping potions.

He was weak and often fell into insensibility. I fed him broth when he was awake and prayed that his strength would return quickly. I knew how Indians dealt with laggard captives.

Black Fox kept his distance from the boy. He did not offer to help with him, and I did not ask. I knew how my son felt about the captive, but I would not abandon him, not now that he was recovering.

The boy was young and quick to get his strength back; with it came his memory. His name was Ephraim Carlton. He was eleven years old, although I had taken him for younger. He asked me what had happened to the people in the settlement.

"Some were killed and some taken."

"What about the place where I was dwelling?"

I remembered the body under the fallen beams, but he was not ready to hear about that.

"No way of telling," I said. "I was not present, so did not see what happened. Killed or captured."

"I'm sorry for it, either one. They was good people. Not kin to me, though they treated me kindly."

"What of your family?"

"I don't remember my ma, and my pa's dead. Kilt in an accident. He was out felling trees when one went the wrong way, caught him on the way down, pinned him right to the ground."

"Had you been long in the settlement?"

The boy shook his head. "Been here, been there. Even spent time in Virginia, but the climate wasn't suiting my pa. Anyways, Mr. Barker took me in after Pa had his accident. I been working for him since. When the attack started, I helped fight off the first wave, but then we ran out of powder. Mr. Barker, he reversed his weapon and stood by the door ready to club the first savage son of a whore that came through the door—them's his words, not mine. He bid me and his wife and little girl to hide in the root cellar. Was they . . ."

"They were not there. Perhaps they were taken."

"P'raps." Tears squeezed from the corner of his eyes. "I pray it be so. Anyways" —he wiped his nose on the back of his hand— "anyways, I stood in front of 'em for when the savages come. We heard the door smashed down and things thrown about and breaking. Then it went quiet and all we heard was the padding of moccasin skins soft across the wood. We could see him through cracks in the boards of the floor. Even the child was hushed by the fear of it. We near didn't breathe, hoping he'll miss us, but then the trap goes up. I steps in front, ready to fight. I see him looking, his face painted, quartered and striped, white, black, and red. I scarce saw a man there, more a devil. Then I see his arm go back and I don't remember no more.

"They must have took Mrs. Barker and the child and left me for dead. It's lucky they didn't scalp me." He touched his head. "Too intent on their other prizes to harvest my hair, most likely."

Ephraim was getting better by the day, but I worried about Black Fox, how things would be between us. I understood his jealousy and knew the wellspring of his enmity, but he had to understand this of me: I was a healer and it was my duty to offer my skill to any in need of it. Friend or foe, it did not matter.

Perhaps he did begin to understand, for I found little gifts of game left outside our hut: a haunch of venison, two fat ducks. I saw it as a sign that he wanted to make peace. Black Fox spent much time with the men of the tribe, hunting and preparing for war, but he came back to eat at my fire. I was glad of that, even though he refused to acknowledge Ephraim's presence.

The rest of the tribe was leaving to go south to join with tribes at Mount Wachusett, where Metacom had set up his winter camp. A great host was collecting together to make war on the English towns.

I would not go with them. I would not join the fighting. I belonged to both sides, and this was tearing the heart from inside me. I wished to see no more killing. It tore my heart further to see my son go with them, but he was a warrior now and a scout of great cunning. Few were as good as he. It was clear where his duty lay.

When the time came for him to leave, I knew better than to tell him to be careful, not to take risks with his life. He was going off to war. All I could do was offer the protection it was in my power to give.

"I will do what I can to watch over you. Meanwhile, I want you to have this." I took the feather White Eagle had given me from my pouch. "Your great-grandfather gave it to me, and now I give it to you. May his spirit be with you."

He took the feather and fixed it in his own scalp lock.

"I hope there will be others watching from the world of spirit." I saw by his eyes he meant his father and Speckled Bird. "And I pray I will not disappoint them. Look out for me, in the evening and in the morning—I will return to you."

He swung up on his horse, then turned in the saddle and gave me one of his rare smiles. Then he was gone, the rest of the band with him. Ephraim and I were alone in the forest.

Ephraim was strong enough to travel now. He walked by my side as we journeyed north.

"I have to tell you, Mary," he announced to me as we went onward. "I see it as my duty to escape as soon as may be and join the fight."

"That is your choice, but I counsel you not to try it yet."

"You ain't going to stop me."

"Neither will I, but the forest might. You are still weak from your injuries, and we travel far from the places you know. You will be lost in a minute. There are few settlements this far north, and if you are found by a war band, they will show no mercy."

"But where, where are we going?" Ephraim looked about the forest.

I did not answer.

I walked in constant sorrow, sick to the depths of my being. My son had taken the war trail. I did not know whether I would ever see him again. Fear for him added to the loss of Jaybird and my pretty one. My heart had no time to heal. Each new dawning tore the wound open afresh. The pain was as piercing as in the first moment of knowing, and with every waking minute a sharp blade turned in my heart.

• Mary •

Quechee—the Place of Quick Whirling Falls

Our roving was stopped by a tall man standing by the white-water rush and surge of a tumbling river. I could see he was Pennacook by the way he dressed his hair and the markings on his skin. He came forward when he saw us, as though he had been waiting.

"You are Eyes of a Wolf." He stepped away from the roar of the water, his hand raised in greeting. He was older than I had first thought, and he limped, shorter in one leg than the other. "I am Sparks Fire."

"How do you know my name?"

"I was told in dream of your coming and guided to this place." He turned and pointed. High on the bluff behind him, an eagle perched on the topmost branch of a white pine. "I knew Jaybird when he was a little boy, before the sickness came to his village. His father's band and mine would join to fish the falls." He smiled and his eyes creased in remembered laughter. "He vexed me greatly, for he was always wanting to join in our games, although he was so much younger. I called him Little Brother, so you will be my sister." He looked down at me, recollected merriment laced with sadness. "I grieve for your loss. Your sorrow is my sorrow."

He said no more. We both looked up. A flapping of wings announced the eagle's departure. It wheeled in the sky above us and flew into the fiery heart of the setting sun.

We wintered in the camp of Sparks Fire's Pennacook band. They welcomed us not as outcasts seeking refuge, but as kin. They gave freely of all they had: food, clothing, and shelter. I bore the mark on my cheek, and space was made in the longhouse of the Wolf Clan. We lived as a family, Ephraim and me. Ephraim did not try to escape. How could he? The winter and the forest held him faster than any stockade. We were much farther north than we had been before, and the weather was ever more bitter. I had not known where we would go when the boy and I commenced our wandering, but now I was glad to have found shelter in the warm smoky darkness where many families lived together.

We wanted for nothing. We were given furs for clothing and bed coverings. The band had food stored from the summer harvest, and game was plentiful in these vast northern woods. I fashioned new clothes for Ephraim, for his were torn, too thin for the winter, and all but worn out. I made him fur-lined moccasins and a jerkin and leggings of soft deerskin. I made sure he was not treated as a captive. He was accepted as my son. I taught him the words for all around him, and Sparks Fire taught him to hunt. When he was not hunting, he was with the other boys, sliding in the snow and on the ice.

Often in the evening, Sparks Fire would come and share our hearth. If he had been hunting, he would bring his kill to us. He came to me as a brother. He was Wolf Clan, and members of the same clan are forbidden to marry. Besides, I was not looking for a husband. After my Jaybird, how could I think of another?

We shared our sorrow. He had lost his own wife to sickness the year before, and he still carried the sadness with him. His daughter was married and lived with her mother's clan. His son Naugatuck was with the war bands in the south. White Deer, Naugatuck's wife, had gone back to her mother until her husband's return. He had no other children living; his two younger ones had joined their mother on the path to the land in the west.

He lit his pipe from the embers. "Truly sickness takes more than musket balls, more and more each time it visits. This war is the last flowering of our power."

"How goes it?"

He drew on his pipe and then exhaled, regarding me through the smoke.

"How am I to know? I am far from Wannalancet's council fire."

"That may be so, but I see messengers come and go."

Wannalancet, *sachem* of the Pennacook, was camped at Lake Winnipesaukee to the north of us. Runners from the south often stopped at our camp on their way to him. One of the messengers was Sparks Fire's son Naugatuck. I had asked him to look for Black Fox with the Pentucket band, and he said he would find him. I sent new moccasins. Black Fox's would be worn through by now, and these were lined with rabbit fur, for it was the deepest part of winter. I told Naugatuck to tell him I did well.

Sparks Fire knew I feared for my son.

"He is safe for the moment. It is the time of the shortest days, when the trees crack with coldness. No one fights now, not even the Englishmen. Naugatuck tells me the warriors are waiting for the sun to gain strength in the sky; then they will move against the English towns."

We sat in silence then, thinking of our sons.

"Why are you so far from Wannalancet?"

"He is Christian. I would not convert to this new religion. To me, the Great Spirit is the Great Spirit— why should I call him God? To me he will always be Manitou."

By mid-February messengers were bringing news of fresh attacks, of towns sacked and abandoned along a wide frontier from north to south. By March, the time of ice melting, Indian bands had penetrated as far as Medfield and even threatened Boston itself. I knew my son would be in the thick of the fighting. Each fresh report made me sick for news of him.

Naugatuck came toward the end of March and told me that Black Fox had come through unharmed. He had to stay in the south, but he sent a token, a little fox head made from the same soft black stone used to fashion pipes. Black Fox had traded for the pipe stone and carved it in the idleness of the winter camps. He was ever clever with his hands, and it was cunningly made, with slanting eyes and a grinning mouth. It was bored behind the ears to be used as a toggle. This made me smile through my tears. Black Fox always liked to make things that could be used.

With the coming of spring, the village moved to their summer site. For a while the war was forgotten in the stripping of the camp. The houses dismantled, the covering mats untied and rolled, and the poles left for next winter.

"If there be another wintering here." Sparks Fire had come to help us. He was loading bundles on his carrying frame. Now he looked thoughtful.

"Why not? Wannalancet is neutral—besides, he's Christian."

I had finished making my pack and was fashioning one for Ephraim to carry. These removals meant a full load for everybody. Even children had to do their share.

"That makes no difference. The Christian Indians have been taken from the praying towns and put all together on an island in Boston Harbor." He tightened a strap viciously. "That is how the English repay loyalty."

I prepared for this new journey with all his uncertainty, and more. I remembered White Eagle's words. The Indians could not possibly win this war. I had sought to escape it, but it was coming nearer. I had not thought to live with my own kind again, but if the Indians were defeated and I was taken back, what would happen to me then?

• Mary •
Second Remove

The journey to their summer place took us up the Merrimack River and then by lesser rivers and portage to the wide expanse of Lake Winnipesaukee.

The site lay behind a screen of willows on the south side of the lake. Within a day the village was made again, and all was peaceful as we picked up the rhythm of the year. I helped the women clear the gardens for planting. I worked with White Deer, Naugatuck's young wife, Sparks Fire's daughter-in-law. Ephraim ran with the other boys, playing stickball and football out on the rough meadow, just as Black Fox had done, just as boys in my village in England had done so many years ago.

With the springtime digging and planting, it was sometimes easy to forget that there was a war going on. It was still far to the south of us, but messengers came and went with greater frequency, and Sparks

Fire was often called to Wannalancet's camp at the other end of the lake.

As spring advanced to summer, the news from the south became increasingly gloomy. The runners no longer spoke of victory. They told of lack of powder and ammunition, of Mohawks creeping from the west now that attention was not on them. Above all, they spoke of hunger and sickness, women too far from their home villages to grow anything, men too busy fighting to hunt. There was scant food in the towns attacked, and what had been taken was fast running out. Starvation stalked the camps.

The war was like a seesaw, and the English side was weighted with men, muskets, and money. With no way for food to be replenished, it was only a matter of time before Metacom's forces were defeated. And so it was to be. The lone messengers were replaced by ragged bands fleeing from the south. They told of a great defeat.

Now muster drums were beating through the Commonwealth towns. Hostile bands would be hunted, harried, and hounded through the country. Any Indian refusing to surrender could expect no quarter. They would be killed. Those who surrendered could expect to be bound as servants or sold into slavery.

The tribes were scattering. Different bands were seeking to make separate peace. News came that

Metacom had gone south to his homeland. He was being hunted through the swamps as boys hunt frogs. Then we heard that he was dead. His head had been taken to Plymouth and displayed on a pole as a warning and an act of vengeance.

Metacom's death did not stop the persecution. Soldiers continued to hunt Indians down like rats in a barn. Many groups fled north to us, seeking refuge. These bands arrived weary from travel, with many sick and most half starved; we offered what help we could. It was a time of fear and weary waiting. Black Fox and Naugatuck had not come back. We scanned each group, asking for any news of them. All we heard was rumor and story. They were with this band, or that band, with Metacom himself. They had been in this fight or that attack. Naugatuck had been wounded, but Black Fox had not a scratch on him—it was as if his life were charmed. Many of these stories were months old; some we'd heard before. When we asked their whereabouts now or when they were coming back, we received blank stares and silence. Each one looked to his own survival. We would just have to wait it out.

Some of the bands held English captives. Most of these had already been redeemed, but I saw a few coming in with their captors hoping for ransom or exchange.

I kept out of the way of any white captives. I

made it my business to see that they were given provisions and treated well, but other than that I kept myself separate. I felt no loyalty to them, no bond of blood or kinship. To make myself known would require explanation, and once they knew my history, I knew what their judgment of me would be.

They were not tethered or bound, they could come and go at will, but they were kept close by the forest. They did not congregate together but were scattered through the camp, staying with the families of those who had taken them.

Although I sought to avoid their company and took care to keep separate, I felt one among their number watching me closely. I clearly vexed and troubled her, and she had the air of one who did not like puzzles. I knew her type from Beulah, always busy about other people's business. She reminded me of Martha's sister, Goody Francis. Her name was Mrs. Peterson. Although thin, her clothes worn almost to rags, she knew how to survive among her captors. I never heard her complain, and she had the knack of making herself useful: in sewing, foraging, running errands. It was just such an errand that brought her to me. One evening she approached my camp on the pretext of borrowing some meal.

"I saw your boy . . ." Even in his buckskins, Ephraim's hair gave him away as English. The summer sun had bleached it to corn silk. "Are you captive?"

She looked around furtively. "Where is your master? How long are you taken? Which town?"

"I have no master. I am not captive. I live here freely."

"How can that be?" Her gooseberry eyes grew wide with astonishment, avid to know more.

"I left a settlement many years ago."

"Of your own free will?"

"Not exactly. I was no longer welcome."

She mulled over this unusual occurrence.

"I have only heard one such story. A visiting minister, I forget his name now, he told us of a girl who bewitched a settlement and ran away to join the spirits in the forest."

"Nothing of that sort happened to me," I added quickly. "I had a disagreement with my mistress, over a personal matter of a delicate nature." I dropped my eyes, sure she would understand.

"Unchastity?" She looked suitably shocked.

I nodded. "My mistress took my master's side against me. I was headstrong in those days and foolish, and ran away. I became hopelessly lost in the forest and was found by a Pentucket band. I have been with them ever since. What's left of them, that is. My husband was killed outside Pocumtuck, and my son—"

"You *married* among them!"

She could no longer look at me. Her hand went to her mouth, as though she might vomit. This was far more shocking than a master's seduction of a servant. This was something far too shocking to countenance. Above her torn and dirty collar, her neck reddened to the color of a turkey's wattle.

"I did."

"I see." She kept her lowered eyes away from me. "And the boy? He is not, not born of . . . , I mean, he is so fair. He can't be *native*?"

"No," I laughed at her stifled outrage. "He's not mine."

I told her where he had been taken.

"He will be returned, God willing. As we all will be."

"He has no kin there, as far as I know. When the time comes, it will be his choice to stay or go."

"To go back to civilization or live with savages?" She looked at me. What choice could there be? "You have no other children?"

"I had a daughter." I stopped for a moment, uncertain that my voice would bear the words. "She is dead."

"I have daughters, too. I am sorry for your loss."

Her look of sympathy was genuine enough, but behind it lay the thought that any daughter of mine would be better off dead, I could see it in her eyes.

"They were taken?" I asked her.

She shook her head. "Their father had removed them to a safe town. I was to follow, but . . ." She stopped for a moment, visited again by all that had happened, all that she'd seen. "He is a captain with the militia. Captain Peterson. You might have heard of him?"

I shook my head.

"He is quite famous among *our* people . . ." Her look mixed pride with contempt. "My girls . . ." Collecting herself, she went on. "My girls were safe away when the savages attacked. I praise God for it. I fear they would not have survived."

"You have been treated badly?"

"Not as such, and I've been offered no insult, but life among them is cruel harsh."

"No more than it is for them."

"There's truth in that." She looked down at her blackened broken nails and dirty hands. "I ask God for His strength that I might endure it."

She hurried away then; her master was calling for her. He was not an unfair man, but she held him in some fear. I sent her food and fresh clothing and did what I could to ensure that her master was not too hard on her, for some captives were cruelly used, although often they brought this upon themselves.

She contrived to visit me again, this time bringing a piece of tattered Bible with her that she'd traded from one of the Indians. She came in great earnestness, quoting Ezekiel, chapter 18, verse 27: "When the wicked man turneth away from his wickedness . . . and doeth that which is lawful and right, he shall save his soul alive."

I told her that my soul did not need saving. I did not consider myself to be wicked and, according to my own lights, I had ever striven to do that which was lawful and right.

She looked at me as though I had uttered a very great blasphemy. I saw little of her after that.

She made no attempt to come near, but I often felt her watching me. Or more particularly Ephraim. She would stop him, calling him to her to run some trifling errand or other, then keep him in conversation. When I questioned him, he said she spoke to him of the Bible and whether he kept strong in his faith.

"And you answered?"

"Yes, as far as I am able."

"Does she ask anything more?"

Ephraim did not answer. He would have saved me from knowing but was ever an honest lad, and his fair coloring made it hard for him to dissemble.

"What else did she say?"

"She asked me . . ." He hesitated, flushing deeper, and then dropped his voice to a whisper. "She asked if you practice sorcery. She had heard . . . heard it spoken about."

I felt the world slide about me.

"And what did you reply?" I tried to keep my voice light, although a lot depended on the answer he had given her.

"I answered, of course not! I told her, I told her you was a healer, and for that you was revered and respected. I said that you had saved my life and the lives of many others. She said, 'You mean among the Indians?' I said, she might call 'em heathens, but you didn't see no difference between them and Christians."

"I see. Did she ask you anything else?"

"Yes, she did. She asked me if you worshiped."

"And how did you answer that?"

"I said of course you do, but in your own way." He paused. "Which I told her you were bound to do, you having been away from church and regular service this long while." He looked at me. "Did I do wrong? Did I say the wrong thing, Mary?"

"I'm sure you did not." I ruffled his silky soft hair. "Don't worry."

"If I did, I didn't mean to." He frowned, thoroughly agitated now. "And I am truly sorry. I only said the truth, though." His brow cleared as a fresh thought occurred to him. "That can't do no harm, can it?"

By harvest time the war was over. Naugatuck and Black
Fox were among the last of the warriors to return to
the camp. They came in dusty and tired from many
days' traveling. They were thin and half starving, their
clothes ragged, moccasins worn through, and feet
bloody, but they were alive. The whole camp came out
to greet them, and it was almost impossible to get near
in the crush. Then the crowd parted and my son came
to me. The months of anxious waiting melted into a
moment of pure gladness, and I did not have to tell
him how happy I was to see him back.

He was taken from me then, going with the other
men to the sweat lodge, to be cleansed and dressed
ready for the celebrations. I sent fresh garments that I
had made during the time of waiting and joined the
other women. We gathered all we could find together
to make a feast of welcome home.

There had been precious little to celebrate in recent months, and all were invited without exception. Not everyone, however, took up the invitation. Mrs. Peterson stayed by her own fireside. At the height of the festivities, I noticed someone else was absent. Ephraim had disappeared. I thought he was with the other boys, who were running here and there in wild play, but I did not find him with them. I found him in Mrs. Peterson's camp. He said that he had felt out of place now that Black Fox was back.

He returned with me on that occasion, but he began to spend more and more time with the English-woman. She welcomed him readily and made a deal of a fuss over him. Perhaps he felt I neglected him in my joy at having my son back again. Perhaps he was wary of Black Fox himself. My son had come back a seasoned warrior with a fierce reputation, and although he held to his promise and showed no unkindness to the boy, he showed no friendship, either, and I could see why Ephraim might fear him.

Now that the war was over, Wannalancet was summoned to Dover to meet with a Major Richard Waldron to formally agree on the peace and to hand over such captives as had lately come into his care. It was Ephraim's decision whether or not to go with them. I would be sad to see him go, sadder than I wanted him to know, but I had said that he could choose when the time came. I had given my word on it, and I am not one to go back on what I have promised.

I still thought that he might stay with me, but on the appointed day, he left with Mrs. Peterson. He would have none to claim him, by his own account having no living relations in the colony, but Mrs. Peterson would take care of him. Although I would hardly call us friends, she promised this to me.

Sparks Fire counseled Black Fox and Naugatuck not to go to the meeting. He thought Wannalancet mistaken in the trust he showed toward the English. "We are all their enemies now." That was how he saw it.

Good that he did and that our sons heeded his warning, for many who went never came back. Although Wannalancet acted in good faith, he was tricked. He went to make peace with the English, nation unto nation, but Waldron saw it otherwise. In his eyes, Wannalancet was harboring fugitives and this was an act of war. Hundreds were killed and many more taken captive to be sold as slaves, either here or in the Indies.

It was an angry band of warriors who came back to the camps. Wannalancet felt that he'd been tricked and betrayed. He had been neutral before, but this made the English his enemies.

Now that Black Fox was with me, I made a new dwelling away from the longhouse. Sparks Fire often came to sit at our hearth, to talk with Black Fox about the war, smoke a pipe, and bring news from the council fire. He was with us one evening, just before night was falling, when there was a knock on the flap of the wigwam. It was one of Sparks Fire's men. He struggled through the door with something clutched in his arms. I thought at first that he held a dog or some injured animal. Then I saw the head cradled on his arm. The fair hair was shorn to stubble, but I knew it was Ephraim. His feet were bloody, the moccasins worn to shreds; his arms and legs were scratched and scored by branch and thorn; his face was puffed and swollen with insect bites. His clothes smelled rank as a dung heap.

I bade the warrior to lay him down, and I cut the filthy skins away from him. Sparks Fire carried him to the sweat lodge, and there the men bathed and tended him. He came back wrapped in furs and was set down to sleep.

He slept until the evening of the next day. He woke ravenous but still so weak that his hands trembled, knocking the horn spoon against the wood of the bowl. I fed him myself, and then undid his bundle to find fresh clothes for him.

"You kept my bundle?"

"I have thrown nothing of yours away."

"Good. Because I reckon I'm going to stay."

"What happened?"

"I didn't like it. Didn't like how they was with me."

"Mrs. Peterson?"

"Not so much her. Her husband. The Captain."

"Did he not treat you well?"

"Weren't just that." He turned from me, his eyes suddenly bright with tears. "There were other things, too."

I waited for him to recover and go on.

"When I seen how it was, I changed my mind. I wanted to go back with Wannalancet, but I was held fast. That woman, Mrs. Peterson, commenced fussing over me. Had me scrubbed, and none too gently, although I weren't in need of a wash. She put me into boys' clothes. I forgot how wool itches next to the skin, and the boots pinched my feet. I asked for my old clothes back, at least my moccasins, but it was like I asked for something dirty.

"They commenced to pray over me and sermonize. I'd forgotten how hard wood benches are, and the minister up there telling lies. Mrs. Peterson, I didn't mind her so much, but her husband had set ideas on how a boy should be, and they did not sit well with me. He begins specifying about order and discipline, and all the time he has a switch and he's beating the words out into his other hand. I looks at the girls, his daughters. They listen with their heads down and don't dare catch his eyes, mine neither.

"That night, I'm in bed and I'm weighing one side along another. My pa weren't that way, and it's bin a long time since anyone told me what to do or ordered me about when I don't see no reason for it. She says I ain't a servant, but that's how it feels to me. So, I creep out dead of night—I can see in the dark and move with no noise. I find my clothes, the ones you made, put on the midden pile. They don't smell so good, but I put 'em on anyways, thinking they will hide my own scent if they send dogs after me. Daylight sees me take the trail north. I'd taken good note of which way we'd come, like Sparks Fire taught me.

"I ain't alone in that. A whole army been on the move. Englishmen on horses. I came across what they'd done. Shot 'em down like dogs. Some were Nashua, I reckon, by the markings on 'em. But some I knew. Been here the whole time, never took the war trail at all, but the soldiers weren't asking, just shooting. They shot some right in the back. That's how much cowards they are. No man would do that. Scalps taken, too—what kind of white folks would do that?"

"How do you know it was not another tribe?"

"They was white all right. I seen the hoof prints milled about in the mud and blood, and I came across their camp later that night. Sight farther on there's a village all burnt. I pushed on past, leaving myself no time to rest. I feared what I'd find. I feared you'd be gone, I feared . . ." He bit his lip to crescent redness, trying to hold his tears back. "Glad you ain't, that's all.

"I came back because . . . all I got by way of family is right here." He looked at me. "You're the nearest I've ever known to a mother. And . . ." He looked at Sparks Fire now, his eyes glittering with unshed tears. "And I figured, since my own pa's dead now, I figured I could choose my own, and it weren't going to be Captain Peterson."

Sparks Fire smiled and reached out his hand to touch the boy's stubbly head.

"A man would do well to have such a one as his son. Naugatuck will be proud to call you brother."

"I, too, would be proud." Black Fox had been listening all the while, resting on his sleeping platform. He rose from his place in the shadows and came toward the boy. "You have showed yourself to be as brave and cunning as any warrior among us. You have suffered much to come back, and you are here because you have chosen your people. You are one of us now."

He took out his scalping knife, testing the thin, finely honed blade as he squatted next to Ephraim. The boy did not even wince as the knife sliced through the flesh at the base of his thumb. Black Fox cut himself in the same manner and clasped their two hands together, binding them around with his head cloth so their two bloods ran together.

"Now we are of one blood. We are brothers, you and I."

Ephraim opened his mouth, but no words came. Instead tears spilled down his cheeks. Black Fox waited until the storm had stilled; then he lifted the boy and carried him to his sleeping place.

Sparks Fire shook tobacco from his pouch and relit his pipe. "Our fires in the south have been quenched with blood. We cannot go back."

"We cannot stay here." Black Fox came back. Ephraim was now sleeping. "I know of this Peterson. Ephraim did well to get away from him, but he is ruthless and he does not like to be beaten. He will come after the boy."

"Wannalancet talks of going north, to the land of the French."

"To Canada?" I asked.

"Some of his people are already there, at a place the French call Saint François." He reached forward and took a brand from the fire to light his pipe. "The French have no love for the English. There can be no peace now."

"We must join them." Black Fox squatted down by the fire.

Sparks Fire grimaced. "The place is full of Blackrobes. They crawl over it like fleas on a dog."

"Blackrobes?" I had not heard the term before,

but I was taken by a sudden coldness, as when a shadow passes over the sun.

"Jesuits." He laughed but there was no mirth in it. "They make your Puritans look like a flock of fat partridges."

"Where will we go, then?" Black Fox was finding it hard to contain his impatience.

"It is for each one to decide. It is a hard thing to leave the land of one's birth, of the birth of one's grandfathers, and their grandfathers. I thought it would be the land of my children, my children's children, but that is not to be. We are torn up like trees in the forest. It is as if a great wind twists us from our roots."

His eyes became dull, like chestnuts left from one season to another. He squatted on his heels, elbows on his knees, head resting on his forearms, and stayed that way for a long time. He rose and left us without another word.

Days passed and Sparks Fire stayed in his state of melancholy. He shunned company, walking by the lake, or taking his canoe out from first light to night falling. Black Fox was all for leaving, but I argued to stay awhile longer. Sparks Fire had been a good friend to me. I would not desert him now.

On the third day, Naugatuck came to me. He was worried about his father.

"He looks to decide what to do. Can't you help him?" the young man asked. "You are strong in spirit, so Black Fox says."

"The future is as closed to me as it is to you or anyone. Sparks Fire seeks solitude because he looks for a sign."

He nodded. The copper disks swinging from his ears and spaced around his neck glowed in the fire-light.

"So do his people. Other bands are leaving. Let us hope the spirits speak to him soon, or he may find that he is the only one left at the lake."

A week went on like this, then Sparks Fire came to me just at sun rising. I knew straightaway that something had happened. His step was light, not heavy and dragging, and when he pushed the flap to my wigwam open, his eyes were full of their old fire.

I bid him break fast with us and then sent Ephraim to join the other boys at play.

I could see by Sparks Fire's face that he had received the sign he wanted. We sat in silence until he was ready to tell me what he had seen.

"Last night as I walked by the lake, I heard the wild geese calling. Later I dreamed I stood in the same place and, looking up, I saw the great lines of them flying over me, spread across the sky like broad-beaten arrowheads. In the dream I could understand their words to me. They spoke of the lake and the Place of the Flint."

I frowned and shook my head. Dreams are of the greatest importance in divining what to do, but I was at a loss to know what this one meant.

"What does it mean?"

"We will go to Missisquoi, the place the Abenaki call Mazipskoik, the Place of the Flint. They have a village there on a great water that they call Bitawbagw, the lake the French have named Champlain."

"Have you told Naugatuck?"

Sparks Fire nodded. "I have told him my dream, and such a plan was in his mind, too."

Black Fox spoke up. "He and I will spend the winter hunting and trapping, getting furs for trading. To carry on this fight, we need powder and muskets; to get them, we must go to the French at Mount Royale."

· Alison ·
Montreal

Alison loved Montreal. It was doubly foreign, being Canadian and French at the same time, and she liked that. It seemed like she hadn't been out of the Institute for months, let alone out of Boston. It was good to get away. She had booked into a hotel in the Latin Quarter. She had to confess to enjoying herself, even if her research wasn't going too well. She was relying on local knowledge, and her contact at McGill didn't sound too hopeful. She was meeting him for dinner; by then he might have something for her. In the meantime, she was free to spend the day sightseeing, walking around the old port and Vieux Montréal and reacquainting herself with the city.

"Your girl is an enigma." That's what her friend Glen told her when she met him in one of the old-town restaurants. "If she was here, there's no trace of her."

Alison poured herself a glass of wine and tried to hide her disappointment.

"But she *could* have come here?"

"It's entirely possible." Glen took a bite of his steak. "Especially if she got caught up in King Philip's War. It was a pretty vicious confrontation. The New England tribes took a pretty good whipping down there, and many of them did come north, some of them bringing white captives."

"But she would not have been a captive."

"White woman with a native band? She'd have been noticed."

Glen finished his *frites* and dabbed his napkin to his lips.

"I'll see if I can find out more for you. I've got a colleague at UQAM. He could know something. It's more his field. I checked with his office. He's been at a conference but is expected back in a day or two."

There was nothing to do but wait. Alison decided that she might as well go up to Quebec. She had friends in the city, and she'd promised herself some time with them. She could stay over and then hit the libraries, searching the archives herself for any reference to Mary.

She returned to Montreal empty-handed and feeling more than a little dispirited. When she got into her room, the message light on the phone was winking. She called down to the front desk.

"Mademoiselle Ellman? We have a fax for you."

Alison stood up, then sat down, then stood again. She paced the room, fax in her hand. Mary had been here. Maybe she'd walked the very same streets Alison had been walking. Glen's friend had given him a reference to a white woman, English, traveling with a native band fleeing New England after King Philip's War. He'd even suggested a possible route they might have taken to get here.

Alison stood at the window, trying to conjure Mary's presence. Ordinarily she liked being near the heart of the city, but now the sounds coming up from the streets all around only served to make her agitation worse. Mary was an enigma; Glen was right. What he'd found out just added to that. It asked more questions than it answered. How did she get here? What happened to her along the way? Where did she go after that? The solution to this, to Mary, did not lie in the modern city; neither did it lie in books, museums, and libraries. It lay with Agnes.

Alison sat down on the bed, pondering the importance of the girl. Agnes had made no contact; Alison didn't even know where she was for sure, but she would have to find her. It was time for their research efforts to come together.

• Agnes •
Looking Glass Lake

Agnes woke again with no idea where she was, or even who she was, but she could remember everything. Scenes came back vivid, newly minted. It was like accessing someone else's memory; there was none left of her own.

She knew she had to do something.

Aunt M was sitting at the table by the window. She came over as soon as she saw that Agnes was awake.

"Are you OK? Do you want anything? Can I fix you something?"

Aunt M knew she was fussing like an old hen, but she was so glad to have her niece back again. Several times tears had leaked from Agnes, seeping from the corners of her eyes, as though whatever she was seeing was too much to bear. Aunt M had been strongly tempted to wake her then, even though she knew such intervention would be dangerous.

"I feel fine."

Aunt M smiled her relief.

"Well, not fine exactly." Agnes frowned, her mind still clouded, her thoughts woolly. "There's something I need you to do."

"Oh, and what's that?"

"I need you to listen."

Her aunt nodded. She understood. When Agnes spoke again, it was to recount the unfolding story, scene by scene. Her aunt listened gravely with the unchanging expression of one long practiced in committing the spoken word to memory.

When Agnes had finished, Aunt M reached up for the maps and spread them out.

"They must have started about here." She pointed with a stubby finger to the ragged-shaped lake on the map. "And gone along these waterways."

She got up from the table and fished about in a can for a Magic Marker. The point squeaked as she made a fat black line on the map's surface. She kept up a running commentary, marking out the route they might have taken. As she spoke it, Agnes saw it, half in her own world, half in another.

They decamped at the time of falling leaves. Canoes laden with everything they had, everything they would need for the winter ahead: food, pots, clothing, furs and coverings, mats to build shelters. Men worked to make the birch-bark canoes ready, resewing seams with black spruce root and caulking each one with resin to make sure that the craft were proof against the water. They built the sides up to take the extra load and decorated the craft from stern to prow, wetting and scraping the bark, marking on signs to protect and preserve. They painted the paddles with resin mixed with dye, then scraped that back to show the things they had seen in their dreams.

The old, the children, dogs, and baggage were placed in the center of the canoes. Women and men sat to the front and rear of them. One in the prow and one aft, to steer and guide; two in the middle to push the craft on. They plied their craft with great skill, gliding in the slipstream, working the ebb to move against the main flow of the water. As they paddled, they sang, chanting out the stories of the tribe, from the first times to this present removal, and every dip of the paddle told the river of their dreams.

Aunt M read off the names of the rivers and mountain ranges, and Agnes saw the water squeezed between great rearing cliffs into white surging torrents, tumbling over rocks and whirled around boulders as big as houses. In some places the rivers became ever narrower and ran ever shallower until they gave out altogether. Then they had to leave the water and carry the canoes and burdens until they found a stream to bear them again.

The journey became a series of flashes: dawn paling the eastern sky, the sun sinking behind the trees, marking the glittering water with bars of darkness. Red campfires sparked on some spit jutting into the flowing stream, or by the shores of some lonely lake where the ducks and geese rested on their way down to the south. Men hunted, barely to be seen in the shadows of the forest. Women scoured for berries, nuts, storing the fruits of autumn against the coming winter, just as the squirrel does. She saw medicine plants close up, turned to nod and smile at a young woman she had never seen in life but knew to be White Deer, Naugatuck's young wife. She felt the need to hurry, to collect nuts, seeds, leaves, roots, and bark, before the land froze and became covered in snow.

She saw the bobbing flotilla follow the flow of rivers great and small until they reached a place where two great rivers joined. From here the pace hastened. In the north, winter comes early. They traveled under blue skies, but the forests were turning; overhanging trees showered them with gold. They were moving up into new mountains, the rivers rushing and wild. Frost rimed the ground and whitened the temporary shelters.

"Guess they'd be about here," Aunt M said quietly, her marker resting at the point on the great divide where one river system gave way to another.

The way was steep and difficult. Everything had to be carried, often taking several journeys, until they reached the head of yet another river. The Winooski. This was the river they sought. It ran downward all the way to the lake.

Aunt M pointed to Lake Champlain, a narrow twisted shape, a blue patch on the map. Agnes felt the swiftness of the river under her. She was taking a gut-wrenching terror ride down to the lake, which was not called Champlain but Bitawbagw, the Door to the Country. She felt almost sick as the swell and movement of the waves caused the canoe to tip and yaw.

Then she was no longer in the craft but soaring up and up, as the sun set, turning the water to a sheet of red. She was looking down now at the thin line of craft turning for the north: frail and tiny, like little leaf boats made by children, on the great expanse of water.

The Abenaki village that the French called Missisquoi had grown into a town, the population swollen by bands fleeing, like us, from the war in the south. The Indian peoples are generous and have a tradition of giving and sharing, helping one another in times of trouble. The Abenaki had extended the hand of friendship to any who wanted to grasp it, and now smoke curled up from myriad cooking fires and hung in the still air, swathed above a sprawling encampment made up of people from many different nations.

I was at a loss to see where we would fit ourselves among this great multitude, but we discovered Pennacook who had come before us and found haven with them.

There were others here besides the native people. Frenchmen. I found them very different from my own countrymen.

Sparks Fire asked me, "How different?"

I told him, "As different as Pennacook from Iroquois."

The first I encountered were called in their own language *coureurs des bois*. They were trappers and fur traders and could be mistaken at first glance for the people with whom they did business. Their skin was burned dark, and they wore their hair long. They dressed in breechclout and buckskin. Only their boots and beards marked them apart from those they called *les sauvages*. Indian men always wore moccasins and plucked the hair from their faces; they considered beards to be ugly. These *coureurs des bois* also differed in another way. Indian men bathe every day, even in winter, breaking ice on a lake or river, scrubbing their bodies with sand or grit, whereas many of the traders stank mightily.

Some of their kind were excellent men who truly admired, shared, and sought to follow an Indian way of life. But others misunderstood what they saw, taking long flowing hair and freedom in dress as an excuse to give themselves over to unkempt filthiness. They attributed the freedom of young girls to bestow favors on whom they chose as moral laxity and were also free with strong liquor, drinking to excess themselves and encouraging it in others. Some of the Indians liked to drink; they said it brought their visions nearer.

221

Anything seen in that way would be false and worthless, but that did little to dissuade those who had already developed a taste for French brandy.

These men were different from any I had encountered before, white or Indian. I went out of my way to avoid them, but Ephraim quickly become enamored. He loved to hear their talk, what he could follow of it. They had journeyed farther than any white man into the deep interior of the continent and would talk long of what they had found there: lakes as great as seas, thunderous waterfalls, endless prairies, and wide rivers that they said led all the way to the western ocean. It was in his heart, even then, to become one of them. I did not prevent him from going to their camp, but it meant sometimes that I had to go in search of him.

It was on just such an errand that I first encountered the one they called Le Frenais. I found Ephraim down by the lake, sitting outside one of their drinking dens. I called him to me and he rose obediently; then one of their number lurched between us. He was a man newly come to the camp and had been celebrating his return from the wilderness, as many of his kind did, with drinking to excess and making free with any woman who came within his compass.

"Who are you?"

"Who are you?" I asked in turn.

At this he staggered, taken aback by my insolence.

"C'm here, you savage . . ."

He went to make a grab for me but was held back by one of his circle. The men around him were from different tribes. There were some from New England among the French and Abenaki.

"She's Yenguese." The man who held his arm spoke Algonquian and looked to be from the south. Pocumtuck maybe, or Nashua. "She travels with a Pennacook band."

"Captive?" He shook off the hand and turned to me.

"I am not a captive." I spoke in the common tongue. I had no French then.

"Who is your master? What does he want for you? I'd take you and the boy together. I could use a woman like you. The boy, too. The English pay well for the return of captives."

"I am not a captive," I said again. "Neither is the boy. There is no price on us."

"I've got plenty." He swayed in front of me. "Pelts, guns, gold."

"Nothing. I have said."

"Even cheaper."

He laughed and leered and made to maul me then, as he was accustomed to do with other native women. I pushed him away. He was so drunk that he lost his balance. He slipped in the mud and went down on his bony backside, knobbed knees bent like a colt's, breech flap knocked aside to show the length of his white skinny thighs. His descent and landing occasioned much laughter among his companions. They made no move to help him as he struggled to rise, and he failed to get a purchase, sliding farther in the mud. The more he fell about, the louder they laughed until he cursed all around him, and then he turned his curses on me.

I looked down at him. "Be careful whom you curse," I said in English. "Lest it come back as three."

In my mind I saw him as a pig. He made to stand but I spun him over on all fours, making him shuffle and snuffle in the filthy ground. All around him the laughter redoubled, until the Indians were wiping tears away. When he went to stand again, I saw him as a dog. He rose on his hind legs, hands bent like paws, and let out a series of barks and then a stream of high-pitched yelps.

Frantic, he looked at me, the fog clearing from his drink-bleared eyes, replaced by fear and panic. He looked about, eyes wide, pleading for help. All around, men backed away from him. The mirth around him died and all eyes turned to me. I heard "*jongleuse,*" their word for sorceress, although I didn't know the meaning then. None of the native men would look me in the eye, and one of them crossed himself.

I turned Le Frenais onto his back again and allowed one of his party to help him upright. He reeled away, helped by his friends, and I went back to my own fire.

This encounter troubled me. I knew that I had made an enemy, but Le Frenais was forced from my mind as winter tightened its grip. There were too many people crowded all together. Already sickness was stalking the camp, striking down native and white alike. I was a healer, and as such my skills were in demand.

One of the first to suffer was the priest. The Blackrobe. He was a Jesuit, a member of the Society of Jesus, whose mission it was to convert the heathen. They were named for the long black cassocks and hooded cloaks that they wore. Abstemious and celibate, fastidious in their habits, devout to the point of martyrdom, these Frenchmen were as unlike to Le Frenais and his sort as bear is to wolf.

This man had come by canoe from Mount Royale, struggling up from the lake with his world strapped to his back. He had set up an altar and a tabernacle to serve those who were already of the Catholic faith and in the hope of converting those who kept to their own belief. He had built a small chapel, distinguished from the other dwellings by two staves lashed together to form a cross.

I don't know how many souls he saved, but he was tolerated. In that he fared better than those of his kind who had tried to spread their faith in England. My grandmother had told me of the fate of a Jesuit harbored at a local manor house. When his presence was discovered, he had been dragged from his hiding place and hanged.

I avoided him. I had reason to dislike priests of any stripe. But White Deer had kin among the Abenaki, and some of them were of the Catholic faith. They came to me because they despaired of him. He was sick but would not allow them to treat him, and he would not eat the food they brought to him. He feared sorcery, no doubt, but all they intended was an herbal concoction for his symptoms. They thought that he might pay attention to me since I was Yenguese, from across the sea.

I did not share their conviction that he would listen; nevertheless, I agreed to visit him.

He was propped up on a rough pallet, writing and sketching in a little book he kept continually by him.

He was newly out of France, by all accounts. Since landing here, he had grown a beard in an attempt to give him gravity, but the sparse dark down did little to disguise his youth. I judged him to be still in his twenties, and he was handsome, although sickness had paled his face to parchment. His brown eyes were sunken, the skin around them gray and thin, but they glittered bright when he saw me. I put this down to the fever that wasted his body, not realizing the zeal that fueled his purpose.

I told him who I was and why I had come.

"I have heard of you." He propped himself up on one elbow and regarded me with a look that mixed curiosity and puzzlement. He spoke in English, but slowly, as if each word was recalled from distant memory.

Although the house was made of bark in the way of the Abenaki, it was full of furnishings from France. A table, a carved casket, metal bowl and drinking cups, an altar cloth richly embroidered. I stood for a moment and gazed around. I had not seen such things for a long time; they were familiar, yet strange to my view. The effect was odd, as if one world was wrapped within another.

"I hear that you are sick." I came up to him as he lay back on the bed.

"I am treating myself." He indicated the lancet and bowl on the table. He was weakening his body still further by bleeding.

"Killing yourself, more like. You would be better to take the remedies that the women offer you."

"I do not trust their remedies, and I have no appetite for their food. It disgusts me."

"Their remedies are as sovereign as any you would find in Paris. As for food, I will prepare that myself— if you promise to eat it."

I treated his illness and prepared food for him. His name was Luc Duval. He came from Normandy, from a wealthy family, but he had always wanted to go into the church. He had found his vocation, inspired by one of his boyhood tutors who had been a Jesuit. This man had spent time in England as a Catholic missionary. Luc had learned English from him and was eager to learn more; in return he taught me some French. He was also striving to learn the common language of the tribes. We floundered to find meaning together, sometimes speaking in three tongues at once, but as time passed we became more fluent and at ease with each other.

As his strength returned, so did his curiosity. He wanted to know about my life and how I came to be here. He wanted to know how I fell among savages.

"I do not find them savage," I replied.

"I have heard much of their barbarity, their rites, and their cruelty."

"Our own rites might seem strange to other eyes. Already they mistrust baptism."

"Why? It is their way to salvation."

"They call it water magic, and they associate it with death, because that is when they see the rite performed most often."

He frowned, unable to understand such misinterpretation of what was for him truth without question.

"What of their cruelty?"

I looked at him. Who was he to speak of cruelty? How were the Indians more cruel than the French, or the English, for that matter? Even as we spoke, Metacom's head rotted on a pike at Plymouth. In his country or mine, how many had suffered? How many had died? Slaughtered in the streets, burned at stakes, hanged, drawn and quartered, racked and tortured, branded with irons, flogged with whips?

"Savagery is everywhere," I said.

"They live in squalor. How could you choose to *live* among them?"

"I have not found that so."

"The discomfort, the smoke . . ."

I laughed, remembering my grandmother's cottage, with one room and one bed between us. "I was not highborn like you. My home held few comforts and was far from free of smoke. Why did you come here, if you find the life so uncongenial?"

"I came because it was my duty," he said simply. "I am not afraid to die. I follow in the footsteps of martyrs. I take as my example Father Jogues, who was killed by the Iroquois, and Father Gerard, my superior, who suffered mightily at the hands of a Mohawk band. Only out of affliction can true glory come. Only through suffering can we know the agony of Christ on the cross."

I had no reply to that. What he was saying was stranger by far than any beliefs I had come across among the Indians. No wonder they treated the Blackrobes with suspicion.

His return to health brought back his zeal.

"I came to baptize, to save souls, to bring them to God, but everywhere I am resisted, even though the church is salvation. The pathway to heaven!"

I tried to explain that a Christian heaven meant leaving kin and comrades, not just on this earth, but for eternity. He could not see how lonely that would be, why after death, most would choose to take the long road west.

"I make slow progress. It is true. Perhaps they cannot understand my message." He suddenly looked at me. "But you . . ."

His glance was shy, but that did not disguise the gleam of fire in his eyes. I was as lost as any he deemed heathen. He was a zealot, every bit as convinced of his rightness as Reverend Johnson, or Cornwell, or any of the Puritans I had known. I was not about to swap one tyranny for another.

"I am not of your religion, nor ever will be. Your energies are wasted on me."

From that time on I was no longer so easy in his company; but the more I avoided him, the more he came after me. One day he caught me by the lake.

"Mary, I must speak with you."

"What is it?"

"Why do you no longer come to me?"

"You are recovered. You no longer need me."

"I thought we were friends."

"Friends do not seek to look into each other's souls."

"What if they fear that one whom they have come to hold in high regard is in danger of being lost forever?"

"What do you mean?"

"You are named for the Holy Mother. Why would you deny her name and take another? It is not just that you are Protestant; I fear that you have slipped into even greater error. I know that you are respected among these people, but I thought that you were revered for your healing skills. But now I learn that it is more than that. They see you as a medicine woman, a sorceress. Even the French here share in this belief. This very day one among the *coureurs des bois* came asking me to hear his confession and to lift a curse he says you put on him."

He meant Le Frenais. In life he kept away from me, but in dreams he had begun to haunt me.

"Such a thing is repugnant." Duval's face twisted in quick disgust. "Horrible."

"Then do not listen."

"You do not deny it?" He looked on me with horror.

"What is there to deny? What I believe is my business."

"I will pray for you."

"You will not be the first to have done so."

"I see that prayer will not be enough." The sadness in his eyes did not quench the zeal. Despite his youth, his belief was absolute and his purpose was of steel. "I will not let this happen. I will save you. I will instruct you . . ."

I did not want to be saved. I just wanted to get away from him. Where once I had found him stimulating company, now he troubled me.

My dreams were full of unease. Sometimes Le Frenais fled from me across a field of howling whiteness. Sometimes a great bird flew above me, overshadowing me, turning all to blackness. Sometimes my path was gathered around with mist and barred by a great palisade of spikes many feet high. I asked Sparks Fire what he thought these dreams might mean, but he was irritable, restless. He suffered badly from the aching sickness, and his strength was further sapped by pain from an old break in his right thigh where the bones had not knitted well together.

I thought I would be safer in the wilderness. I thought to go with Black Fox and Naugatuck on their winter hunt, but there is no swerving destiny. It was clear that Sparks Fire would not stand a winter in the forest. His bad leg would make him more a burden than a help, and besides, his people needed him here. Then White Deer came shyly and told me that she was with child. Whatever my doubts, I would have to lay my fears aside and think of other people, but when Black Fox and Naugatuck went to their winter camp, I begged them to take Ephraim with them. I did not want him getting into mischief or falling into bad habits. He still visited the French traders, despite my prohibition. For many of them, drink offered a ready escape from the idleness and boredom of a winter camp. They would be happy enough for Ephraim to join them, even though he was only a boy.

I thought to avoid trouble. I kept to my own paths well away from the little bark-clad chapel and the fetid lakeside hovels, but one afternoon, near the time of the shortest days, when night was falling quickly, my way took me near to the shore. The figure of a man loomed out of the gathering darkness, and suddenly Le Frenais was there.

I went to step around him, but he blocked my way. I could smell the liquor on his breath and his blue eyes barely focused, but he moved quickly for a man the worse for drink.

"Touch me and it will be the worse for you."

He leered at me, showing brown and broken teeth.

"I will teach you a lesson. Come here, witch!"

I could see from his eyes what he intended, and that he'd had this in mind for some time. He was a weak and despicable creature, but he was a man, and he knew the best way to avenge himself on a woman.

There was no one about to help me; even if there had been, I doubted that any would come to my aid. I slipped from his grasp and fled, knowing what he would do if he caught me. I ran toward the lake, which was a field of ice now, many feet thick. Night was falling, and with it snow was coming, a great gray bank of it blowing down from the top of the lake with unbelievable quickness. I could almost believe that Hobbomok—dark spirit of the deep waters, of the night, of the northeast wind—was swooping down toward us in a great storm of snow.

Soon white was swirling all around us, spinning the world to nothing. Fear of Le Frenais was lost in my urgency to find shelter. Storms like this leave the world with no margins; it is easy to lose all sense of direction and die mere yards from a safe haven. I stumbled across an upturned canoe by the lakeside and hid under it, waiting there for the tempest to abate.

I emerged to land and water indistinguishable from each other under a deep mantle of snow. There was no sign of Le Frenais, no sign of anyone, as I made my way back home.

Le Frenais had gone. Some said he'd taken a sled to go hunting, but his gear was still in his cabin. He was not mourned greatly, but his disappearance was a mystery. Some said he'd been seen on the ice, shrieking and screaming, running from some dark pursuing thing. There was talk for a time, but winter tightened its grip and each one turned to his own survival. Le Frenais was soon forgotten.

Fishermen found him at the time of the ice melting, floating among the floes. They knew him by the cross he'd started wearing about his neck, the one the Blackrobe gave him. They took him up to the church for the Blackrobe to bury and put the cross sticks over him, but the little bark chapel was deserted. Duval had been lately recalled to Mount Royale, so they did the best they could.

Never had I watched so avidly for spring's return, even though the first gift from the lake's breaking ice was Le Frenais's bloated, fish-nibbled body. Perhaps I should have taken it as an omen, but I did not. I turned my mind from that. The changing year would bring the hunters back to camp.

A winter hunt holds many dangers, and we had heard nothing since they left us. Sparks Fire and I watched every day, both of us trying to hide our fear from the other. Then on a day warm with the promise of summer, a runner came up from the lake. Canoes had been sighted. We hastened to the dockside, and this time we were not disappointed. Black Fox and Naugatuck were coming in safe to land, their craft piled so high with furs that there was scarcely room for Ephraim. My heart swelled at the sight of them. They looked thin after a winter in the northern forests, and Ephraim appeared in need of a good scrubbing, but they were safe and for that I gave thanks.

They had done well; their haul was wondered at by all. We scraped together what we had left from the winter and feasted them into the night, listening to their stories, drinking in their presence. Black Fox and Naugatuck were modest in the face of general admiration and full of praise for the part Ephraim had played in the hunt. The two young men laughed as Ephraim took over the telling time and again, declaring that if it were not for him, they would have returned with nothing. He gave me a necklace of claws from a bear that he swore he'd killed himself. Black Fox ceased laughing then and said that it was true; Ephraim had proved himself a brave and fearless hunter. They called him Lynx for his parti-colored hair and for his stealth in the forest.

Black Fox spoke with pride, and gladness filled my heart to see them together. They were truly brothers now, showing the absolute trust and deep companionship that grows between those who have depended on each other for their very lives. Their care of each other pleased me far more than any number of beaver pelts.

They had returned with many skins to sell, but they soon learned that the traders at Missisquoi were not to be trusted. They had heard that they would get a better price if they took their furs to Mount Royale.

I agreed to go with them, for even there the traders might seek to cheat them. I could understand the language and the marks made on paper. They needed me to accompany them, and I was glad to go. It was a relief to leave the overcrowded winter camp, which the springtime thaw was fast turning into a fetid sea of mud.

We left Sparks Fire, White Deer, and the rest of the band to strike camp. It had already been decided that once the furs were traded, we would come back with the trade goods and return to the Pennacook homelands in the south. Some would not be making the journey. They had already chosen to stay with the Abenaki. Sparks Fire grieved long over this, but all were free to choose, and he was determined to go back.

We went by canoe, following the waterways, until we came to the city the French were building between river and mountain. It was like no town that I had ever seen. It was stoutly palisaded as if expecting attack at any moment, and although most of the buildings inside were of wood, some were of stone, making the town seem even more like a fortress. Threats from outside were real. The town was subject to attack from the Iroquois, and soldiers kept constant vigil.

The inhabitants were just as alert to assaults of a spiritual kind. A great wooden cross looked down from the slopes of the mountain, and churches were being built by the harbor and along the newly laid-out streets. Nuns and priests mingled with adventurers, soldiers, traders, trappers, and Indians of many different nations. Apart from the nuns, there were few women about, and even fewer children. It seemed to be a town made up of men.

The fur traders had their warehouses down by the river and were as great cheats as any at Missisquoi. The goods we were offered were paltry and did not include muskets, shot, and powder. The trader raised his arm high, smiling with sneering contempt, indicating many more pelts were needed. Black Fox and Naugatuck stared down at him, their expressions unreadable. They had already put fathoms of distance between him and them. I watched these two young men standing straight and tall, their handsome faces unblemished, being insulted by a filthy, twisted, misshapen wretch barely half their size with hardly a tooth in his head. His breath smelled of brandy laced with the grave. They had risked their lives for these pelts, and I would not see them cheated.

I stepped forward and spoke to him in French.

"Now their women speak for them?" He turned as if to an audience, then hobbled forward, peering up into my face. "But you are not one of them, are you?" He extended a filthy half-gloved paw toward me, touching me on the breast. He twisted his face around to Naugatuck. "How much?"

"Too much for you, Devois."

A Frenchman who had been watching us stepped forward. His movements were slow, almost feline in their laziness. He was not dressed for the wilderness, nor did I take him to be a military man, although he had a sword and pistol about him. He wore velvet and lace and had a jewel in his ear. His hair hung in oiled ringlets, and his close-cut beard was carefully barbered. As he came close, I caught the spiced scent of his perfume. He looked at me and smiled.

"You must come with me."

Although he did not look to be a soldier, he was accompanied by such. He signaled to them now, and two stepped forward, flintlocks at the ready. Naugatuck and Black Fox tensed, their hands reaching for their weapons. They were ready to fight, but I warned them off with a shake of the head. They were in a place full of enemies: soldiers and traders, Indians from different nations. They risked losing everything, including their lives, if they fought back.

Black Fox was trembling in every muscle, but eventually he took his hand from the hilt of his knife.

"Sensible lad." The man smiled; his eyes were of a dark, cloudy lapis blue. They held a fleeting glitter of amusement but were as cold as stones. "Now, for myself, I would not see you cheated."

He raised a finger to the trader, and the goods doubled and doubled again. Now they included the precious muskets. When he was satisfied, he signaled that the trade was done.

"Take them before I change my mind."

Naugatuck and Black Fox stood unmoving. They had traded for the goods, but it would be shaming to take them.

"Now. Or you have nothing."

Black Fox would have refused, but I nodded to him to take the goods offered. It was no bribe. They had traded for these things squarely. They belonged to them now.

"This is yours." He spoke to Naugatuck. "You understand?"

Naugatuck inclined his head.

"Not this." He laid a hand on my shoulder. "You must come with me. The boy, too."

He looked around, but Ephraim had learned much in his time in the forest. He could come and go as quietly as any native boy, and he was nowhere to be seen.

"No matter, we will find him later. *Petit sauvage* with hair like an angel, we can hardly miss him, can we? Now, madame, if you are ready?"

His tone was polite, but full of menace. It was plain that I was captive. Soldiers accompanied us before and behind.

Black Fox leaped forward, Naugatuck with him, but the soldiers crossed muskets and forced them back. I called out to Black Fox, ordering him to let alone. I did not want to see my son's brains dashed out in front of me. Naugatuck was a fine young man, the son of my friend, and his pretty young wife was big with his child. I would not have his blood spilled for me either. I would have to go with the Frenchmen; there was no other way.

My captor's name was Le Grand, but that was all he told me. He offered no other information, about himself or why I had been taken. I was conducted to a chamber; a Huron girl brought food, and water for me to wash, but when she left, the door was locked. I went to the window. There was no way down, and soldiers stood sentry in front of the building. I was a prisoner. Escape would not be easy.

That night I slept between sheets for the first time in seventeen years, but I dreamed of the forest. I was a girl again, and Jaybird was chasing me. I could hear him calling and his laugh echoing as I ran from him. He was gaining on me; I could hear him getting closer and closer. I slowed deliberately for him to catch me, whirling around with quick anticipated desire, but he just smiled and turned away. I chased him now, but he kept just out of my sight.

I came upon a cave and entered, thinking I might find him there, following down a winding labyrinth of tunnels until I became lost in the maze. At the center sat White Eagle in his Chamber of Visions. He looked up from the fire burning before him. He stood when he saw me, and his shadow became a monstrous bird on the wall behind him, wings spread like a thunderbird.

I cowered back and felt the shadowing of great wings over me. I thought to see an eagle, but the cloaking feathers were dusty black and ragged like a raven. I struggled and fought, but great scaled claws, talons as sharp as razors, held me pinioned, and the great bird settled upon me as a crow settles on carrion. The long beak struck at me, ripping open my deerskin shift, seeking to tear the very heart from my breast.

I woke in a sweat, at a loss where I was. In a room, in a house—the very idea was strange to me after so many years sleeping under bark and matting. I lay back staring at the close-worked wood of the ceiling. A fire glowed in the hearth. I rose by its light, thinking to dress, and found that my clothes had been removed while I slept.

When the Huron girl returned to my chamber, I spoke to her in the common tongue. I did not know if I could trust her, but I asked her to get word to Black Fox. I wanted her to tell him where I was, that I was closely guarded but no insult had been offered me, and no harm had come to me—yet.

She did not reply but nodded as if she understood. I did not say more, not knowing how far I could rely upon the girl, but I'd said enough for my son to know that I could not easily escape on my own and that any kind of direct assault was pointless. All I could do was see what awaited me and glean what information I could from the Frenchman. Other than that, I had to trust in Black Fox to find a way. The thought of my son brought comfort to me, for he had great cunning and was as wily as his name. If anyone could get me out of here, he could.

The Huron girl filled a tub for me and laid linen for me to dry myself; then she left. To bathe in warm water was a very great luxury, and I own that I lingered long in the perfumed water. She returned with clothes for me: a dress with full skirt and petticoats, slashed sleeves, and a tight-fitting bodice. The European garments felt strange and restricting to my body, but I had to don them or go naked. My moccasins had been taken along with my clothes, but I would rather go unshod than squeeze my feet into the shoes I was supposed to wear.

I spent the day alone, locked in my room. Then toward evening the girl returned. She had come to conduct me to her master, but she also carried word from Black Fox. She told me that although Naugatuck had returned to Missisquoi, Black Fox and Ephraim were keeping near. They were staying hidden. Le Grand's men were searching for Ephraim, and word had gone out that Le Grand was offering a reward for him.

"Your son said, 'Do not worry, they will not find him.' He also said . . ." She frowned as if trying to remember something that made no sense to her. "He also said to remember Coos and the autumn hunt."

He'd been no more than a boy of nine or ten. Coos had forbidden him from joining his hunting party, saying his lack of experience would scare off the game. Black Fox had followed them anyway, stealing into their camp, taking not only their choicest pelts but also Coos's fletching knife. His stealth had become a matter of legend. I smiled at the memory, but I was struck full of fear for him. This house was a fortress, and getting in here might prove too much even for Black Fox.

The Huron girl said she would find out more that night, but she was anxious not to keep her master waiting. She brought me into his presence with her eyes cast down.

Monsieur Le Grand—Jean Le Grand—sat at the head of a long table in a large room set with many candles. The light shone warm on polished wood and winked off glass, brass, and silver. The walls were

hung with richly colored tapestries. I had never seen
such luxury, or thought that it existed in any of these
rough-hewn colonies. He invited me to dine with
him. We ate off tableware finer than any I had ever
seen before and drank from glasses of great thinness,
but I found the food not to my taste, at once too
salted and too refined, and the wine made me giddy.

"I will not stay here. You cannot make me."

He spread his ringed hands. "You will find that
I can."

"Who are you?"

"I am a merchant, a trader, an entrepreneur,
although your own countrymen have other names for
me. They call me a privateer."

"A buccaneer?"

He grimaced as if he found the term offensive.

"I act on behalf of France, but I have been known
to stop ships outside Boston Harbor and divert their
cargoes elsewhere." He leaned back in his chair. "You
are my guest here until such time as your fate is
decided. The governor is very interested in your presence. It was he who asked me to look out for you and
entertain you here."

"How did you know about me?"

"We have been watching out for you. The boy, too.
A Captain Peterson came to Quebec asking if any captives were among the bands fleeing from the south. I see
you know the name." He had been observing me

closely. I saw no reason to deny it. "He particularly asked for any news concerning a woman and a boy who traveled together but were of no kin to each other."

"Why would that be?"

Le Grand half smiled at me. "He seemed to think the boy might be in jeopardy."

"How could he be?" I stared at Le Grand in astonishment. "I would no more harm him than my own son."

"Exactly. Your son is *sauvage*. You mated among them and have taken to their heathen ways, so Peterson says. Peterson is a righteous man and fearful for the boy's soul. He is most anxious to remove him from such a ménage and return him to his kin."

"The boy has no kin."

"That is not what Peterson says. There is an uncle in Rhode Island, anxious to trace him. He is offering a rich reward." He smiled. "Peterson's concern does not stop at the boy. His anxiety runs to you, too. It is an offense to him—to all Englishmen—that you should live as you do."

"What does he want with me?"

"He wants your return. What he plans for you then, it is not for me to say." Le Grand laughed. "Do not look so alarmed. You are in French territory, and English captains hold no remit. Your fate has not been decided."

Despite his words, my mind ran on apace. If I was

taken back, how soon would it be before my whole story was discovered? The colony was a small place. There were those who would know of my flight from Beulah, the reasons for it, and the suspicion that had centered on me there. What judgment would fall on me once my error was compounded by living with savages?

I sat lost in thought. A servant entered and whispered in Le Grand's ear. He nodded quickly, as though this was intelligence for which he had been waiting. The servant withdrew and Le Grand turned to me.

"There is someone come who wishes to speak with you. Father Gerard."

"A Blackrobe?"

"He would prefer to be called Jesuit. He is head of the order here. He wants to convert you." He regarded me steadily. "I'd say he would have more luck trying to convert the wild beasts in the forest, never mind the savages, but these Jesuits are stubborn. He is another who wants to save your immortal soul. You are honored, Mary. Come. He is waiting in the library."

He rose from his seat, indicating for me to follow.

We went into a room lined with shelves of leather-bound books and set with tables for study. A priest sat by a fire blazing high in the wide stone-built hearth. The burning logs gave out great heat, but he leaned forward as if he craved more. His chair was drawn up close enough to scorch the skirts of his robe. He was gray haired and bearded, his drawn face grooved with deep furrowed lines of the kind etched by chronic pain over a long period of time. He did not seem discomforted now, although he did not rise to greet me. He kept a stout stick close by his side. His hands lay along the arms of the chair—one curled into a fist, half hidden inside his robe; the other hung down heavy with rings that glistened in the firelight.

"I am Father Gerard."

He indicated that I should sit opposite him. I knew now the cause of the pain etched in his face. He was missing all the fingers on his left hand. What I had taken to be a fist was knuckle covered in puckered pink skin. I had seen this mutilation before, a result of torture employed by the Iroquois. Each finger had been sawn off using the sharpened edge of a piece of shell. It took a very brave man to endure this ordeal without screaming or crying out. I looked at the Jesuit with new respect. He must have remained silent or he would not be with us now.

"I have been waiting for you, Mary." He pronounced my name the French way. "If you had not come to us, we would have come for you."

"How do you know my name?"

"Father Luc Duval. His field notes alerted us to your presence in the territory." He held up a small, stained notebook that had been resting on his knee. "At first, he was concerned for your welfare. For a white woman to be living among savages is not, ah . . ." He searched for the correct word. "Satisfactory."

"I live with them by choice," I said simply. "I do not want to be rescued. Where is Father Luc?" I looked around expecting to see him, fresh-faced and clean-shaven.

"He is not here. He has gone on another mission. This time to the Iroquois." A look passed between the two Frenchmen. "I fear that he seeks martyrdom. Before he went, however, he wanted me to look out for you. He was most insistent upon it." The Jesuit's black eyes flickered over me. "He fears for your immortal soul, you see. Certain, certain events described here"——he thumbed through the buckled water-stained pages—"have to be taken very seriously. If, if they were true, or were *proved* to be true . . ."

I looked from him to Le Grand.

"I'm sorry, I do not understand."

The priest looked at me, his eyes bright, beady as a raven's in his ravaged face.

"Let me put it more plainly. They say that you are a sorceress. That you killed a man. A man called Frenais."

"*Le* Frenais." I corrected.

"You know him, then?" the priest asked.

"Of course."

"So? Is this true? Did you have a hand in his death?'"

"I did not touch him. Life here is dangerous, in the winter even more so. A mistake, any mistake, can be fatal. Le Frenais drank. Drink makes men stupid and careless of themselves, their lives, and much else besides."

"Hmm." The Jesuit regarded me steadily. "They say there is more to his death than that. The Indians say that he was seen running over the ice at the height of a storm, shrieking as if the Devil himself were after him, fleeing from some dark pursuing thing."

"Why wouldn't they? It is a good story to tell around a winter fire. The Indians like a good tale. They do not differ from us in that."

The Jesuit snapped the book shut. "I am not here to try you, Mary. I hope it won't come to that. The native people are credulous and superstitious. Your fame has spread among them. To have a white woman among them revered as a sorceress? It will not do. We have enough trouble converting them as it is. There are some"—he glanced at Le Grand—"who would hand you back to the English, but I am not sure anymore how that will serve. I am arranging for you to stay with the holy sisters while I decide what is to be done. I know the sisters will do their best to bring you

252

to the church. Listen well to their teaching, for your life may depend on it."

He stood up, leaning heavily on his stick, using his good hand for leverage. He hobbled toward the door, shrugging off any help from Le Grand. The Jesuit's gait was grotesquely skewed. From the way he walked, I judged he had been born with one foot clubbed and that leg much shorter than the other. To come to this place in that state, to live the life, to bear the hardship! These Jesuits were tough, as tough as the natives they sought to convert.

"What did he mean?" I asked Le Grand. "Why will my life depend on it?"

I knew well what was meant, but in order to decide what to do, I needed his confirmation.

"To convert such a one as you would bring others flocking to the fold. Otherwise . . ."

"Otherwise what?"

He did not answer directly. Instead, he picked up the notebook Gerard had left and waved it in my face.

"They call you Loup-Garou."

I recognized the words. I had heard them before at Missisquoi.

"A werewolf? That is a creature of mere superstition." I felt beset by great weariness. How little they know of such things. "I do not walk the night and wake naked in some ditch, my jaws slathered with blood."

He held up Duval's book.

"They say you killed a man through sorcery."

"As I said to the priest, life here is dangerous enough. You do not need sorcery."

"You *are* a witch, then? You know what we do with them?" I made no reply, so he supplied the information for me. "We burn them. *That* is the fate that awaits you if you do not convert. We have saints here in the making, both French and native. Perhaps Father Gerard wants you to join their company as a prized convert, or . . ."

"Or?"

"You will be his very own Jeanne d'Arc."

"So you will give me over to him?"

I divined from his face that he would not but took small comfort from that. It seemed I would but leap like a flounder out of the frying pan into the fire.

He sat down in the chair Gerard had just vacated.

"The Jesuits are powerful here, 'tis true, but I have other plans for you. I have a ship leaving soon, in a day, two at the most, and you will be on it."

"And what do *you* intend for me? To take me back to Peterson?"

"I have not decided. To leave you to the sisters and the Jesuits would be a waste. I have a friend who is held captive in Boston, a privateer, like myself. The authorities there would be interested in trading. That is the idea of Captain Peterson. But I might not do that."

"What might you do instead?"

He paused, as though considering. "I would be willing to trade the boy, once we catch him, and we will catch him soon enough. I have put a good price on him, and the inhabitants of Montreal, French or native, would trade their grandmothers for gold. But I do not think I will give *you* to Peterson."

"What will you do with me?"

"I have a mind to take you to France." He smiled, his teeth white against the black of his beard. "You are quite a beauty underneath all that native dirt, and with such an exotic history. *La belle sauvage.* The court craves diversions of all kinds. You would be a sensation." His tone hardened when I did not reply. "It is either me or the nunnery. Think on it well."

"What if I choose neither?"

"You know what is left." He shrugged his elegant shoulders. "There is always the stake."

I clutched my arms to me as though I already felt the flames licking about my feet.

He smiled. "But it may not come to that. You are shivering. Here." He rose to throw more logs on the fire and rang a bell to summon a servant. "I will order some heated wine for us. The nights are still chilly at this time of year."

"You interest me, Mary," he said when the wine arrived. He had the air of a man who had seen much and was surprised by little. "I have known many women in my life before, but I have never met one like you." He stirred the bowl that had been set before him, ladling some of the steaming liquor into a silver cup. "Drink this! It is made to my own recipe—I think you will like it."

He handed me the cup and watched as I drank from it. The brew was warming, a mix of brandy and wine, heady with the scent of spices: nutmeg, clove, and cinnamon. As I sipped, I thought I tasted an undertone of something else, something heavy and powerful. I looked at him, questioning.

"It is best drunk slowly." He smiled again. "It contains a strong spirit; I traded from the Dutch for it—they call it *genever*. Now tell me, how did you come to be with the savages? I want to know more. And do not worry. In my family we are no strangers to magic. Whatever you tell me will not pass beyond these walls."

Whatever the drink contained, I found my tongue loosening. I found myself telling him everything. All that had befallen me. When I had finished, he leaned forward, replenishing my cup.

"I knew you would not disappoint me. We make a pair, you and me." He grinned wide, showing gold teeth on either side of his jaw. This time the smile reached his dark blue eyes. "They call me Loup de la Mer—Wolf of the Sea. Now it is my turn to tell you about myself."

He came from a noble family, although he did not use his title.

"I am what you call the black sheep. My brother is a priest, like Gerard, although he prefers to stay in France; my other brother is at court, but I find life there dull and stifling. I was destined to be a soldier, but grew tired of killing Dutchmen in the mud of Flanders. I wanted adventure and found it on the sea. I have interests everywhere—here, and in the East, and in the West Indies." He smiled again, this time more gently, as if at some inward scene only he could see. "You would love it there, Mary. It is so warm, not like this cursed cold, and so green, but the green is bright and there is a different light, not like in these dark gloomy forests. The islands are full of color. Flowers and fruit grow everywhere, both at the same time, as like Eden. Birds flit between them, blue, red, yellow, some as small as this." He made a walnut shape in the hollow of his fist. "They hover like bees, taking nectar through a beak as fine as a needle."

"It sounds truly a wonderful place."

"Oh, it is. It is. The sea is as warm as blood, a clear aquamarine with sand as white as linen. I have a place that I have built, a special place down by the shore where I can be alone. I love to watch the ocean." He paused. "I had thought to take you to France, but now I think to take you there. What do you say, Mary? Is what I have described to your taste? You can live free, as free as you have lived here. Won't you come with me?"

His thought had taken a different turn from any I had expected. I'd judged him an adventurer, ruthless and cold, his heart turned to ice by a harsh and pitiless world. Now I saw the fire within his soul and the reason for his roaming. I wanted to reply to him, but my own thoughts refused to form. I found my tongue thick in my mouth. Suddenly it was hard to move. The heat from the fire, the spiced wine had caused a creeping languor to spread through my limbs. I tried to stand and staggered.

He was there to catch me, putting his arm around me. He pushed my hair back with his other hand and touched the clan mark on my cheek.

"Belle sauvage," he whispered, his wine-scented breath warm on my skin as he turned my face to his.

I had not felt the touch of a man in a long time. Perhaps it was the wine, or whatever drug he had put in it. Perhaps it was the strength of his kiss. But I did not resist as he held me, and when he took me to his chamber, I went freely enough.

• Mary •
Ephraim Arrives

I woke in his bed between sheets of finest linen. I was alone, and I could tell by the sun that it was late. He must have left to attend to his business. I lay back against pillows of goose down and tried to make sense of what had happened, but my mind was slow and my senses dulled. The taste in my mouth told me that the heated wine had been laced with poppy.

The Huron girl came in bearing a tray, which she set down on a table near the bed. I tried to speak to her, but she did not look at me and retired immediately. I rose and donned a silk robe that had been laid out for me. My clothes of the night before were gone, and in their place had been put much finer stuff, silk and velvet. To my mind came an old rhyme: "Three in worsted, three in rags, three in velvet fine . . ."

The food laid out for me tasted like manna. Warm rolls of white bread as meltingly fine as cake, curls of rich yellow butter, and a bowl of some thick dark drink with a taste both rich and sweet. I had never tasted such before, but I knew this to be chocolate. The girl came again, to fill my bath and remove my tray. I spoke to her in French, then in the common tongue, but it was as if she suddenly understood neither. She hastened from the chamber, giving me a look as she left, letting her eyes speak for her.

I spent the day in deep thought. I had never known such riches before. They could be mine forever. All I had to do was consent to his offer. I paced around the house, weighing one life against the other. If I looked for signs, one at least was clear. I had never been shown such deference, but I could not leave. The soldiers on the door would not let me pass. The snare might be silken, but it was still a trap.

Le Grand returned toward evening, announcing that we would be leaving on the morning tide. I had been alone all day, and the shame brought on by the demeanor of the Huron girl had grown in me with each passing hour.

I was set to defy him, but I had forgotten his charm, his handsomeness, his ability to beguile. He toasted me with golden wine as we dined, and afterward he fed me sweetmeats and talked of our life together. I was caught again in his spell, even I who knew something of the skill. By the time we retired for bed, I could well believe he came from a house of magicians.

We were woken by a commotion coming from below. A voice called up to Le Grand. He threw on shirt and breeches and pulled on his boots, while I donned a robe and went to the window to see what was the matter.

Two soldiers stood at the great front door; between them they held a buckskin-clad figure. They had him gripped by the scruff like a struggling cat. They were near twice his size but were having trouble holding him nonetheless. The big doors were opened wide, and Ephraim was pitched onto the flags of the hall. I heard scuffling below and then the thud of feet on the stairs and Ephraim calling me. I went to the door of the chamber to find him in front of me. He stopped in midcareer.

"Mary!"

"He fights like a wildcat." Le Grand came panting after him. "My men are all cut and kicked and scratched about."

"Lynx, that's what they call me," Ephraim announced, smiling. He turned to Le Grand. "I came of my own free will. Your men got no call to treat me that way."

"They name you well." Le Grand grimaced, and

held out his arm. The cuff of the shirt was torn, and his arm showed deep scores already welling up and dripping blood.

"I must see to this. I will be back."

He left then, leaving me alone with Ephraim.

"Are you hurt?" I asked the boy.

"Not hardly." He came into the room, unable to take his eyes off me.

"What are you staring at?"

"You look different," he said in simple wonder. "Like a lady. I got to tell you, Mary, you scrubbed up real good."

"Never mind that." I turned on him. "Why did you come here and let yourself be captured like this?"

"It was the only way to get to you. Black Fox sent me. He has a plan."

I guessed at what it was. Sometimes warriors would allow themselves to be deliberately captured and taken to an enemy camp. Once inside they would work with their comrades on the outside to help prisoners break out. It was a clever idea but full of risk.

"This is extremely foolhardy."

"But, Mary—"

"Listen to me. There is reason behind Le Grand's search for you. You have walked yourself right into a trap."

"How is that?"

"Why did you not tell me you still had kin in the colony?"

"What kin?"

"Le Grand says an uncle seeks for you."

"What uncle? I know of no uncle."

"Captain Peterson has been to Quebec. He says an uncle of yours from Rhode Island wishes to claim you."

Ephraim's face clouded for a moment as memory and realization came together.

"He became Quaker. Him and Pa came to the colonies together. Pa didn't hold with his new belief and there was a falling-out. Pa never spoke of him again." He shrugged. "That's all I know. It happened before ever I was born. What does he want with me?" Ephraim sat on the bed and looked up at me. "He never wanted me before."

"Well, he wants you now. We are to go back. Le Grand is going to trade you to the English for some buccaneer friend of his."

"What about you?"

"He has other plans for me."

Ephraim looked around, at me, at the bed behind, at Le Grand's jacket draped over a chair, at my clothes lying there. He stiffened like an animal suddenly alerted to some danger it had not perceived before.

"*Now* I see the way of it."

He rose to stalk the room, inspecting every corner.

"What if you do?"

He sank down to squat on the floor, resting his head on his hands.

"The Huron girl got word to us. That's why we had to act so quick and desperate. She said Le Grand wanted to take you away with him, but she didn't exactly say what as."

He grinned at me then, his face twisting into leering contempt, an expression he'd copied from the French trappers when they spoke about women. I should have struck him for showing me such insolence, but his scorn scorched my soul. I deserved it. I felt myself flush red.

"Black Fox," Ephraim went on, "can't get in here. The house is too closely guarded; such a thing is impossible. So he figured the time to take you was when you go down to the docks. He's going to be waiting there. He thinks they won't notice him, all Indians looking the same to them. He has all prepared and was going to look for a chance to get you away. But now? Seems hardly worth anybody's effort." He looked up at me. "How could you do this to him?"

"He is a warrior now. A man. He does not need me."

But even as I spoke, I knew that was not true. I had no answer to Ephraim's question. It was as if I had been walking in a dream. He said not a word further, but his blue eyes spoke most eloquently, more eloquently than he knew. I turned away, tears of my own starting, as I remembered another parting in the upstairs room of an English inn many long years ago.

"Ain't going back to Peterson," he said at last. "Nor no uncle I don't know. I'd rather die. I'm going with Black Fox, or I'll be killed getting to him. I give you warning, Mary."

How could I break such a heart? I thought of Black Fox, waiting out in the dark somewhere. They had risked all for me. How could I have countenanced such betrayal as this? I marveled now that I'd ever thought to stay with Le Grand—truly I must have been bewitched.

• Mary •
To the River

It was near sun rising, and Le Grand had already departed for the harbor. The last and most precious cargoes were loaded last, and he didn't trust the clumsy oafs and pilfering rogues from the trading house. He wanted to be there to supervise the doings himself. We were to follow along afterward in time to catch the morning tide.

Ports are busy places, and when a boat is about to depart, there is always much confusion. At the quay-side was a great melee of passengers and sailors mixed with traders who had come to see their goods safe onboard. A scattering of natives moved among the throng, some acting as porters, some to trade, some merely curious. Canoes bobbed near the hulls of the ships. Ephraim ran to the edge of the quay, as if overcome with boyish excitement at sights and sounds new to him. He came back to tell me in English that Black Fox's canoe was down there in the water.

A pair of soldiers escorted us, but they seemed to know that I was special to Le Grand, so although we were watched, it was none too closely, and they were careful to take no liberties. I looked around as if in wonder at the crowd, and soon saw Black Fox at a distance, milling with the other natives, carrying a pack of furs as if to sell. He did not need to come closer. He used the silent signaling language of the woods that hunters use when they can make no sound. Ephraim signaled back, and Black Fox melted out of the crowd to reclaim his craft.

There was no sign yet of Le Grand. The soldiers set to mind us were slow, sluggish from a night's carousing. They stood fidgeting and yawning, talking to each other, drinking brandy to keep out the chill coming up from the river, taking hair from the dog that bit them the night before. I sidled closer, talking low as one might to gentle a pair of horses. They were already fuddled and slow from drink and the cold and the early hour. It was easy enough to lull them further until they noticed us no more.

"How did you do that?" Ephraim asked as we melted into the crowd.

"Magic." The two soldiers sat on a barrel staring straight in front of them, as still as statues. "Talking magic. White Eagle taught me."

We stole away through the throng. With each person on the docks intent on his own business, no one noticed our going, or heeded the quick dip of a paddle and the slight sound of a native craft cutting through the water. Patchy mist was coming up off the river. I hoped that it would obscure our escape still further as we flitted along the line of wharves until we found a deserted mooring. There we hid among dripping piles, set as close as a forest, and waited for Black Fox to come gliding toward us.

"I won't ever speak of it again," Ephraim said as we huddled together, "not if you tell me one thing."

"What thing is that?"

I knew what he was talking about.

"Why did you do it, Mary? Why did you think to stay with him over Black Fox and me?"

"It wasn't because of you; Black Fox, either. I can't explain, not really. Besides . . ." I looked down at his wide-set child's eyes, his puppy-furrowed brow. "You're too young yet. One day you'll understand."

"Was it a kind of madness?" Ephraim was reluctant to leave it; he did not like a puzzle.

I laughed. "You could say that. Perhaps he used a kind of magic."

"And it worked? Even on you?" Ephraim stared at me, eyes full of wonderment.

"Yes." I smiled, still savoring the taste of it: a mix of bitter and sweetness, like his chocolate. "It worked. Even on me."

The tide was nearly high, lapping at our feet. Soon it would be turning. I wondered if Le Grand had missed me yet. He was most anxious to leave; that much I knew. He would not want to wait for another tide with the ship ready and loaded; there was other business besides, which meant he would want to leave immediately.

Would he risk all for me? A cannon boomed as if in answer. I hoped that it signaled the ship's departure, but voices were hallooing along the docks and getting nearer. They were calling my name. He was searching for me.

I looked back to see him high on the rail of the ship, directing his men to fan out through the milling throng. His sailors were swarming up the rigging, taking lookout, their sharp eyes casting all up and down the shore for any sign of us. They were looking to the river. Le Grand was no fool. He would have told them to search for a native canoe. A couple of small craft pushed off; they were after Black Fox, too.

"See there!"

Ephraim pointed to where men were running along; they showed like a line of ghosts through the gray mist. They were following the route we had taken. Soon we would hear the beat of their booted feet on the wooden dock. Another group was coming upon us from the other direction, and all the time the incoming tide was creeping up the piles, forcing us to retreat back toward the riverside. I looked at the river, peering through the swirls of mist, hoping to see Black Fox paddling toward us. There was no sign of him. Perhaps he was caught or had been forced to alter his course to avoid his pursuers. Perhaps the strong current had swept him into the center of the river. We were trapped. If we stayed, we risked being swamped by the rising water; if we broke cover, they would see us for sure.

A call came from the water. An eerie seabird cry,
Ephraim answered with another, and a canoe came
gliding into view. We boarded quickly, each taking a
paddle, for we were pursued. Black Fox guided the
canoe out into the main stream. Native canoes and
longboats were after us, some following strongly, others joining the river from the docks strung along the
shore.

We played hide-and-seek, in and out of the
patchy mist, but the other boats were gaining on us,
threatening from different directions. Use what magic
is to hand, that is what White Eagle had told me. I
conjured the mist to murky fog. Men shouted and
cursed as boats bumped and collided, and we struck
out for the main river channel, trusting that the swift-
flowing currents would take us away from danger.

The shouts and cries faded. Town and docks slipped behind us, replaced by towering cliffs and the silent, brooding presence of the woods. Black Fox pulled for a small inlet, and I changed out of my foreign clothes into native garb. I left the dress Le Grand had given me on the gritty sand. The wide skirts and petticoats lay at the edge of the water, looking for all the world like a woman drowned and cast up on the shore.

We paddled on, using the river's flow to make our way to the Richelieu River, which would take us back to Lake Champlain. We would travel the length of the great waterway and then strike off to the east following the route that Sparks Fire, Naugatuck, and the rest of their band were taking back to their homeland. That was our intention, but fate had a different future ordained for us. We would never see our Pennacook friends again.

We were out on the lake proper, tiny as flecks of ash on a mirror, when the storm struck. A sudden rushing wind came from behind, and we turned to find no margin between air and water. The lake was as black as the sky. It was as if the two elements would marry together. Water twirled in great whirling spouts, while waves as huge as any on the ocean rose up and threatened to swamp our frail craft.

We drove for the eastern shore, but it was as if a great hand were forcing us westward. We were powerless. The storm was like some howling beast coming over the lake toward us. The rain was falling in such torrents that we could see neither land nor sky nor water. Black Fox muttered that Hobbomok must truly be angry. It was as if the stories of the people were coming to pass; as if some great lake-dwelling serpent had awakened and was about to arise scaly and dripping from the water, to devour us whole.

We lost all. Even the clothes were near torn from our bodies as we were tossed up on the shore. We must have seemed as dead, sprawled among the logs and leaves, covered in mud from the lake.

I woke to voices harsh to my hearing, speaking a language I had never heard before. I was jabbed in the ribs and the back with a stick or the butt of a lance, and then a foot turned me over. The sole was soft, moccasined. These were native people, whoever they were. I opened one eye and saw beading I had not seen before. These people wore leggings to the knees, quilled deerskin, red broadcloth traded from the Dutch, and long fringed breechclouts. One was kilted with a broad belt, richly decorated, with a wide woven sash loosely knotted at the shoulder. They carried a formidable array of weapons: war clubs, tomahawks, and scalping knives. One carried a lance. He leaned on it as he looked down at us.

Their faces were painted red, yellow, blue, and

white, but I did not know the designs. Their hair was dressed differently also, and two of them wore head-dresses like caps with a swivel of three feathers.

They drew apart and their talk was low. The tone was one of curiosity rather than hostility. I had never seen any in life, but I knew who they were, and I knew their reputation. These were Iroquois warriors, possibly Mohawks, and as such feared above all others. Even the names used for them: Iroquois, Mingo, Mohawk, Maquas—adders, treacherous, cannibals, cowards—spoke of the terror that they inspired. But I knew we were safe. For the moment, at least. They would not kill us as we lay in this state, for to do so would be cowardly.

After a brief consultation, they came back. One of them seized Ephraim by the hair. Not to scalp him. To take a scalp in such a way would be like eating carrion. He was marking the color. Two went to the lake with wooden buckets to collect water to dash upon us. I could not lie in dog's sleep forever. I shivered at the second drench and sat up.

They threw more water over Black Fox, dragged him to his feet, and slapped him hard about the face, making his nose bleed. I called for them to stop in all the languages I could muster.

One of them came over to me.

"*Français?*"

I shook my head. "English."

"Kiohensaka?" His eyes widened in surprise. "Him?" He asked in French, pointing toward where Black Fox lay struggling on the ground. One of the warriors hit him again while another bound his hands.

"Pennacook. He is my son."

"This other?"

He pointed to where Ephraim lay, still half insensible.

"My son, also."

He nodded, taking in this information, then stood in one fluid movement. He pointed at himself and his men.

"Haudenosaunee. Iroquois. Kahniakehaka. Mohawk. You will come with us."

• Alison •

At the Reservation

Hau-den-o-sau-nee. Alison spelled the words out to
herself. People of the Longhouse. Kah-nia-keh-aka.
People of the Flint.

"May I help you?"

"Oh!" Alison looked around from the board she'd
been studying. "Oh, I'd like to have this." She grabbed
a dream catcher from a stand next to her elbow. "And
I'm trying to find someone."

"Who would that be?" the woman asked as she
wrapped the item and rang the price up.

"A girl. Her name is Agnes Herne."

"That'll be ten dollars."

Alison handed over the money. "Do you know
Agnes?"

"Maybe." The woman looked wary. "What do
you want with her?"

"She's a student of mine," Alison improvised

quickly. "She's helping me with some research. She came to interview her aunt?"

"That'd be Miriam. Store over yonder." The woman jerked her thumb at the window. "Ain't there, though. Been shut all week."

"Where is she?"

"No way of telling." The woman shook her head. "Miriam's a law unto herself. Sim'd know. He's her son."

"Where can I find him?"

"I can direct you to his house. But he likely isn't there right now. He's probably up at the casino."

Alison thanked the woman and left. The casino was farther up the same road. The neon-pink sign was paled by the bright light of the morning, but you still couldn't miss it. It was the tallest thing for miles around.

Sim came to the front desk to meet her. He did not seem that surprised to see her, but when she explained her mission, he had to tell her that he was just about to go to work.

"I've got a car. Tell me where it is; I'll go up there."

Sim shook his head. "Better if I take you. You gotta take logging roads. You could get lost."

"I'll wait, then. When do you get off?"

"I could get a relief to come in. Say around noon?"

"OK."

"What will you do till then?"

Alison gazed around. "I've never been in a casino before. It looks exciting."

"Hey, now . . ." Sim's forehead wrinkled. "You be careful. You could lose everything. I mean it! Just play the slots. No branching out to the bigger stuff. . . ."

"I'll be fine."

"OK. See you later."

When they met again, Alison was beaming. She had a sack of change to cash in.

"Pretty impressive place you've got here," she said as she counted her dollars.

"It's small compared with some operations, but we're getting bigger and there's plenty of room for expansion. Right now we're looking at the possibilities of gambling on the Net."

"So it's a good thing?" Alison asked as they walked out to the parking lot.

"Most people think so."

"Including your mom?"

Sim scowled, scratching the side of his face with his thumb.

"Let's say she has issues."

"She sounds like quite a strong character."

Sim grinned. "You could say that."

"Agnes certainly seems fond of her."

"Yeah, they're very close."

"Agnes said you grew up together. That you were like a brother."

Sim smiled in surprise. "She say that?"

"Yeah, she said that."

"Her mom more or less dumped her here. It was a shame. She was hurting so that she'd get in fights all the time at school, wouldn't talk to no one. I had to look out for her, you know?"

"What about her mother?"

"Oh, Agnes don't want a whole lot to do with her right now, but Mom says give her time. Mom says it was not really her fault, that Dina, Agnes's mom, was not much more'n a kid herself when she had Agnes. She thinks when Agnes grows up some, she'll come around."

"What do you think?"

"I think maybe. Agnes has had a tough time; she's kind of wary." He paused. "She likes you, though."

"Oh?" Alison felt strangely pleased by that. "How do you know?"

"Can just tell. You're honored. She don't trust many people. 'Specially not from outside. You learn not to."

"What? Even now?"

"Even now."

Sim held her door as she got into the driver's seat.

"My pickup's the black one over there. You follow close."

"Boy, that Alison. Is she ever persistent! She's been chasing Sim all over the reservation. Now he's bringing her up here."

"How do you know? More shaman stuff?"

"Not really." Aunt M cackled and held up the cell phone. "Was just looking at this thing while you were sleeping, and it started beeping. It was Sim. He's bringing her up here."

"When will they be here?"

"Soon. I could wish for better timing. I almost sent them right back again."

"How's that?" Agnes wanted to see Alison. She wanted to know what she'd found out and was eager to tell her what had happened here.

"Because it isn't finished and I don't want interruptions. We gotta follow it all the way, as far as she will take us, and I don't think we're there yet, do you? I don't want you here when they come."

"Why not?"

"Break your concentration. They won't be long now. I've a mind to send them right back again. You go out for a spell."

Agnes left the cabin, as instructed. She had long ago given up trying to fathom Aunt M. Besides, for the moment she had taken the role of shaman's apprentice, assistant sorceress, and as such she had to do as she was told. She took the track that led above the cabin. From here she had a view of the road and could see people come and go. From the distance came the drone of one engine, then another, a car behind something bigger. It must be them. She quickened her step to get to a better vantage point. Maybe she'd go down anyway, just to say "hey." They could pick up when Alison left again. Nothing was going to happen right now.

Her legs felt heavy and her back ached, as if she'd been walking for days. Suddenly she felt impossibly weary as though even one more step would be too much for her. She sank down, resting her back against a great forest tree, and closed her eyes.

They had bound us with black spruce root and then tied us together with a halter made from twisted vine. They marched us onward, two before us and two behind. They kept a cruel running pace through the paths in the forest, and it was hard to keep up with them. We were weakened by our near drowning, and we had not eaten for a night and a day. Black Fox was as tireless as the Mohawk warriors, but Ephraim was worse than me. He was at the end of his strength. He was reeling, his steps weaving, his face pallid, sweating, the skin tinged blue all around the mouth. He might swoon at any minute. Such weakness would render him valueless, and his life would be forfeit. I sank down, my back against a tree, and swore that I could go no farther. Even though I knew I might well die for it, I had to call a halt.

Our captors retired some distance to talk among themselves. One was minded to kill us there and then, but their leader overruled him. It was not long to night falling, so the halt was timely. He ordered the others to make a camp. They left us tethered to a tree, hobbling us like beasts to be sure that we did not get away.

They brought us water and fed us with dried cornmeal, moistened a little to make it palatable. It was standard fare for warriors on the trail and the same as they ate themselves. It was parched stuff and there was little of it, but it gave some nourishment and brought strength back to all of us.

Ephraim crawled over to me. "Can't you use the talking magic like you did on the soldiers?"

I shook my head, pointing to the amulets they wore at neck and chest. It would not work on them.

We went on in this way for three more days. On the fourth night we stopped for only the briefest halt, and we went on as soon as light showed in the eastern sky. We were close to their home village, and this day was a special day for them; they were in haste to get home. The way was difficult, boggy underfoot and tussocked with rush and coarse grass. They hurried us on, forcing the pace, cuffing us with clubs, jabbing us with lances, scolding any stumbling. We went on reluctantly. Journeying was better than arrival. There was no telling what they intended, and if it was death, then it would not be quick.

The day promised heat, but mist curled from the marshy ground. The way we took was eerie, passing through a cemetery land where clothing streamed from the trees like tattered banners and the blind-eyed antlered skull of some great horned creature watched over all.

Beyond this burial ground lay the camp. It was set on higher land; a great stockaded settlement bristling with sharpened staves made from tall trees criss-crossed against each other. It rose before us, hunched like a porcupine. I faltered and would have stopped had I not been shoved roughly onward. I had seen this place in dreams, and every sight, every sound was ominous, from the pebbles on the path to the grunts of our guards and the creak of their moccasins.

Lookouts on high platforms saw us approaching and called out, announcing our presence to those within the stockade. The way in was through a double line of staves set to overlap each other. We wound through this narrow way and into the village proper. Before we entered I could hear drums beating, and chanting, and the stamp of feet dancing. We had come upon them at a time of festival or ceremony, but as soon as we appeared, all sound stopped.

The whole village was there foregathered. Our captors untied our bonds, allowing us to chafe the feeling back into wrists and hands. They did not fear our escape now.

Small children dashed out of the jostling crowd to throw stones and insults. They showed particular attention to Ephraim, attracted by his hair, his difference. If they sought a reaction, they were to be disappointed. He knew what was expected and how to behave. He stood, arms folded, adopting the faraway stare of Black Fox, his brother. Black Fox was already composing himself, preparing his mind for what might happen. He had to show that his courage was equal to any trial. To show weakness, to cry for mercy, would mean that they could take his soul and his strength would go to them; or else he would become an earthbound spirit and never reach the plains of heaven. He must be able to withstand anything. They could put him to the most excruciating torture designed to test his fortitude beyond measure. They could do the same to us and make him watch. They could take us all to a place where death would come as a most merciful friend. It would take us three days to die.

The men who brought us in stepped back and left us for inspection. Three women came out of the crowd and looked us over as a master might a servant at a hiring fair, or a farmer buying cattle. The women wore clan marks on their cheeks: turtle, wolf, bear. These were the clan mothers, rulers of the longhouses that dominated the village. They would decide our fate.

The women stood in front of us. One of them turned my head, noting the wolf mark on the left side of my face. It matched hers. She looked into my eyes and smiled.

The other women bade Black Fox and Ephraim strip and stood back in frank appraisal, taking in the lithe power of Black Fox's body, marveling at the shocking whiteness of Ephraim's skin in contrast to the brown of his face and hands. At length they turned, and at a nod from them, the people ceased from milling and began to line up.

The women walked back down the forming corridor, retreating to their longhouses. These were impressive bark-clad dwellings, greater than any I had ever seen before, of ten to fifteen fires, large enough to take twenty to thirty families. The houses were marked as lodges by the clan insignia above the doors.

The women stationed themselves with the other leaders at the doors of the different houses. The women chose what happened to prisoners. The village must have sustained losses, for we were not to be tortured and burned. We were to be adopted. But first we would have to run the gauntlet.

The people stood in two lines now: men, women, children, all holding whips, clubs, sticks, anything they had at hand with which to beat us.

We had to gain the door of the house. To falter, to fail, to fall would render us worthless, and we would be put to death.

Black Fox went first. Club and stick came striking out at him, but they struck thin air as he streaked on, feinting right and left, dodging feet and legs stuck out to trip him. He was through before most of them knew that he had even gone past. The man who had taken us smiled in broad admiration. He beckoned Black Fox to the Turtle Lodge. The men standing at the door came forward to greet him, clapping him on the back, hugging him about the shoulders, welcoming him in like a brother.

Next it would be Ephraim. He stood next to me, straight-backed, and stared forward, ignoring the renewed taunts of the dung-flinging children, but he was trembling like a yearling colt before its first race.

"I will take care of you," I whispered.

He nodded and set off as swiftly as Black Fox, but he was younger and he had been weakened by the journey and his ordeal on the lake. He soon caught heavy blows to back and shoulder, and this slowed him further. He was about to falter, a blow to the thigh buckling his leg under him, but he staggered on, crouching lower, body skewed over his weakened leg, soaking up blows from left and right. I thought he would make it on his own. Then a small boy, his face full of chuckling malice, stuck out his foot. Ephraim was about to pitch over it and fall face forward into the mud. I stared down the row. Everything slowed. The child overbalanced and tumbled in front of Ephraim, who stepped over him and stumbled onward. He had only a little way to go now, and the other boy on the floor was proving a distraction, causing people to mistime their blows. They flailed at thin air or clashed with one another. They looked at their weapons in wonder, but Ephraim now was through them and staggering up to the lodges.

He would have followed Black Fox, but the clan mother from the Wolf Lodge caught him. She took him in her arms and near carried him to her door.

Her gaze came back to me. It was my turn to walk

between the lines of people. Women do not have to run the gauntlet. The people lowered their weapons and stepped aside to let me through.

We were bathed, feasted, given new clothes. We had proved ourselves worthy, and we were Kahniakehaka now. People of the Flint. Adoption is common among many nations, to replace people lost to them through sickness or war. I soon saw why we had been taken into the tribe.

Sickness was present in the Wolf Clan longhouse. It was midday, but there were still people on the sleeping racks, throwing off their robes in the grip of fever or lying in scarce-moving torpidity. I went closer and saw that their hands and faces were covered with weeping sores and erupting pustules. They had the spotted sickness, what the English call smallpox.

The clan mother watched from her place at the central hearth, and her face was troubled and full of sorrow. Such sickness can kill near all before it has run its course.

She spoke to a smaller woman, who jumped from her place and came over to join me.

"They call me Wahiakwas, Picking Berries. I am Pennacook, like you. I was taken in a raid on my village many years ago. I was brought here at this time of year, in the moon of strawberries, and adopted by the

Kahniakehaka." She glanced around at the bodies spread about. "These fell ill when a trader came. He was Dutch, what they call *asseroni*, maker of knives. They did not know he was sick, or else he would never have been allowed in, but now . . ."

"How long?" I looked at her. "How long since he came here?"

"Not long. A week since he fell sick—"

"How many are ill like this?"

"Four or five in each house . . ."

It was late, but it might still be of benefit, and it might stop others from getting it.

"Tell the clan mother I wish to speak to her."

The clan mother took me to the chief man. He would have to approve my plan.

He stood at the head of his lodge, awaiting my approach. His face was stippled with markings, his head hung round with weasel skins and topped with a coronet trailing eagle feathers. He was richly girdled about with wampum belts. He was not tall—his men on either side dwarfed him—but they left careful space about him. He wore his power like a cloak.

He listened in silence as my plan was explained to him.

"Why?" he asked Picking Berries. "Why would she do this?"

"They are sick and I am a healer," I replied through her. "Your people are my people now."

"Very well." He looked to the warriors flanking him. "It is done."

The house was made away from the village, outside the bristling palisade. The sick were brought on pallets to me and then I was left. I asked them to gather fresh flowers, as many as they could find, to make the house fresh and wholesome, and to bring the herbs and medicines I needed, gathering them from the forest. Then I told them to leave me, only coming to bring any others who fell ill from the sickness. Food and fresh water were to be left outside the fence I ordered made.

I already had fifteen patients, including several children. I set about caring for them as best I could, hoping that the task would not be too much for me.

I built a fire and put a pot to boil to prepare an herbal infusion to bathe their sores and to help prevent infection. I set to pounding and grinding, preparing ointments and decoctions to bring down fevers and purify the blood. I sang as I worked, an old tune in my own tongue, "So early, early in the spring . . ." It was one my grandmother used to sing about the cottage. I felt her spirit around me, and I called on her to send strength to me now.

Light was fading on the first night as I sat before my fire, surrounded on all sides by the cries of the sick and the groans of the dying. Suddenly, I felt the

291

air in the house change. The door flap was pulled back and someone was entering. I heard the tick and scratch of a turtle rattle, and a face loomed out of the flickering darkness. Any ordinary woman would have bolted. I truly thought this was a spirit, the earthly manifestation of a god. My heart jumped in my chest and I bid it stop. I was no ordinary woman. I was a *powwaw*. I was a sorceress.

I waited, staying quite still, and watched him circle, as a great cat might circle its prey. The body and clothing were those of a man, but the coat was of fantastic design—cloth, skin, and fur all sewn together, and set about with disks of shell and copper and iron. The coat clinked as he danced around me, and the face turned toward me was huge, twisted, and distorted, with ragged hair like raven's wings, the eyes great cavernous spaces, the skin the very color of blood.

I reached into my pouch and offered him tobacco. He stepped away from me with his arching catlike tread and began to pass among my patients, dancing down the rows and chanting, shaking his rattle over them, hovering his hands above their bodies. Even the most restless grew quiet as he passed, and when he returned, the whole hut seemed full of peace and tranquility.

He came to where I was standing and stood

before me. I could feel the power coming from him like heat from the fire.

He removed the mask to show a face almost as ugly and twisted as the guise that had concealed it. One eye was closed and drooping. A great cut, made by a tomahawk or hatchet, cleaved that side of his face from forehead to jaw, carving through the Bear Clan mark he wore on his cheek. The other side was whole. The dark eye was bright with intelligence, but the skin was deeply pitted and badly pocked. He stood before me, a man now and a flawed one, but I felt no diminution of his power.

"I am Satehhoronies, Tall Sky, because I see as far as a bird flying high." He turned his blind eye to me. I understood his meaning: you do not need eyes to see. "I am Ronaterihonte, Faith Keeper. I am also a healer, as you are." He raised the mask he held between his hands. "This is who I become when I perform the ceremonies. This is who brings me the healing power. This is carved from the living basswood; it has much *orenda*, what you would call *manitou*."

He spoke in the tongue used by the tribes of New England. When I looked at him, he replied to my thought.

"I speak many languages." He repeated the phrase in English, then French, and then in what I took to be Dutch. Next he smiled and his face changed to almost beauty, showing what it must have been before being so ravaged and scarred by disease and war. "I have come to help you." His fingers went to his cheek, reading the pitted skin. "As you can see, I have had this sickness before."

"Those who have had it once do not generally fall sick."

"Just so. And you? For this sickness kills white men too."

"When I was a child, I suffered a milder kind. Cowpox my grandmother called it. She gave it to me."

"*Gave* it to you?"

I nodded. "She took some matter from one of the sores on the hands of a milkmaid, then made a little cut in my skin. Any who suffered from that sickness never got the worse one, that's what she said, and I believe it to be true."

"There could be wisdom in that." He rose from the fire and held his hand out to me. His grip was warm and strong. "It is a good thing that you do, Mary."

"How do you know my name?"

"I know much." He made his look distant and mysterious. Then he smiled his lopsided smile. "I could say through magic, but in truth the boy told me. You have a new name now, did you know?"

"What do they call me?"

"They call you Katsitsaionneh, which means Bringing Flowers. Come, there is much to do."

So he stayed and helped me fight the sickness, and I own that without him, I would have joined the dead whom he took daily from the house. He helped heal the sick, and he gave comfort to the dying. When they went beyond us, he buried their bodies with all due ceremony. But still they came, more and more of them.

One day he asked me again for my grandmother's healing wisdom about this plague.

I told him and he sat in thought for a long time.

"Perhaps we can do the same. Take matter from one near recovered, introduce it beneath the skin of the others in the tribe."

"What if they die?"

"If this goes on"—he looked at me bleakly—"they all die. I will talk to my brother healers. We can raise it in council, then the people will decide."

I did not think that they would agree to such a drastic plan, and it was discussed long around the council fire, but at last it was approved.

Neither of us knew if our treatment would work. At first it seemed to make things worse, but gradually the cases became fewer and fewer, until one day none was brought to us. The time stretched on to a week, then two. No one else came in with the sickness. Our remaining patients recovered. After months of working until we were ready to drop with tiredness, we had nothing to do.

We came out when the leaves were no longer green, and the people hailed us; they hailed us both.

All my patients had gone. The house that had been
made for them was empty. I set about cleansing it,
raking out and burning the bedding, then burning
juniper and tobacco to purify. There were no flowers
now, so I gathered spruce and pine for their fresh,
sharp smell. As I worked, the idea came to me as clear
as a striking bell. I would not join the others in the
Wolf Clan longhouse inside the palisade. I would stay
here. The sick would come to me. I would care for
them, just as my grandmother told me the sisters did
long ago, before King Henry's men turned them out
and left their priory, infirmary and all, to fall into
ruin.

I explained to Satehhoronies that this was what I
intended to do. He thought for a while, then he said,
"The people respect me, but they fear me, too." He
stroked the mask propped next to him. "They fear

this." Then his hand went to his ruined face. "And they fear this." He shook his turtle rattle. "They fear this, *ohtonkwa*, the spirit, but you fear nothing. I will stay with you."

I did not want for company. Wahiakwas, Picking Berries, often came to visit me, bringing other women, and we would sit and work together. They showed me how they worked birch bark and hide with dyed moose hair. I showed them the way I had been taught to embroider, using steel needles they had traded from the Dutch, and we worked together, making ordinary objects fine.

The first thing I made was a box for my special things; the second was a knife sheath for Ephraim to wear at his naming ceremony. Ephraim came to visit me often. He liked to talk to Satehhoronies, for the medicine man had traveled far in his life, and the boy loved to hear about the places he had visited.

Satehhoronies chose Ephraim's new name. He was to be called Kaheranoron, Rare Cornstalks. The name had belonged to one who had departed to the spirit world, and the naming ceremony was held at the festival of ripe corn. It was an important occasion, marking not just Ephraim's acceptance into tribe and clan, but his passage to young manhood. It was time for him to leave his mother's side. I would have worried for him, for he had no father now that Sparks Fire was gone, but Black Fox would be there. He would help him.

Black Fox also had a new name. He was now Tekaionhake, Two Rivers—a name he had been given from another who had come from beyond Kani-atarakaronte, the Door to the Country, the Mohawk name for Lake Champlain. He was accepted and admired for his strength, bravery, and prowess with weaponry. Ephraim could ask for no one better to guide him in the world of men.

Ephraim grew taller by the day, just like the cornstalks of his new name, and he grew strong, skilled in hunting and the ways of the warrior. I watched him with the pride any mother feels, and I felt a mother's grief, although I did not show it. I knew he would not take the war trail and for that I gave thanks, but I also knew that he would not stay here. The rhythms of village life were too slow for him. He craved excitement, and as he got older, his restlessness grew stronger.

In the spring, groups of warriors went to Kahnawake, the Mohawk village outside Mount Royale. They went to collect beaver from the people living there, to sell in Albany because Dutch prices were higher. A party went every year; it was one such that had found us half drowned on the shores of the lake. Ephraim was eager to go with them. He came back, safe and sound, but I knew that the year would come around when the warriors would return and he would not be with them. He had never forgotten the stories he had heard at Missisquoi told around the smoky fires by the *coureurs des bois*. I knew it wanted only time before he would go and join them. The distance was already there in his eyes, the longing for wide horizons and faraway skies.

"I'm going north again, Mary," he came to tell me just before the party was leaving. He still used my English name when we were alone.

"And this time you won't be coming back?" I asked, guessing what his answer would be.

He didn't reply immediately.

"Remember when I gave you this?" He caught the string of bear claws that I still wore around my neck. "I was so proud. I so badly wanted to be a son to you, to do anything that Black Fox could do . . ."

"You have been a son to me. And I'm proud of you."

I reached up to touch his face. He was tall now and his cheek was sanded with fine fair stubble. His body had a man's hard finish to it, but he had a boy's wide smile and his eyes were full of hope and expectation.

"And I'll make you prouder yet, Mary. I'm minded to join them French boys. I hear they're traveling far to the west." His eyes took still more light at the thought of this adventure. "Following the lakes, one going into another, until the last one is as big as the sea. I've been talking to Satehhoronies, too, and he says that there are great mountains beyond that where no white man has ever been, and plains and forests and rivers that no white man has ever seen. Maybe they'll name a river after me, or a lake, or a great mountain peak. Or maybe I'll name one after you." He smiled down at me again, but his blue eyes were blurring with visions of the future and thoughts of farewell. "Anyway, that's where I want to go, Mary. *Voyageurs*, that's what they call them, and that's what I want to be."

"Then you must follow your destiny. Before you go, I have something for you."

Knowing this day was coming, I had fashioned a bandoleer for him to go with his knife sheath. He held it up, studying the patterns I had worked into it, showing our life together: wolf, lynx, fox; in forest, lake, and mountain; all set around with a border of rippling water and flowers and tall cornstalks. He put it over his head and arranged it across his chest.

"Thank you," he said. "Thank you, Mary. I will wear this always; that way I'll keep you with me."

Ephraim left me then, and he did not return from Kahnawake with the rest of the men. He joined a French expedition heading west. He became a *voyageur*. He came to visit when the trail led him back this way. He'd arrive with a pack full of gifts and a fund of wondrous tales to tell. He'd stay a month, maybe more, but then he'd become restless to resume his wandering ways. He never lived a truly settled life again.

I had one son remaining, Black Fox, now Tekaionhake. He would always call Ephraim brother, but he did not intend to go from the village. Already his eyes were turning toward a young woman, Kanehratitake, Carrying Leaves. It was clear that soon there was to be a wedding. I set about preparing, trading red cloth from the Dutchmen, curing skins to the softest whiteness, and tanning hide to velvet blackness. Then I began fashioning and embroidering garments for him. I did all the work myself, determined that my son would be the handsomest of grooms. She was daughter to the *sachem*, and theirs was the finest of weddings. Tekaionhake joined his bride in her mother's longhouse. His life was with the tribe now.

Tekaionhake's young bride did not have an easy life. She feared for him as I had done and did still, for he loved the war trail. He was proving a fearsome warrior, renowned for his stealth; he was brave to foolhardiness and so ruthless that he won admiration among a people famed for their warlike qualities. He was valued, and his value would grow. War was coming between France and England. These two nations would pit the native people against each other, but the Kahniakehaka have ever loved a fight, and there was no keeping them out of it. Tekaionhake fought with the rest of his tribe on the side of the English, the people who had killed his father. Such is the strangeness of life.

War kept us busy, but Satehhoronies and I treated all alike: sick, wounded, warrior, or prisoner—it made no difference. Our lodge became famous. Not just among the Haudenosaunee, the People of the Longhouse, but among other nations. Many came and from all the four directions: young, old, men, women, Indian, African, and European. They came to learn, from us and from one another. We taught them all we knew of the healer's skill. All we asked of them was that they came in peace and laid all hatred and difference aside, leaving it like their weapons outside the door.

That is the way I lived my life.

Agnes felt released. The sensation was almost physi-
cal. She rose as the sun was sinking over the water and
set out for the cabin, her step quicker and lighter than
it had been for some time.

Sim's truck had gone, but Alison's car was still
there. Light spilled onto the porch from the half-open
door. She could see Aunt M sitting at the table.
Opposite her sat Alison. They were deep in conversation. The oil lamp cast soft light onto a chaos of
papers and maps spread out between them. Agnes faltered; then she halted, looking in from the outside.
Up until now it had been just her and Aunt M, no
one else involved.

Aunt M solved her dilemma. She pulled herself
up from her chair and came to the door.

"Come on in here, Agnes. It's getting cold and I
want to shut the door."

Agnes sat down at the table to begin the last part of Mary's story. Alison listened to her with rapt attention right through to the end, stopping Agnes only now and then to change the tape in the little recorder she had brought with her.

"They founded a secret medicine society open to men and women alike, and to every tribe, even whites." Agnes finished: "And that's it. That's how she lived her life."

Alison's finger hovered over the "off" button. She looked up at Aunt M, ready to ask if this secret medicine society was still in operation today. Something in the older woman's eyes told her that might be one inquiry too far.

"Alison should tell you about what she found out in Montreal." Aunt M could feel the question coming on and was anxious to deflect it. Secret medicine lodges were not to be discussed.

"Oh, well . . ." Alison laughed. "I guess I thought it was quite a big deal, but it rather pales compared to what you guys have discovered." She looked at Agnes. "Will you write it down for me?"

"Sure, of course."

"That's wonderful." Alison smiled. "I want to put it all in 'as told to Agnes Herne.'"

Aunt M got up then and pulled a trunk from under the bed. She opened it up and reached in for something, bringing it back to them cradled in her cupped hands as if she were carrying a nest full of bird eggs.

She put it in the center of the table. A birch-bark box decorated with moose hair embroidery. Agnes recognized it immediately.

"Could it be the same one Mary made?" Alison asked, her voice hushed, her eyes wide as if it were something alive.

Aunt M shook her head. "Most likely not." She smiled when Alison looked a little disappointed. "I don't see that it matters." She turned the box around in her hands. "Like on a quilt, the patterns are what's important, not the fabric. They would remain, worked in by each woman who made it again. That way they stay fresh." She offered the box to Agnes.

Agnes leaned across the table. The toggle fixing the lid was a little black head of a fox. She hadn't noticed that the first time; it had just been a toggle back then. It was still stiff to work. She twisted it out of the loop of plaited grass and lifted the top, tilting the box so Alison could see in as well.

Agnes had not seen these things since childhood. She had not asked for them when she first came to visit. There had been more pressing matters. She had not wanted to see them then. Now she did. She leaned over, looking closer. They seemed smaller, more human scale and battered, in the way of things remembered or imagined, or long anticipated but never seen. They were no less special for that.

"Pick 'em up," Aunt M said. "We ain't in a museum."

Agnes shook her head. No. She did not want to touch them. To look was enough just now.

Alison didn't feel it was her place to touch them, either, not before Agnes, but she was having a hard time keeping her hands on the table.

"They could definitely be hers," she said, her voice rising in excitement. "That slip of paper would be all the proof needed. And the half of a silver shilling in the center of the gorget?" She craned her head closer. "It has to be a match. I'd have to take them back to test—" She turned to Aunt M, suddenly anxious, mindful of what Agnes had told her, not wanting to seem to take anything for granted. "That's if, that's if, well, if you don't mind. If you'll give your permission."

"Ain't mine to give." Aunt M shrugged.

"I'm sorry?" Alison looked utterly mystified now.

"Ain't mine to give. I ain't the owner." She nodded to Agnes. "Better ask her."

"Oh, no, Aunt M." Agnes put up her hands.

"I'm not taking no." She pushed the box toward her niece. "You have them. You've earned them. They are yours now."

"No, they're not." Agnes smiled, carefully fitted the lid, and pushed the box across the table. "Not for a while, at least. I want Alison to have them for now, so they can be verified. Then I want them to go to her exhibition."

Alison reached out and their hands met in giving and receiving. Alison had been all but overwhelmed when she first saw the box opened. Now to think that it was being given into her keeping—it made her feel quite faint. These things were being lent to her, and it was a very great honor. She'd been talking all day— talking and asking questions. Now she could think of nothing to say. All she could do was look at Agnes and smile back her wonder and thanks.

"You got that little tape machine running, Alison?" Aunt M turned to the younger woman. "Story ain't finished yet, y'know. Now . . ." She settled in her seat, folding her hands on the table. "Tekaionhake, her son, the one they called Black Fox, had a daughter. She was called Ojijiagauh, Little Flower, because she was like her grandmother. She had her looks, her ways, her laugh. She grew into a beautiful young woman and followed the medicine way.

"When Katsitsaionneh, Bringing Flowers, was finally laid to rest, her granddaughter released a white bird above her grave, as was the custom in those days, to bear her spirit aloft and speed it on to the plains of heaven. As she let the bird go, a jay darted out of the forest. They flew away together, up and up, until they were just specks in the great blue of the sky, until they could be seen no more. That was the story told to me. That is the story of the grandmothers."

Agnes listened to her aunt tell it, and it was as if she were meeting herself coming back. The story she'd seen unfold and the one that had just been told, they were one now. That should have brought some kind of closure; instead it made her feel lonely. With Mary gone from her, she felt bereft and even more lost than she had before. She frowned and looked up at her aunt, her gray eyes pleading for help.

"Sometimes its hard." Aunt M stood up. "It's hard for us to find our place, to know where we fit in the world. The way I see it is like this."

Aunt M opened another box and took out a wampum belt. It was about two feet long and four or five inches broad, made up of many small white and purple beads worked into a repeating pattern.

"Ever seen one of these?" she asked Alison.

"Only in a museum, but I know how important they are."

She knew the belts were very special, sacred. Laws, treaties, were talked into them. They held the history of the people.

"Glad you do." Aunt M looked stern.

She did not like the way wampum, *gehsweda*, had been dishonored, devalued, and disrespected over the years. First by the Europeans who had mistaken value for money, then by collectors, and now by ignorant people who used it as a slang term.

"Wampum was never used by native peoples as money. These belts carry the word, the code, the law. They are sacred and a living part of us. They are still used now and always will be. Each bead is treated with great reverence, but each bead is very small." She put forefinger and thumb a quarter of an inch apart.

"On their own they fall and scatter." She opened her palm and turned her hand. "Put them together, though, and you've got something else. Together they make up something big. Together they preserve the words." She looked over at Agnes. "This is how I figure it: you, me, Mary, the people in her life, the folk Alison has found out about, Alison herself—we're like the beads on this belt. Look at us apart and you can't tell a lot. But put us together and then you can read the whole story."

BACKGROUND NOTES

Note 1—Elias Cornwell (1631?–1713)

The Reverend Elias Cornwell was a prolific writer. His archive contains many publications, including pamphlets and sermons, although it is the diaries that interest us here. These run to many volumes, spanning the clergyman's whole life, from his days at Cambridge to his eventual career as an established and well-respected minister in Boston. The entries referring to his time in Beulah are interesting because they provide a very different perspective on Mary's flight from Beulah and also offer additional information about the fates of others involved in her story and the fate of the community itself. The relevant passages are included here.

Excerpt from Elias Cornwell's Journals (from volumes 6 and 7)

November 1st, 1660

I must recount certain doleful and terrible events
lately occurring here in Beulah. They concern the
orphan Mary Newberrie. This girl (I hesitate to call
her by that name, besmirching, as she does, all
womankind, not least the spotless maidens, the very
flowers of our community, that she has used so cruelly), this girl was welcomed among us with most
Christian charity. All unknowingly, we sheltered in
our bosom a serpent, a servant of the Evil One
Himself. Only God knows what havoc she might
have wreaked if she had not been discovered. But
He ever watches over us, like to a father, and I truly

believe that He sent His servant, Obadiah Wilson, as an holy Angel to deliver us from harm.

November 2nd, 1660

The wicked flee when no man pursueth (Proverbs 28:1) and so it was with her. She has fled the town. And although we have searched most thoroughly, for a night and day ranging far and about, no trace of her has been found.

The men came back from searching. The weather has turned freakishly severe even for this harsh climate, with great cold and snow flying too fast to see anything. The searching parties risked losing men, or dogs, or both. They have found nothing. No trace. No tracks in the snow lying thick on the ground. Some say she brought the snow on in order to hide her flight and fill her tracks as she made them. Others say there are none to find. They say she flew, as her kind are said to be able to do.

November 3rd, 1660

The snow blew and the wind howled all last night. With daylight the storm at last abated, but snow lies to the eaves of the houses. I deem it fruitless to hunt more, but Reverend Johnson sends the men out again and orders them to take every dog they have with them. He is determined that she shall not escape.

The men come back and report still no sign of her.
It is as if she has vanished. The more superstitious
hold yet more strongly to the notion that she has
flown on a stick or been borne off by devils. The
less fanciful are inclined to believe that she lies
buried in snow, frozen in the forest, or that she has
been taken by wolves or some other of the fierce
wild creatures that dwell in its depths. I fervently
pray that this is so and that this perfidious creature,
this limb of Satan, has indeed perished.

That I ever entertained tender thoughts in
her direction! My blood runs chill in my veins to
think on it. The Reverend Johnson, wise in so much
else, was wise in this also. For he did warn me even
as I sought to protect her and protested her inno-
cence, quoting to me from Proverbs, chapter 5,
verses 3 to 5:

> *For the lips of a strange woman drop as an*
> > *honeycomb, and her mouth is smoother than oil:*
> *But her end is bitter as wormwood, sharp as a*
> > *two-edged sword.*
> *Her feet go down to death; her steps take hold on*
> > *Hell.*

Those were his words to me, but I was too blind to
see. I own that I was a credulous fool to be near
ensnared by her wiles, but I must not use myself

too harshly. I was cruelly duped. For her words were honeyed, and winning were her smiles. She was indeed fair, and as subtle and beguiling as the very serpent. I have truly escaped a terrible fate and thank God most fervently for delivering me from this female fiend, this very Lilith.

"And I find more bitter than death the woman, whose heart is snares and nets" (Ecclesiastes 7:26).

December 2nd, 1660

A thaw came, swift and unexpected, taking much of the snow. This has been followed by a sharp frost, freezing the roads and making it easier to travel. Obadiah Wilson is anxious to be gone, feeling that his work in Beulah is done.

December 4th, 1660

Obadiah Wilson has been persuaded to stay for a little time longer. There is concern over one of the afflicted girls. Hannah Vane continues to do poorly. It is feared that others in our midst are still busy about the Devil's business and that they do come upon the unfortunate girl, to the very great impairing of her strength and wasting of her spirits.

My own fear is for Obadiah himself. For this is the season for rheums and colds, and he is frequently wracked with coughing and daily spits blood.

December 20th, 1660

The frost holds, turning all to iron. Again I find truth in Proverbs 28:1, viz. "The wicked flee when no man pursueth," for Martha Everdale and Jonah Morse are gone. Even though this is not the season for it, they are travelling on. Obadiah Wilson smiles between his coughing. There is no smoke without fire, he says, and witches seldom work alone.

January 6th, 1661

Perhaps Obadiah Wilson was right, for little Hannah is somewhat recovered. Wilson says that this is a sure sign that the evil has gone from us, and I pray that it is so. He himself is preparing to leave. His work here is done, but he will be needed in other places if the Devil is not to break forth again in our fair New England. Although this is a bad time for travelling, the roads are firm and there is little snow. I have offered to go with him to Salem, for I do not think that he would survive the rigours of the journey if he travels alone. His coughing is no better. He is little more than skin and bone, and lately a violent fever wracks his body and spots his cheeks. He needs the services of a doctor, and we have none here, nor apothecary now, nor any skilled in herbs and healing. If he does not seek help soon, I fear that it will be too late.

Obadiah Wilson has been taken from us, God rest his soul. He died yestereve, seized with a fit of coughing that would not stop. He died of haemorrhage, choking and gargling, drowning in his own blood.

At last the year is turning; the thaw has set in now, heralding the spring. The afflicted girls have all but recovered. The Reverend Johnson has been tending to the Vane sisters, Deborah and Hannah, since the curse of affliction fell heaviest upon them. Deborah, the elder of the two, does especially well. All afflictions left her some time ago, and she fairly blossoms in his presence.

I am also most pleased with the progress that I have made with Sarah Garner. She has become my particular responsibility, and I pride myself on how well she does under my care. All fits and afflictions having ceased some time ago, she prospers mightily. Indeed, I would think my work done, except she implores me so to see her still in case the evils come again. She weeps when I am leaving, and her mother says she pines most piteously for my return. For my part, I own that I have grown fond of her. She is a most sweet child, so different from *that other*, as innocent and guileless as the day. As soon as I feel that she is recovered sufficiently to take up wifely duties, I hope that she will make me the happiest of men.

August 14th, 1661

The weather stays hot and sultry, most unpleasant. My fears grow for the Reverend Johnson. His new young wife has failed to lift his mood, and he has become ever more melancholy. He sits in his room and broods. His beard and hair are streaked with white and grow increasingly unkempt. When he does not keep to the house, he has taken to wandering far and wide. I fear that he is falling victim to a distemper of the brain. Certainly, he neglects his duties most shamefully. I have to visit the sick on his behalf and have taken Sunday services four weeks in a row.

September 8th, 1661

Terrible news this day. I hardly have the strength nor the will to write. The Reverend Johnson has been found drowned. He was discovered this morning, facedown in the swamp.

September 26th, 1661

The Reverend Johnson has been laid in the Burying Ground, next to the wife he lost a year since
and those of his children taken unto God,
although some do mutter that he has no place
there at all and should be put outside the wall.
Rumours abound that the melancholy he had
lately suffered seized his mind entirely and that
he is guilty of self-murder. This is a terrible
accusation and one that I have taken care to
repudiate most vigorously. How could any man
of Reverend Johnson's virtue commit such a
hideous sin? How could he turn his back on our
Lord and follow the path of the despised Iscar-
iot out to the Judas tree? It is a double crime
against God and Commonwealth; it is not in his
nature to do such a thing, but still the rumours
persist. He was found in a pool both brackish
and shallow, where the water is scarce a foot
deep.

October 5th, 1661

The Reverend Johnson's death, most especially the
manner of it, has come as a very great shock to
Beulah. Many have been deeply affected by it. Not
least little Hannah Vane. It seems to have turned
her wits entirely. She refuses to eat or drink and
loses flesh by the day. She has not left her bed since

the news of his death, but lies curled with her face
to the wall. Sarah thinks her not long for this world.

October 14th, 1661

Reverend Johnson's death has thrown all into doubt.
Many of the people here came with him from
England, crossing the seas at his bidding, following
him into the Wilderness, as the Israelites followed
Moses. Others came later, as I did, in very great
faith and belief in him and his vision of a City on
the Hill.

Now many are saying that vision was false. They
say now that Reverend Johnson did not choose well
when he planted this settlement. He was no farmer
and his visions blinded him to the poorness of the
land: the soil is hard to work, every acre must be
wrested from the forest, and the presence of the
swamp gives off an evil miasma and brings mosqui-
toes in summer and bothersome flies.

October 20th, 1661

John Rivers has received news of his brothers,
whom he came here to seek. Harvest is done and he
prepares to leave. With the Riverses go Tobias
Morse and his wife, Rebekah, and their little child.
I do not know where they go but have heard that
they mean to travel south and west, even as far as
Connecticut.

321

October 24th, 1661

Reverend Johnson's widow, Deborah, wastes no time in finding a husband. My good wife, Sarah, tells me that she is to marry Ned Cardwell, a man inferior in station, an erstwhile hireling of Deborah's uncle. I express my very great surprise. I tell Sarah that Caldwell must be marrying her for money. I know that Reverend Johnson left his wife well provided for. Sarah says that must be so, but I have lately learned that Deborah and Cardwell long had an understanding, perhaps more than that. I would not, of course, repeat this to Sarah. Such talk would offend her modesty and bring the blood rushing to her cheeks.

October 26th, 1661

Hannah Vane did not live to see her sister's nuptials. She died this day, wasted away.

October 27th, 1661

Deborah and Ned Cardwell are married, but Sarah tells me that they plan to leave for Gloucester. Ned is done with farming, so he declares, and wants to use his newfound wealth to open a tavern. Gloucester is a seaport and thus has opportunities for enterprises of that sort.

Others talk of leaving also. A new settlement has grown up to the north where our little river joins a greater. Reverend Johnson frowned upon any intercourse with our neighbours, fearing ungodly influences, but now he has gone and news comes that this other township is seeking for settlers and that good land abounds, with fishing aplenty where the river falls and copious meadowland.

November 1st, 1661

I myself have resolved to leave Beulah. I intend to take Sarah and the babe she expects (for we are blessed!) to Boston and seek for a ministry there. I have ever found the people here to be of a poor sort, ignorant and for the most part uneducated. I wish to live in a community more congenial, which will provide proper sustenance to both mind and spirit. Even so, I would have stayed to do the Lord's work here in Beulah, had the people seen fit to choose me as their spiritual leader. Instead they seek another. So be it.

Note 2—Deborah Vane

A search of the Essex County records shows that Deborah Vane failed to prosper after she left Beulah. After she married Ned Cardwell, they moved to Gloucester and bought a tavern. It was not long before they began to appear in the court records for violent behavior, often directed toward each other. Ned was often the complainant.

1. Offered in evidence by Ned Cardwell against Deborah Cardwell on a charge of common assault, Essex court records, 1665:

> She took me by the throat & with her fist did punch me in the
> breast so that I was faint with wont of breath. Then she came
> upon me with a hatchet, forcing me to flee . . .

2. Evidence offered by Deborah Cardwell on a plea of self-defense:

> After he hath given me several blows, threat'ned me with whip
> and knife, and altogether used me most barbarosely.

Court decision: defendant found not guilty, but both warned to mend their ways for "their several riotous behaviours" under threat of fines and the whipping post. Further indictments for drunkenness (both of them) in 1667 and 1668, and for keeping a disorderly house. In 1669 they both stood accused:

> For having received into your house and given entertainment
> unto disorderly Company and ministering unto them wine and

strong waters unto Drunkenness and that not without some iniquity both in the measure and pryce thereof.

License revoked.

Deborah Cardwell's name occurs on a 1670 passenger list manifest on the ship *Fortune* bound for Virginia. No Ned Cardwell on the passenger list.

In 1673 Mistress Cardwell, late of Massachusetts, appeared before the justices for allowing her premises to become "a veritable baudie house and meeting ground for rogues, whores, desolate and rooking persones." This is the last documented reference to Deborah.

Note 3 — The Fate of Beulah

Beulah disappeared from the historical record sometime in the 1660s. This disappearance is not all that surprising. Many towns sprang up about that time; while some grew, others decayed and died. This could happen for any number of reasons: some were too isolated from other communities, vulnerable to local Indian hostility; others had been established in inauspicious places. In still others the inhabitants had fallen out among themselves. Sometimes the ruling regime was too rigid or too lax, causing settlers to leave and not be replaced. If the population fell below a critical mass, then the settlement was no longer viable.

Without historical record, there can only be archaeological evidence.

Beulah? Could be
fwd fr Toni T:
FROM: InHouse Archaeology
http://www.InHouseArch.com/editorial/20010408/1047257.asp

Latest Finds

A site between Lowell and Billerica has been yielding interesting finds. Site Director and Associate Professor of Anthropology Ed Jordan reports on last summer's dig. Jordan and his students spent two weeks last summer in digging a site that provided the local university with a chance to examine what life was like for European settlers in the middle of the seventeenth century. While some of the sites that have been examined have been thousands of years old, the program's summer 2000 dig examined the "Dowell Site" in the Billerica area. The site was believed to have been an English community that existed between about 1650 and 1670, said Jordan. The discoveries from the site are now on display in the local library.

Jordan determined to examine the site after amateur archaeologists in the 1970s found what they believed to be the remains of a meetinghouse. The foundations of this building have since been excavated. Most of the finds are European in origin and date from the colonial period. These include: clay pipe bowl and stem pieces, rusted keys and hinges, a belt buckle, pottery, glass, and lead musket balls. But in an interesting development, stone materials incorporated into the building have been tentatively identified as being of Native American origin. Other finds dating from the Late Woodland period include shell and midden remains, beads, and arrowheads.

Funding has been allocated for this coming summer, much to the relief of Site Director Ed Jordan and his team. Ed comments, "This is an exciting opportunity to examine continuity of use on one particular site. There is still a lot of work to do. To fully explore the site could take years."

Note 4—Jonah and Martha Morse

Married 1662. Settled in Boston. Jonah set up as an apothecary in what is now the North End, choosing an advantageous spot on an important thoroughfare between the Old Mill Cove and the Town Dock.

Landownership sources show he bought a property that combined house and shop, with a back yard where he probably planted a physick garden.

Broadsheet advertisement, owned by Boston Historical Society:

Drugs and Medicines
Mr. Jonah Morse
has lately received a general assortment
of Drugs and Medicines
of the best quality
which he sells wholesale

and retail from his shop on the way
from Cove to Cove
Also
Various Chymical Tinctures
Newlie arrived from England

The Society also possesses a small pamphlet, "Certain Receipts":

For Coughs
*Take one ounce of meadow cabbage, one ounce of lobelia, half
an ounce of indian turnip, one-fourth ounce of blood root,
handful of hoarhound and the same of coltsfoot. Add the weight
of the whole of purified honey, pulverise the ingredients and
mix them up, and let the patient take what the stomach can
bear. Continue until well.*

For Jaundice
*Take equal parts of white snake root, burdock, narrow dock,
dandelion and coweslip heads, steep them together, and drink
until well. This cure is certain.*

Note the combination of plants of English origin—coltsfoot, dandelion, cowslip—and those native to America: both white and black snakeroot, skunk cabbage, Indian turnip.

The will of Jonah Morse, dated 1672, includes:

Sundry jars
1 copper alembic
1 glass alembic
1 pottery alembic
2 pestle & mortar (one great of stone, one small of brasse)
1 scale
1 cabinete and contents
to my wife, Martha (or profite from the sale of such)

Martha continued to live and trade in a small way until her own death in 1674. The will of Martha Morse included: "*2 ashwood stools, 5 oak chaires (one carved very fair), one great oak table, one greate oakwood chest, one fireside settle, a bed, a silver bowl, spoones and candlesticke*" to Tobias Morse. "*My Best Red Kersey Petticoate, My Sad Grey Kersey Wascote, my white Holland Appron with a small lace at the bottom*" to Mistress Humphries, neighbor. To Rebekah Morse: "*My black silk neck cloath and 2 yards of lace and Sixe yards of Redd Cloth, A wooden boxe carved on top and quilte contained within it.*"

Jonah and Martha Morse are buried together in the Copp's Hill Burying Ground.

Note 5 — The Rivers/Morse Family

From the Rivers/Morse private family papers:

Letters between Sarah Rivers and Rebekah Morse

July 1675

My dear daughter,

I do heartily enjoin you to come to us. War has bro-ken out between settler and Indian. The trouble lies to the south, to be sure, but still we live in very great fear that it will spread to the tribes who live hereabout, despite their seeming friendliness.

Your loving mother,

Sarah Rivers

August 1675

My dear daughter,

The news we hear serves to feed my fear for you. Quabog [present-day Brookfield] has been laid waste and all are readying themselves for further attacks. John, Joseph, and Joshua have been called to join the muster. Only Noah is with me now. Whatever he might think, he is too young to fight. Susannah and Rachel are with me here, their husbands being away, and I wish you would come to me too. Hadley is by no means safe from attack, but safer than where you are now. I worry so about you and the little ones.

Joseph is to accompany a troop that is being sent to Pocumtuck to strengthen the garrison. If all stays quiet, his plan is to escort you and your children back to Hadley. I do entreat you to allow him to do this.

Your loving Mother,
Sarah Rivers

August 1675
My dear Mother,

I trust this letter finds you well and safe still. I am grateful for your concern for me, and well know the danger we stand in here. Others are leaving for Hadley and Hatfield, and I trust my children to your care.

Joseph says he will see them safely to you before he rejoins his company. I own my heart ached to see him again, and will ache afresh to see him go, my little ones with him, but I honour my vows to Tobias. My place is with him. He will not leave all he has built here and, besides, there is much work to do, what with the beasts to tend and harvest coming. He cannot do it all alone, and if I do not stay to help him, we will have nothing for the coming year. He will not leave the place empty, for then the indians will sack and burn it for sure.

With Joseph and the children, I send also my box with its precious contents. I earnestly pray to God that all arrive safe.

I remain ever your obedient & loving daughter,
Rebekah Morse

September 1675

My dearest Mother,

 I received your letter and thank God that Joseph brought the children to you safe and well.

 I write this in haste. We are in desperate straits here. Many have crowded into our house, it being the strongest hereabouts. We have come under attack. The assault was repelled, but we fear another. We were set to leave for the greater safety of Pocumtuck, but that is no longer possible. We fear that the enemy is all about, and it would be as dangerous for me to leave as to stay. So I do what I can. I will load muskets and fire them if need be. Meanwhile I provide sustenance, and tear sheets into bandages in readiness for the attack that all expect hourly.

 The attack came at dawn. A small group, part of a larger party, fell upon us, hoping to find us sleeping no doubt, but we maintain a constant lookout. The Indians were few in number and easily repulsed, although we lost two men: one to a musket ball to the head, the other with an arrow through the throat as he tried to regain the house. Several others were wounded, although only slightly. They lost men also. Four bodies lay strewn about after the attack.

 I went to see what help I could give, but all were dead. Among them a man who I took to be their chiefest warrior. I name him such by the stature of his person and by the paint he wore upon his face and by a fine gorget he wore at his throat, woven of white and purple wampum beads, interspersed with discs of silver and beaten copper. One of our men bent to rip

332

this from him and raised his sword as if to hack off his head, declaring, "This must be Philip himself!"

I held the man's arm and begged him to desist. He was disposed to argue with me, saying that he "would have his head for that is what the Indians do to our dead," but I bid him stay his hand and ordered the bodies removed to the edge of the forest.

We expected another attack, but it did not come. The Indians appeared merely to remove their dead. Then they melted back into the forest, and we have not seen them since.

We know not if they are still lurking there, but we must take our chance. Tobias does not think we could survive if they return and attack in any numbers. We leave today for Pocumtuck, hoping to be safer there, from whence this will be dispatched onwards.

I do not look for the worst to come to pass, but I have given thought to what I wish to happen if it does. My intentions are thus:

I hope and trust that you will care for my children. Such of my goods that survive should be kept for them. In particular, the box that Joseph conveyed is for Mary Sarah, to be kept for her and handed over on the occasion of her marriage. It and its contents are to be preserved by her, to be passed on to her daughter, and her daughter after, and, if she has none, to the wife of her oldest son. Tell her what you will of the history of the quilt, but tell her, and this most strongly, that it should not be used for everyday purpose. It should serve, as it served me, as cover and comfort to mother and newborn child.

333

If it is God's will, then we will meet again.
   Until then, I trust in his Great Goodness and remain
ever your loving daughter,
   Rebekah

Extract from Alison Ellman's notes on Rebekah Morse

Rebekah survived, although the settlement she left did not. Pocumtuck stood alone, the last of the frontier outposts. The other towns around it lay deserted, burnt, and wasted. The women and children were evacuated, Rebekah with them, leaving only the men behind to stay and fight. After a vicious skirmish at a place known ever after as Bloody Brook, Pocumtuck was abandoned, its houses burned, its crops taken. It became a town "inhabited by owls."

Tobias survived to join his wife and children in the comparative safety of Hadley. The loss of home, farm, and business must have been a bitter blow to this ambitious young man, but at least he was alive and he meant to build again.

Rebekah and Tobias eventually went back with others to rebuild their devastated town. Somewhere in the process it was renamed Deerfield. The town was not without future troubles, but the Morse family stayed on and prospered. Some of them live there still.

Extract from *Sewing Serendipity* (1916):

> *Eveline Travers Harris adds to our occasional series*
> *"Old Quilts of New England" with a fascinating family*
> *tale about an extremely unusual quilt from her very fine*
> *collection.*

The Morse Quilt

It may not be much to look at, being all of one
color and a drab one at that, but it is not color or
pattern, cleverness of working, or intricacy of
stitching that makes the Morse quilt (as we call it)
something special. Its age does that, and what it
means to us. It has been in our family forever, and I
do mean ever. It was not manufactured here in the
United States—or the colonies, as it would have
been called back then. The quilt started life in
England, so family tradition tells us, sometime in
the seventeenth century, so it is of very great
antiquity.

It came here with one of the first families.
Some say a Morse brought it with them, some say a
Rivers, and some say that it originally belonged to
someone else entirely, but one thing we do know
for sure. It has been in the family ever since that
time and is always passed down on the female side.
It has seen every conceivable threat and danger,

Indian wars and rebellion, not to mention the War of Independence and the Civil War, and survived them all, just as our family has.

So it means a lot to us, not least in the family traditions that go back to those "first times." It is said that Rebekah Rivers Morse (1643–1714) of Deerfield was the first owner. When she gave it to her daughter Mary Sarah on the occasion of the girl's marriage, it was with the instruction that the quilt was to be passed on to her daughter, and so on. If there was no daughter, then the quilt was to go to the wife of the oldest son. Curiously nearly all of the mothers had daughters, right down to this current generation.

The quilt was never used for its original mundane purpose. Right from the start it was treasured. It was kept in its original box, and only brought out at the birth of a child, when it was spread over mother and offspring in the belief that it would protect both of them in those first few perilous weeks, childbirth being a risky business for both mother and babe until relatively recent times. Now, what with antiseptics and anesthetics, it might be said that we are no longer in need of the quilt's protection, and many might feel inclined to dismiss the tradition as mere superstition. To them I would reply that no baby ever died who had the quilt spread over it; all of them thrived, and no mother lost her life to the fevers that claimed so many after the birth of a child.

I certainly intend to carry on the family tradition. I look forward to the day when I can give this wonderful quilt to my daughter, Etta May, on the occasion of her marriage.

Eveline Travers Harris, September 17, 1916

Eveline Travers Harris died in 1981. The quilt was bought by J. W. Holden in 1985. On his death (1996), it became part of the Holden Collection at the Holden Foundation Museum.

Note 7 — Jack Gill

Transcript of interview with Richard Gill of Nantucket, April 6, 1999:

AE: I'm interested in a man called Jack Gill. Are you any relation?

RG: Sure am. Been Gills on this island since pretty near the time of the first settlement. I'm Richard Gill. Jack'd be my great-great-and-some-grandfather going way back. [Pause] Well, now. Old Jack Gill. Jack Gill was from off island. He weren't first family. But he came pretty near when the colony started. From Long Island, so they say, but he'd been up and down the eastern seaboard from Nova Scotia to Virginia, to the West Indies and back again.

He'd gotten together a goodly sum in the process, but he couldn't rest, couldn't settle—it was like he was looking for something, someone. Then his ship called here, caught in a storm she was, running for shelter. He came ashore and met up with an island girl. A pretty thing by all accounts, eyes as gray as a winter sea and hair as gold as the sands. Maybe he was ready to stop his roving, maybe he left off looking, but anyways, he fell in love and she fell in love right back.

Now she *was* first family, and Quaker over that, so when she married him, she married out—that's what we call it. He didn't turn Quaker, but he never left the island again.

AE: So what did he do?

RG: He didn't want to do trading no more, so he turns to whaling. There was whaling, even back then, carried on in a small way compared with what came later. The boats operated from the shore. Lookouts were set along the coast, and when a whale was sighted, a crew would go out in pursuit.

AE: What kinds of whales were they hunting?

RG: Right whales, mostly. Called that because they was the right kind to kill. They came past every autumn, migrating to their breeding grounds in the south. Still do, matter of fact, what's left of 'em, that is. Well, old Jack, he goes along with this for a while, but he has bigger ideas. He takes his craft farther and farther out into the deep ocean, way offshore, out of sight of land. Here he catches him a sperm whale, probably by accident first time around. Now sperm whale oil is better quality than right whale oil. In particular the oil in its head—they call it the case—is light and pure and worth a whole lot more. That's what Jack is after. He dreams of having a fleet of sloops—these'd be judged small by later standards, thirty, forty tons, but they'd be capable of going to the deep waters. He has big plans, but he's getting to be an old man. He can't do it himself no more. He can't manage the steering oar, or handle the killing lance. He's too old to go to sea.

[Pause]

AE: Too old to go to sea?

RG: What I said, be in his sixties by this time.
[Pause]

AE: OK. So, so how did he die, then?

RG: Old Jack? He died in his bed.

AE: Really?

RG: What's wrong with that?

AE: Nothing. Go on. Go on with his story.

RG: He hands the business on to his son Ichabod. He will take the sloops out to the deep ocean where Jack dreamed to go. There he'll hunt the great sperm whales.

Now, these beasts are a different prospect from the right whales they've been used to hunting. These are bigger, grander—more valuable, yeah, but a whole lot faster and harder to catch. And mean. You read *Moby-Dick*? They've been known to stove a ship.

[Pause]

Anyways. Where was I?

AE: Ichabod?

RG: Oh, yeah. Ichabod was a Quaker, like his mother had been before she "married out." He joined the Meeting, something Jack never did, and he married into one of the island's Quaker families. He was as ambitious as his father, but he lacked Jack's spirit of adventure, his wayward streak. Ichabod left nothing to chance. He was as strict as they come, and chance is a thing Quakers don't have no truck with. No truck with superstition either, so before the voyage, when the old man pressed his lucky piece into his hand, Ichabod gave it right back, saying he got no need for it.

AE: This lucky piece—what was it?

RG: Half a silver coin, given to Jack by the captain of some ship he served on. Jack swore by it all his life, never went to sea without it.

AE: What happened to the other half?

RG: Never would say. My guess was he gave it to a sweet-heart—it's what sailors did in them days. Anyways, Ichabod sails out without the lucky piece and he doesn't come back. His whaleboat was stove, the whole crew lost. When the sad

340

news came back, his only son dead like that, the old man never got over it. He took to his bed and his soul went out on the very next tide. They found him cold in the morning, his fist closed tight around that half a silver shilling.

AE: So it was Ichabod who was killed by the whale, not Jack at all?

RG: Yeah. That's what I been telling ya.

Note 8 — Ephraim Carlton

Brass plaque set into stone by the side of the Missouri River:

> This plaque is dedicated to the memory of *voyageurs* EPHRAIM CARLTON, JEAN DUPRÉ, and TONSA, their native guide, who passed this spot in February 1695 and were among the first explorers to open the way for the exploration and subsequent settlement of the vast American continent.

Additional Information on Mary's Mother, E. G.

Provisionally identified as Elinor Garfield, wife of Colonel Garfield, a commander in Cromwell's army and signatory to Charles I's death warrant.

Contemporary sources describe Elinor as a woman of exceptional intelligence, courage, and resourcefulness, "above the ordinary pitch of women." She served the Common-wealth cause with great loyalty and stuck with her husband through great adversity, saving him from execution when the monarchy was restored.

Although a great deal is known about her adult life, little is known of her girlhood and young womanhood, save that she lived in a large manor house outside the town of War-wick, deep in what was then the Forest of Arden. Her own mother died when Elinor was born, so she would have been given over to a wet nurse (who may or may not have been Eliza Nuttall). Her father and brother were among the first to join on the side of Parliament on the outbreak of the Civil War. They were both soldiers in Cromwell's New Model Army. Before her marriage to Colonel Garfield, a friend of her father's, Elinor would have been alone in the house while her menfolk were away at the war.

We can only surmise that it was during the time of soli-tude that Elinor conceived and Mary was born. As for the father? We have no information about him. I personally believe he *was* the Erl King.

Alison Ellman, August 31, 2001

Acknowledgments

This is a work of fiction and I take full responsibility for everything in it. I have tried to make it as accurate as possible and would like to thank those who have helped me with this.

In order to write this book, I undertook a research trip to America. I would like to thank Karen Lotz and Candlewick Press for their kindness and hospitality to me and my family. During the trip I had the good fortune to meet John Fadden on a visit to the wonderful Six Nations Indian Museum near Onchiota, New York. The museum was founded by his father, Ray, and is now run by John and his son, David. It is a fascinating place and I spent a long time there talking to John, who was kind enough to offer his help and advice on all things to do with the Iroquois and Mohawk, past and present. I would like to thank him for the considerable patience he has shown in dealing with my questions and inquiries, as well as his invaluable comments on the manuscript. I would also like to thank his wife, Eva, and Eva's mother, Elizabeth Thompson, for their generous help with names and language.

As to other research undertaken, I would like to thank Gillian Irving of the Herbert Art Gallery & Museum, Coventry, for advice about conservation; and Dr. Mary M. Brooks, head of Studies & Research, Textile Conservation Centre, University of Southampton, for advice about textile conservation.

Finally, I would like to thank Sarah Odedina for her support and enthusiasm, and for seeing two books where I saw only one.

Celia Rees

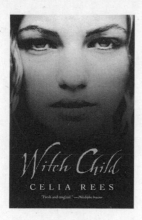

Witch Child

Celia Rees

"Journal entries, found and pieced together from pages
stitched inside a seventeenth-century quilt, are said to
be the basis of this captivating tale. As her grandmother
is executed as a witch by English village folk, Mary
Newbury is abducted by a wealthy woman and
shipped off to America. . . . The healing skills Mary
learned from her grandmother make her useful, but
also a target for suspicion." —*School Library Journal*

"An expertly written, potent novel." —*The Horn Book*

"The text is haunting. . . . Sure to be in high demand
for a long time." —*Kirkus Reviews*

Paperback ISBN 978-0-7636-4220-8

www.candlewick.com